Hezekiah Butterworth

True to His Home

A tale of the boyhood of Franklin

Hezekiah Butterworth

True to His Home
A tale of the boyhood of Franklin

ISBN/EAN: 9783337343972

Printed in Europe, USA, Canada, Australia, Japan

Cover: Foto ©Andreas Hilbeck / pixelio.de

More available books at **www.hansebooks.com**

TRUE TO HIS HOME

A Tale of the Boyhood of Franklin

BY

HEZEKIAH BUTTERWORTH

AUTHOR OF

THE WAMPUM BELT, IN THE BOYHOOD OF LINCOLN, ETC.

The noblest question in the world is, What good may I do in it?

POOR RICHARD

ILLUSTRATED BY H. WINTHROP PEIRCE

NEW YORK

D. APPLETON AND COMPANY

1897

PREFACE.

THIS volume is an historical fiction, but the plan of it was suggested by biography, and is made to include the most interesting and picturesque episodes in the home side of the life of Benjamin Franklin, so as to form a connected narrative or picture of his public life.

I have written no book with a deeper sympathy with my subject, for, although fiction, the story very truthfully shows that the good intentions of a life which has seemed to fail do not die, but live in others whom they inspire. Uncle Benjamin Franklin, "the poet," who was something of a philosopher, and whose visions all seemed to end in disappointment, deeply influenced his nephew and godson, Benjamin Franklin, whom he morally educated to become what he himself had failed to be.

The conduct of Josiah Franklin, the father of Benjamin Franklin, in comforting his poor old brother in England by naming his fifteenth child for him, and making him his godfather, is a touching instance of family affection, to the memory of which the statesman was always true.

Uncle Benjamin Franklin had a library of pamphlets that was very dear to him, for in the margins of the leaves he had placed the choicest thoughts of his life amid great political events. He was very poor, and he sold his library in his old age; we may reasonably suppose that he parted with it among other effects to get money to come to America, that he might give his influence to " Little Ben," after his brother had remembered him in his desolation by giving his name to the boy. The finding of these pamphlets in London fifty years after the old man was compelled to sell them was regarded by Benjamin Franklin as one of the most singular events of his remarkable life.

Mr. Parton, in his Life of Franklin, thus alludes to the circumstance:

A strange occurrence brought to the mind of Franklin, in 1771, a vivid recollection of his childhood. A dealer in old books, whose shop he sometimes visited, called his attention one day to a collection of pamphlets, bound in thirty volumes. dating from the Restoration to 1715. The dealer offered them to Franklin, as he said, because many of the subjects of the pamphlets were such as usually interested him. Upon examining the collection, he found that one of the blank leaves of each volume contained a catalogue of its contents, and the price each pamphlet had cost; there were notes and comments also in the margin of several of the pieces. A closer scrutiny revealed that the handwriting was that of his Uncle Benjamin, the rhyming friend and counselor of his childhood. Other circumstances combined with this surprising fact to prove that the collection had been made by his uncle, who had probably sold it when he emigrated to America, fifty-six years before. Franklin bought the volumes, and gave an account of the circumstance to his Uncle Benjamin's son, who still lived and flourished in Boston. " The oddity is," he wrote, " that the bookseller, who could suspect nothing of any relation between me and the collector, should happen to make me the offer of them."

It may please the reader to know that "Mr. Calamity" was suggested by a real character, and that the incidents in the life of "Jenny," Franklin's favorite sister, are true in spirit and largely in detail. It would have been more artistic to have had Franklin discover Uncle Benjamin's "pamphlets" later in life, but this would have been, while allowable, unhistoric fiction.

Says one of the greatest critics ever born in America, in speaking of the humble birth of Franklin:

That little baby, humbly cradled, has turned out to be the greatest man that America ever bore in her bosom or set eyes upon. Beyond all question, as I think, Benjamin Franklin had the largest mind that has shone on this side of the sea, widest in its comprehension, most deep-looking, thoughtful, far-seeing, the most original and creative child of the New World. For the last four generations no man has shed such copious good influence on America, nor added so much new truth to popular knowledge; none has so skillfully organized its ideals into institutions; none has so powerfully and wisely directed the nation's conduct and advanced its welfare in so many respects. No man has so strong a hold on the habits or the manners of the people.

"The principal question in life is, What good can I do in the world?" says Franklin. He learned to ask this question in his home in "beloved Boston." It was his purpose to answer this all-important question after the lessons that he had received in his early home, to which his heart remained true through all his marvelous career.

This is the seventh volume of the Creators of Liberty Series of books of historical fiction, based for the most part on real events, in the purpose of presenting biography in picture.

The former volumes of this series of books have been very kindly received by the public, and none of them more generously than the last volume, The Wampum Belt. For this the writer is very grateful, for he is a thorough believer in story-telling education, on the Pestalozzi and Froebel principle that "life must be taught from life," or from the highest ideals of beneficent character. H. B.

28 WORCESTER STREET, BOSTON, MASS., *June, 1897.*

CONTENTS.

LIST OF ILLUSTRATIONS.

TRUE TO HIS HOME.

CHAPTER I.

THE FIRST DAY.

It was the Sunday morning of the, 6th of January, 1706 (January 17th, old style), when a baby first saw the light in a poor tallow chandler's house on Milk Street, nearly opposite the Old South Church, Boston. The little stranger came into a large and growing family, of whom at a later period he might sometimes have seen thirteen children sit down at the table to very hard and simple fare.

"A baby is nothing new in this family," said Josiah Franklin, the father. "This is the fifteenth. Let me take it over to the church and have it christened this very day. There should be no time lost in christening. What say you, friends all? It is a likely boy, and it is best to start him right in life at once."

"People do not often have their children christened in church on the day of birth," said a lusty neighbor, "though if a child seems likely to die it might be christened on the day of its birth at home."

"This child does not seem likely to die," said the happy tallow chandler. "I will go and see the parson, and if he does not object I will give the child to the Lord on this January

day, and if he should come to anything he will have occasion
to remember that I thought of the highest duty that I owed
him when he first opened his eyes to the light."

The smiling and enthusiastic tallow chandler went to see
the parson, and then returned to his home.

"Abiah," he said to his wife, "I am going to have the
child christened. What shall his name be?"

Josiah Franklin, the chandler, who had emigrated to Boston town that he might enjoy religious freedom, had left a
brother in England, who was an honest, kindly, large-hearted
man, and "a poet."

"How would Benjamin do?" he continued; "brother's
name. Benjamin is a family name. and a good one. Benjamin of old, into whose sack Joseph put the silver cup, was a
right kind of a man. What do you say, Abiah Folger?"

"Benjamin is a good name, and a name lasts for life. But
your brother Benjamin has not succeeded very well in his many
undertakings."

"No, but in all his losses he has never lost his good name.
His honor has shown over all. 'A good name is rather to be
chosen than great riches, and loving favor rather than silver
or gold.' A man may get riches and yet be poor. It is he
that seeks the welfare of others more than wealth for himself that lives for the things that are best."

"Josiah, this is no common boy—look at his head. We
can not do for him as our neighbors do for their children.
But we can give him a name to honor, and that will be an
example to him. How would Folger do—Folger Franklin?
Father Folger was a poet like your brother Benjamin, and he

did well in life. That would unite the names of the two families."

John Folger, of Norwich, England, with his son Peter, came to this country in the year 1635 on the same ship that bore the family of Rev. Hugh Peters. This clergyman, who is known as a "regicide," or king murderer, and who suffered a most terrible death in London on the accession of Charles II, succeeded Roger Williams in the church at Salem. He flourished during the times of Cromwell, but was sentenced to be hanged, cut down alive, and tortured, his body to be quartered, and his head exposed among the malefactors, on account of having consented to the execution of Charles I.

Among Hugh Peters's household was one Mary Morrell, a white slave, or purchased serving maid. She was a very bright and beautiful girl.

The passengers had small comforts on board the ship. The passage was a long one, and the time passed heavily.

Now the passengers who were most interesting to each other became intimate, and young Peter Folger and beautiful Mary Morrell of the Peterses became very interesting to each other and very social. Peter Folger began to ask himself the question, "If the fair maid would marry me, could I not purchase her freedom?" He seems somehow to have found out that the latter could be done, and so Peter offered himself to the attractive servant of the Peterses. The two were betrothed amid the Atlantic winds and the rolling seas, and the roaring ocean could have little troubled them then, so happy were their anticipations of their life in the New World.

Peter purchased Mary's freedom of the Peterses, and so he bought the grandmother of that Benjamin Franklin who was to "snatch the thunderbolts from heaven and the scepter from tyrants," to sign the Declaration of Independence which brought forth a new order of government for mankind, and to form a treaty of peace with England which was to make America free.

Peter Folger and his bride first settled in Watertown, Mass., where the young immigrant became a very useful citizen. He studied the Indian tongue.

About 1660 the family removed to Martha's Vineyard with Thomas Mayhew, of colonial fame, where Peter was employed as a school teacher and a land surveyor, and he assisted Mr. Mayhew in his work among the Indians. He went to Nantucket as a surveyor about 1662, and was induced to remove there as an interpreter and as land surveyor. He was assigned by the proprietors a place known as Roger's Field, and later as Jethro Folger's Lane, now a portion of the Maddequet Road. Their tenth child was Abiah, born August 15, 1667. She was the second wife of Josiah Franklin, tallow chandler, of the sign of the Blue Ball, Boston, and the mother of the boy whom she would like to have inherit so inspiring a name.

Peter Folger, the Quaker poet of the island of Nantucket, was a most worthy man. He lived at the beginning of the dark times of persecution, when Baptists and Quakers were in danger of being publicly whipped, branded, and deported or banished into the wilderness. Stories of the cruelty that followed these people filled the colonies, and caused the Quaker's heart to bleed and burn. He wrote a poem entitled A Looking-glass for the Times, in which he called upon New England to pause in her sins of intoleration and persecution, and threatened the judgments foretold in the Bible upon those who do injustice to God's children.

"Abiah," said the proud father, "I admire the character of your father. It stood for justice and human rights. But, wife, listen:

"Brother Benjamin has lost all of his ten children but one. I pity him. Wife, listen: Brother Benjamin is poor through no fault of his, but because he gave himself and all that he was to his family.

"Listen: It would touch his heart to learn that I had named this boy for him. It would show the old man that I had not forgotten him, but still thought of him.

"I can not do much for the boy, but I can give Brother Benjamin a home with me, and, as he is a great reader, he can instruct the boy by wise precept and a good example. If the boy will only follow brother's principles, he may make the name of Benjamin live.

"And once more: if we name the boy Benjamin, it will make Brother Benjamin feel that he has not lost all, but that he will have another chance in the world. How glad that would make the poor old man! I would like to name him as the boy's godfather. I do pity him, don't you? You have the heart of Peter Folger."

There was a silence.

"Abiah, what now shall the boy's name be?"

"Benjamin."

2

"You have chosen that name out of your heart. May that name bring you joy! It ought to do so, since you have given up your own wish and breathed it out of your heart and conscience. To give up is to gain."

He took up the child.

"Then we will give that name to him now, and I will take the child and go to the church, and I will name Brother Benjamin as his godfather."

"It is a very cold day for the little one."

"And a healthy one on which to start out in the world. There is nothing like starting right and with a good name, which may the Lord help this child to honor! And, Abiah, that He will."

He wrapped the babe up warmly, and looked him full in the face.

Josiah Franklin was a genial, provident, hard-sensed man. He probably had no prophetic visions; no thought that the little one given him on this frosty January morning in the breezy town of Boston by the sea would command senates, lead courts, and sign a declaration of peace that would make possible a new order of government in the world, could have entered his mind. If the boy should become a good man, with a little poetic imagination like his Uncle Benjamin, the home poet, he would be content.

He opened the door of his one room on the lower floor of his house and went out into the cold with the child in his arms. In a short time he returned and laid little Benjamin in the arms of his mother.

"I hope the child's life will hold out as it has begun,"

he added. *"Benjamin Franklin, day one; started right. May Heaven help him to get used to the world!"*

As poor as the tallow chandler was, he was hospitable on that day. He did not hold the birth of the little one—which really was an event of greater importance to the world than the birth of a king—as anything more than the simple growth of an honest family, who had left the crowded towns and a smithy in old England to enjoy freedom of faith and conscience and the opportunities of the New World. He wished to live where he might be free to enjoy his own opinions and to promote a colony where all men should have these privileges.

The house in which Franklin was born is described as follows:

Its front upon the street was rudely clapboarded, and the sides and rear were protected from the inclemencies of a New England climate by large, rough shingles. In height the house was about three stories; in front, the second story and attic projected somewhat into the street, over the principal story on the ground floor. On the lower floor of the main house there was one room only. This, which probably served the Franklins as a parlor and sitting-room, and also for the family eating-room, was about twenty feet square, and had two windows on the street; and it had also one on the passageway, so as to give the inmates a good view of Washington Street. In the center of the southerly side of the room was one of those noted large fireplaces, situated in a most capacious chimney; on the left of this was a spacious closet. On the ground floor, connected with the sitting-room through the entry, was the kitchen. The second story originally contained but one chamber, and in this the windows, door, fireplace, and closet were similar in number and position to those in the parlor beneath it. The attic was also originally one unplastered room, and had a window in front on the street, and two common attic windows, one on each side of the roof, near the back part of it.

Soon after this unprophetic event Josiah Franklin and Abiah his wife went to live at the sign of the Blue Ball, on what was then the southeast corner of Hanover and Union Streets. The site of the birth of Franklin was long made notable as the office of the Boston Post, a political paper whose humor was once proverbial. The site is still visited by strangers, and bears the record of the event which was to contribute so powerful an influence to the scientific and political history of the world.

Wendell Phillips used to say that there were two kinds of people in the world—one who went ahead and did something, and another, who showed how that thing ought to have been done in some other way. The boy belonged to the former class.

But I doubt if any reader of this volume was ever born to so hard an estate as this boy. Let us follow him into the story land of childhood. In Germany every child passes through fairyland, but there was no such land in Josiah Franklin's tallow shop, except when the busy man sometimes played the violin in the inner room and sang psalms to the music, usually in a very solemn tone.

There were not many homes in Boston at this period that had even so near an approach to fairyland as a violin. Those were hard times for children, and especially for those with lively imaginations, which gift little Benjamin had in no common degree. There were Indians in those times, and supposed ghosts and witches, but no passing clouds bore angels' chariots; there were no brownies among the wild rose bushes and the ferns. There was one good children's story in every home—that of " Joseph " in the Bible, still, as always, the best family story in all the world.

CHAPTER II.

UNCLE BENJAMIN, THE POET.

Mrs. Franklin has said that she could hardly remember the time in her son's childhood when he could not read. He emerged almost from babyhood a reader, and soon began to " devour "—to use the word then applied to his habit—all the books that fell within his reach.

When about four years old he became much interested in stories told him by his father of his Uncle Benjamin, the poet, who lived in England, and for whom he had been named, and who, it was hoped, would come to the new country and be his godfather.

The family at the Blue Ball was quick to notice the tendencies of their children in early life. Little Benjamin Franklin developed a curious liking for a trumpet and a gun. He liked to march about to noise, and this noise he was pleased to make himself—to blow his own trumpet. The family wrote to Uncle Benjamin, the poet, then in England, in regard to this unpromising trait, and the good man returned the following letter in reply:

To my Namesake, on hearing of his Inclination to Martial Affairs. July 7, 1710.

> " Believe me, Ben, it is a dangerous trade;
>   The sword has many marred as well as made;
>   By it do many fall, not many rise—
>   Makes many poor, few rich, not many wise;
>   Fills towns with ruin, fields with blood beside;
>   'Tis sloth's maintainer, and the shield of pride;
>   Fair cities, rich to-day in plenty flow,
>   War fills with want to-morrow, and with woe;
>   Ruined estates, victims of vice, broken limbs, and scars
>   Are the effects of desolating wars."

One evening, as the tallow chandler was hurrying hither and thither in his apron and paper cap, the door opened with a sharp ring of the bell fastened by a string upon it. The paper cap bobbed up.

" Hoi, what now?" said the tallow chandler.

" A letter from England, sirrah. The Lively Nancy has come in. There it is."

The tallow chandler held the letter up to the fire, for it had been a *melting* day, as certain days on which the melting of tallow for the molds were called. He read " Benjamin Franklin," and said: " That's curious—that's Brother Ben's writing. I would know that the world over." He put the letter in his pocket. He saw Dame Franklin looking through the transom over the door, and shook his head.

He sat down with his large family to a meal of bread and

milk, and then took the letter from his pocket and read it over to himself.

"Ben," said he, "this is for you. I am going to read it. As I do so, you repeat after me the first letter of the first and of every line. Are you ready? Now.

"' *Be to thy parents an obedient son.*'"

"B," said little Ben.

"' *Each day let duty constantly be done.*'"

"E," the boy continued.

"' *Never give way to sloth, or lust, or pride.*'"

"N, father."

"' *Just free to be from thousand ills beside.*'"

"J, father."

"' *Above all ills be sure avoid the shelf.*'"

"A, father."

"' *Man's danger lies in Satan, sin, and self.*'"

"M, father."

"' *In virtue, learning, wisdom, progress make.*'"

"I, father."

"' *Ne'er shrink at suffering for thy Saviour's sake.*'"

"N, father. I know what that spells."

"What?"

"Benjamin."

"' *Fraud and all falsehood in thy dealings flee.*'"

"F," said the boy.

"' *Religious always in thy station be.*'"

"R, father."

"' *Adore the Maker of thy inward heart.*'"

"A, father."

" ' *Now's the accepted time, give him thy heart.*' "

" N, father; and now I can guess the rest."

" ' *Keep a good conscience, 'tis a constant friend.*' "

" K, father."

" ' *Like judge and witness this thy acts attend.*' "

" L."

" ' *In heart with bended knee alone adore.*' "

" I."

" ' *None but the Three in One forever more.*' "

" N."

" And to whom are all these things written?"

" ' To BENJAMIN FRANKLIN,' sir."

" Well, my boy, if you will only follow the advice of your Uncle Benjamin, the poet, you never will need any more instruction.—Wife, hear this: Brother Ben writes that he is coming to America as soon as he can settle his affairs, and when he arrives I will give over the training of little Ben to him. He is his godfather, and he takes a great interest in a boy that he has never seen. Sometimes people are drawn toward each other before they meet—there's a kind of sympathy in this world that is felt in ways unseen and that is prophetic. Your father was a poet, and Uncle Ben, he is one, after a fashion. I wonder what little Ben will be! "

He put on his paper cap and opened the door into the molding-room. The fire was dying out on the hearth, and the candles in the molds were cooling and hardening. He opened the weather door, causing the bell attached to it to ring. He stood looking out on the bowery street of Boston town.

On the hill rose the North Church in the shadows near the sea. A horn rent the still air. A stage coach from Salem came rolling in and stopped at the Boston Stone, not far away. A little girl tripped down the street.

"A pound of candles, sir."

"Hoi, yes, yes," and he took some candles out of a mold and laid them in the scales. The girl courtesied, and the tallow chandler closed the door with a ting-a-ling.

Then Josiah sat down with his family and played the violin. He loved his brother Benjamin, and the thought of his coming made him a happy man.

One day the old man came. Soon after there happened a great event in the family.

It was a windy night. The ocean was dashing and foaming along the sea wall on the beach where Long Wharf, Lewis Wharf, and Rowe's Wharf now are. The stars shone brightly, and clouds flew scudding over the moon.

Abiah Franklin opened the weather door and looked out. She returned to her great chair slowly with a cloud in her face.

"It is a bad night for those on the sea," she said. "It is now nine years since Josiah went away. Where he found an ocean grave we shall never know. It is hard," she added, "to have hope leave you in this way. It is one long torture to live in suspense. There hasn't been a day since the first year after Josiah left us that my ear has not waited to hear a knock on the door on a night like this.

"Josiah, you may say that I have faith in the impossible, but I sometimes believe that I shall hear that knock yet.

There is one Scripture that comforts me when I think that; it is, ' Commit thy way unto the Lord; trust also in him, and he shall bring it to pass.' "

Josiah Franklin sat silent. It was now indeed nine years since his son Josiah had left home against his will and gone to sea—" run away to sea," as his departure was called. It was a kind of mental distemper in old New England times for a boy " to run away and go to sea."

There had been fearful storms on the coast. Abiah Franklin was a silent woman when the winds bended the trees and the waves broke loudly on the shore. She thought then; she inwardly prayed, but she said little of the storm that was in her heart.

" I shall never see Josiah again," at last said Josiah Franklin. " It is a pity; it is hard on me that the son who bears my name should leave me, to become a wanderer. Boys will do such things. I may have made his home too strict for him; if so, may the Lord forgive me. I have meant to do my best for all my children.—Ben, let Josiah be a warning to you; you have been having the boy fever to go to sea. Hear the winds blow and the sea dash! Josiah must have longed to be back by the fire on nights like these."

Josiah went to the window and tapped upon the pane. He did that often when his mind was troubled. To tap upon the pane eased his heartache. It was an old New England way.

Josiah took his violin, tuned it, and began to play while the family listened by the fading coals.

" I thought I heard something," said Abiah between one of the tunes.

"What was it, Abiah?" asked her husband.

"It sounded like a step."

"That's nothing strange."

"It sounded familiar," she said. "Steps are peculiar."

"Oh, I know of whom you are thinking," said Josiah. "May the Lord comfort you, for the winds and waves do not to-night."

He played again. His wife grew restless.

"Josiah," said she when he ceased playing, "you may say that I have fancies, but I thought I saw a face pass the window."

"That is likely, Abiah."

"But this one had a short chin and a long nose."

She choked, and her eyes were wet.

There came a rap upon the door. It was a strong hand that made it; there was a heart in the sound.

"I'll open the door, Josiah," said Abiah.

She removed the wooden bar with a trembling hand, and lifted the latch.

A tall, rugged form stood before her. She started back.

"Mother, don't you know me?"

"Yes, Josiah, I knew that you were coming to-night."

She gazed into his eyes silently.

"Who told you, mother?"

"My soul."

"Well, I've come back like the prodigal son. Let me give you a smack. You'll take me in—but how about father? I thought I heard him playing the violin."

"Josiah, that is your voice!" exclaimed Josiah the elder.

"Now my cup of joy is full and running over. Josiah, come in out of the storm."

Josiah Franklin rushed to the door and locked his son in his arms, but there was probably but little sentiment in the response.

"Now I *know* the parable of the prodigal son," said he. "I had only read it before. Come in! come in! There are brothers and sisters here whom you have never seen. Now we are all here."

Uncle Benjamin wrote a poem to celebrate young Josiah's return. It was read in the family, with disheartening results. Sailor Josiah said that he "never cared much for poetry." The poem may be found in the large biographies of Franklin.

CHAPTER III.

BENJAMIN AND BENJAMIN.

An old man sat by an open fire in a strange-looking room with a little boy on his knee. Beside him was a middle-aged man, the father of the boy.

"Brother Josiah," said the old man, "I have had a hard, disappointed life, but I have done the best that I could, and there has nothing happened since my own children died and my hair turned gray that has made me so happy as that letter that you sent to me in England in which you told me that you had named this boy for me."

"It makes me happy to see you here by my fire to-night, with the boy in your lap," said the father. "Benjamin and Benjamin! My heart has been true to you in all your troubles and losses, and I would have helped you had I been able. How did you get up the resolution to cross the sea in your old age?"

"Brother Josiah, it was because my own son is here, and he was all that I had left of my own family. But that was not all. In one sense my own life has failed; I have come down to old age with empty hands. When your letter came saying that you had named this boy for me, and had made me his godfather, I saw that you pitied me, and that you had a place for me in your heart. I thought of all the years that we had passed together when we were young; of the farm and forge in Ecton; of Banbury; of the chimes of Nottingham; of all that we were to each other then.

"I was all alone in London, and there my heart turned to you as it did when we were boys. That gave me resolution to cross the sea, Brother Josiah, although my hair is white and my veins are thin.

"But that was not all, brother; he is a poor man indeed who gives up hope. When a man loses hope for himself, he wishes to live in another. The ancients used to pray that their sons might be nobler than themselves. When I read your letter that said that you had named this boy for me and had made me his godfather, you can not tell how life revived in me—it was like seeing a rainbow after a storm. I said to myself that I had another hope in this world; that I would live in the boy. I have come over to America to live in this boy.

"O brother, I·never thought that I would see an hour like this! I am poor, but I am happy. I am happy because you loved me after I became poor and friendless. That was your opportunity to show what your heart was. I am happy because you trusted me and gave my name to this boy.

"Brother Josiah, I have come over to America to return your love, in teaching this boy how to live and how to fulfill the best that is in him. A boy with your heart can succeed in life, even if he have but common gifts. The best thing that can be said of any man is that he is true-hearted. Brother, you have been true-hearted to me, and the boy inherits your nature, and I am going to be true-hearted to him and to do all I can to make his life a blessing to you and the world. We do no self-sacrificing thing without fruit."

The old man put his arm about the boy, and said:

"Ben, little Ben, I loved you before I saw you, and I love you more than ever now. I have come across the ocean in my old age to be with you. I want you to like me, Ben."

"I do, uncle," said little Ben. "I would rather be with you than with any one. I am glad that you have come."

"That makes me happy, that makes my old heart happy. I did everything a man could do for his wife and children and for everybody. I was left alone in London, poor; I seemed to be a forsaken man, but this makes up for all."

"Benjamin and Benjamin!" said the younger brother, touching the strings of the violin that he held on his lap— "Benjamin and Benjamin! Brother Benjamin, how did you get the money to cross the ocean?"

"I sold my goods and my pamphlets. *They* were my life; I had put my life into them. But I sold them, for what were they if I could have the chance to live another life in little Ben?"

"What were your pamphlets?" asked little Ben.

"They were my life, and I sold them for you, that I might make your life a blessing to your father, who has been a true brother to me. I will tell you the whole story of the pamphlets some day."

"Uncle, I love you more than ever before, because you sold the treasures for me. I wish that I might grow up and help folks, so that my name might honor yours.

"You can make it that, my boy. If you will let me teach you, you may make it that. There can nothing stand before a will that wills to do good. It is the heart that has power, my boy. My life will not have been lost if I can live in you."

"I have not much time for educating my children," said the younger brother. "I am going to give over the training of the boy to you. True education begins with the heart first, so as to make right ideas fixed in the mind and right habits in the conduct. It may be little that I can send him to school, but it is what you can do for him that will give him a start in life. I want you to see that he starts right in life. I leave his training to you. I have a dozen mouths to feed, and small time for anything but toil."

He tuned his violin and played an old English air. There were candle molds in the room, long rows of candle wicks, great kettles, a gun, a Bible, some old books, and a fireplace with a great crane, hooks, and andirons.

Little Benjamin looked up into the old man's face- and laid his hand on his shoulder.

"I am glad father did not forget you," said he.

The old man's lip quivered.

"He has been a true brother to me. Always remember that, boy, as long as you live. It is such memories as that that teach. His heart is true to me now as when we used to leave the forge and roam the woods of Banbury together in springtime, when the skylark rose out of the meadows and the hedgerows bloomed. It is good for families to be so true to each other. If one member of a family lacks any-

3

thing, it is good for another to make up for it. Yes, boy, your father has a good heart, else you would not now be in my arms."

"Why do you cry, papa?" said the boy, for his father's eyes were filled with tears which coursed down his cheeks. Something that aged Benjamin had said about the forge, the nightingale, or the thorn had touched his heart.

"We can never be young again, brother," said Josiah Franklin. "I shall never see the thorn bloom or hear the nightingale sing as I once did. No, no, no; but I am glad that I have brought you and Ben together. That would have pleased our old mother's heart, long dead and gone to the violets and primroses. Do you suppose the dead know? I sometimes think they do, and that it makes them happy to see things like these. I will talk with the parson about these things some day."

The younger brother smiled through his tears and straightened himself up, as though he felt that he had yielded to weakness, for he was a plain, hard-working man. Suddenly he said:

"Brother, you remember Uncle Tom?"

"Yes, yes; he set the chimes of Nottingham ringing in the air. I can hear them ringing now in my memory. Brother, I think little Ben favors Uncle Tom."

"Who was Uncle Tom?" asked the boy.

"They used to say that he was a wizard. I will tell you all about him some day. Let us listen now to your father's violin."

The house was still, save that the sea winds stirred the crisp autumn leaves in the great trees near and the nine o'clock bell fell solemnly on the air. A watchman went by, saying, " All is well! "

Yes, all is well in hearts like these—hearts that can pity, love, forbear, and feel.

CHAPTER IV.

FRANKLIN'S STORY OF A HOLIDAY IN CHILDHOOD.

As barren as was the early Puritan town in things that please the fancy of the child, Josiah Franklin's home was a cheerful one. It kept holidays, when the violin was played, and some pennies were bestowed upon the many children.

Let us enter the house by the candle-room door. The opening of the door rings a bell. There is an odor of tallow everywhere. One side is hung with wickings, to be cut and trimmed.

When the tallow is boiling the room is very hot, close, and the atmosphere oily.

There is a soap kettle in the room. The odor of the lye is more agreeable than that of the melted tallow.

Little Ben is here, short, stout, rosy-faced, with a great head. Where he goes the other children go; what he does, they do. Already a little world has begun to follow him.

Look at him as he runs around among the candle molds, talking like a philosopher. Does he seem likely to stand in the French court amid the splendors of the palace of Versailles, the most popular and conspicuous person among all the jeweled multitude who fill the mirrored, the golden, the blazing halls except the king himself? Does he look as though he would one day ask the French king for an army to help establish the independence of his country, and that the throne would bow to him?

Homely as was that home, the fancy of Franklin after he became great always loved to return to it.

In his advanced years he wished to prepare a little story or parable that would show that people spend too much time and money on things that could be more cheaply purchased or that they could well do without. He wrote out an anecdote of his childhood that illustrated in a clear way, like so many flashes, how the resources of life may be wasted. The story has been printed, we may safely say, a thousand times. Few stories have ever had a wider circulation or been more often quoted. It has in it a picture of his old home, and as such we must give it here. Here is the parable again, as in the original:

"When I was a child, at seven years old, my friends, on a holiday, filled my pockets with coppers. I went directly to a shop where they sold toys for children, and, being charmed with the sound of a *whistle* that I met by the way in the hands of another boy, I voluntarily offered him all my money for one. I then came home, and went whistling all over the house, much pleased with my *whistle*, but disturbing all the family. My brothers and sisters and cousins, understanding the bargain I had made, told me I had given four times as much for it as it was worth. This put me in mind what good things I might have bought with the rest of the money; and they laughed at me so much for my folly that I cried with vexation, and the reflection gave me more chagrin than the *whistle* gave me pleasure.

"This, however, was afterward of use to me, the impression continuing on my mind; so that often, when I was tempted to buy some unnecessary thing, I said to myself, *Don't give too much for the whistle*, and so I saved my money.

"As I grew up, came into the world, and observed the actions of men, I thought I met with many, very many, who *gave too much for the whistle.*

"When I saw any one too ambitious of court favor, sacrificing his time in attendance on levees, his repose, his liberty, his virtue, and perhaps his friends, to attain it, I have said to myself, *This man gave too much for his whistle.*

"When I saw another fond of popularity, constantly employing himself in political bustles, neglecting his own affairs, and ruining them by neglect, *He pays, indeed*, says I, *too much for this whistle.*

"If I knew a miser who gave up every kind of comfortable living, all the pleasure of doing good to others, all the esteem of his fellow-citizens, and the joys of benevolent friendship for the sake of accumulating wealth, *Poor man*, says I, *you do, indeed, pay too much for your whistle.*

"When I meet a man of pleasure, sacrificing every laudable improvement of mind, or of his fortune, to mere corporeal sensations, *Mistaken man*, says I, *you are providing pain for yourself instead of pleasure; you give too much for your whistle.*

"If I see one fond of fine clothes, fine furniture, fine equipages, all above his fortune, for which he contracts debts, and ends his career in prison, *Alas!* says I, *he has paid dear, very dear, for his whistle.*

"When I see a beautiful, sweet-tempered girl married to an ill-natured brute of a husband, *What a pity it is,* says I, *that she had paid so much for a whistle!*

"In short, I conceived that great part of the miseries of mankind were brought upon them by the false estimates they had made of the value of things, and by their giving too much for their *whistle.*"

CHAPTER V.

THE BOY FRANKLIN'S KITE.

LITTLE Ben now began to lead the sports of the boys. As there came to Froebel an inspiration to found a system of education in which the playground should be made a means of forming character when life was in the clay, so to young Franklin came a desire to make sports and pastimes useful. This caused him to build the little wharf in the soft marsh whence the boys might catch minnows and sail their boats.

Boys of nearly all countries and ages have found delight in flying kites. A light frame of wood, covered with paper, held by a long string, and raised by propelling it against the air, has always peculiar attractions for the young. To see an object rise from the earth by a law of Nature which seems to overcome gravitation to the sky while the string is yet in the hand, gives a boy a sense of power which excites his imagination and thrills his blood.

In Franklin's time the boy who could fly his kite the highest, or who could make his kite appear to be the most picturesque in the far-away blue sky, was regarded as a leader among his fellows, and young Franklin, as we may infer, made his kite fly very high.

But he was not content with the altitude to which he

could raise his kite or its beauty in the sky. His inquiry was, What can the kite be made to teach that is useful? What can it be made to *do?* What good can it accomplish?

Ben was an expert swimmer. After he had mastered the art of overcoming the water, he sought how to make swimming safe and easy; and when he had learned this himself, he taught other boys how to swim safely and easily.

One day he was flying his kite on the shore. His imagination had wings as well as the kite, and he followed it with the eye of fancy as it drifted along the sky pulling at his fingers.

It was a warm day, and the cool harbor rippled near, and he began to feel a desire to plunge into the water, but he did not like to pull down his kite.

He threw off his clothes and dropped into the cool water, still holding his kite string, which was probably fastened to a short stick in his hand.

He turned on his back in the water and floated, looking up to the kite in the blue, sunny sky.

But something was happening. The kite, like a sail in a boat, was bearing him along. He was the boat, the kite high in the sky was the sail, between the two was a single string. He could sail himself on the water by a kite in the sky!

So he drifted along, near the Mystic River probably, on that warm pleasant day. The sense of the power that he gained by thus obeying a law of Nature filled him with delight. He could not have then dreamed that the simple discovery would lead up to another which would enable man to see how to control one of the greatest forces in the universe. He saw simply that he could make the air *work* for him, and he probably dreamed that sometime and somewhere the same principle would enable an inventor to show the world how to navigate the air.

The kite now became to him something more than a plaything—a wonder. It caused his fancy to soar, and little Ben was always happy when his fancy was on the wing.

There was a man named Jamie who liked to loiter around the Blue Ball. He was a Scotchman, and full of humor.

"An' wot you been doin' now?" said Jamie the Scotchman, as the boy returned to the Blue Ball with his big kite and wet hair. "Kite-flying and swimming don't go together."

"Ah, sirrah, don't you think that any more! Kite-flying and floating on one's back in the water do go together. I've been making a boat of myself, and the sail was in the sky."

"Sho! How did that come about?"

"I floated on my back and held the kite string in my hand, and the kite drew me along."

"It did, hey? Well, it might do that with a little shaver like you. What made you think of that, I would like to know? You're always thinkin' out somethin' new. You'll get into difficulties some day, like the dog that saw the moon in the well and leaped down to fetch it up; he gave one howl, only one, once for all, and then they fetched *him* up; he had nothing more to say. So it will be with you if you go kiting about after such things, flyin' kites for boat sails."

"But, Jamie, I think that I am the first boy that ever sailed on the water without a boat—now don't you?"

"Well, I don't know. There's nothin' new under the sun. People like you that are always inquirin' out the whys and wherefores of things commonly get into trouble. Ben, wot will ever become of you, I wonder?"

"Archimedes made water run uphill."

"He did, hey? So he did, as I remember to have read. But he lost his life broodin' over a lot of figers that he was drawin' on the sand—angles and triangles an' things. The Roman soldier cut him down when he was dreamin', and they let his tomb all grow up to briers. Do you think, Ben, that you will ever make the river run uphill? Perhaps you'll turn the water up to the sky on a kite string, and then we can have rain in plantin' time. Who knows?"

He added thoughtfully:

"I wouldn't wonder, Ben, if you invented somethin' if you live. But the prospect isn't very encouragin' of your ever doin' anything alarmin'."

"Did you ever hear what Archimedes exclaimed when he discovered the law that a body plunged in water loses as much of its weight as is equal to the weight of an equal volume of the fluid, and applied it to the alloy in the king's crown?"

"No. Wot did he exclaim?"

"*Eureka! Eureka!*"

"Wot did he do that for?"

"It means, 'I have found it.'"

"Maybe you'll find out something sometime, Ben. You all run to dreams about such things, and some boys turn their dreams into facts, as architects build their imaginations and make money. But the fifteenth child of a tallow chandler, who was the son of a blacksmith and of a woman whose mother was bought and sold, a boy whose wits are off kite-flyin' instead of wick-cuttin' and tallow-moldin', has no great chance in the future, so it looks to me. But one can't always tell. I don't think that you'll never get to be an Archimedes and cry out 'Eureka!' But you've got imagination enough to hitch the world to a kite and send it off among the planets and shootin' stars, no one knows where. I never did see any little shaver that had so much kite-flyin' in his head as you."

"Archimedes said that if he only had a lever long enough he would move the world."

"He did, hey? Well, little Ben Franklin, you just put up your kite and attend to the candle molds, and let swimmin' in the air all go. Whatever may happen on this planet, *you'll* never be likely to move the world with a kite, of all things, nor with anything else, for that matter. So it looks to me, and I'm generally pretty far-sighted. It takes practical people to do practical things. Still, the old Bible does say that 'where there is no vision the people perish.' Well, I don't know—as I said, we can not always tell—David slew a giant with a pebble stone, and you may come to somethin' by some accident or other. I'm sure I wish you well. It may be that your uncle Benjamin, the poet, will train you when he comes to understand you, but his thoughts run to kite-flyin' and such things, and he never has amounted to anything at all, I'm told. You was named after him, and rightly, I guess. He would like to have been a Socrates. But the tape measure wouldn't fit his head."

He saw a shade in the boy's face, and added:

"*He's* going to live here, they say. Then there will be two of you, and you could fly kites and make up poetry together, if it were not for a dozen mouths to feed, which matters generally tend to bring one down from the sky."

An older son of Josiah Franklin appeared.

" James," said Jamie, " here's your brother Ben; he's been sailin' with the sail in the sky. He ought to be keerful of his talents. There's no knowin' what they may lead up to. When a person gets started in such ways as these there's no knowin' how far he may go."

Brother James opened the weather door at the Blue Ball. The bell tinkled and Ben followed him in, and the two sat down to bowls of bread, sweet apples, and milk.

" What have you been doing, Ben? " asked Brother James.

Little Ben did not answer. He got up from the table and went away downhearted, with his face in his jacket sleeve. It hurt him to be laughed at, but his imagination was a comforting companion to him in hours like these.

He could go kite-flying in his mind, and no one could see the flight.

" One can not make an eagle run around a barnyard like a hen," said a sage observer of life. There was the blood of noble purposes in little Ben Franklin's vein, if his ancestors were blacksmiths and his grandmother had been a white slave whose services were bought and sold. He had begun kite-flying; he will fly a kite again one day.

CHAPTER VI.

LITTLE BEN'S GUINEA PIG.

BEN loved little animals. He not only liked to have them about him, but it gave him great joy to protect them. One of his pets was a guinea pig.

"There are few traits of character that speak better for the future of a boy than that which seeks to protect the helpless and overlooked in the brute creation," said Uncle Benjamin to Abiah Franklin one day. "There are not many animals that have so many enemies as a guinea pig. Cats, dogs, and even the hens run after the harmless little thing. I wonder that this one should be alive now. He would have been dead but for Ben."

Abiah had been spinning. It was a windy day, and the winds, too, had been spinning as it were around the house. She had stopped to rest in her work. But the winds had not stopped, but kept up a sound like that of the wheel.

"You are always saying good things about little Ben." said Abiah. "What is it that you see in him that is different from other boys?"

"*Personality,*" said Uncle Ben. "Look at him now, out in the yard. He has been protecting the pigeon boxes from the wind, and after them the rabbit warren. He is always seeking

to make life more comfortable for everybody and everything.
Now, Abiah, a heart that seeks the good of others will never
want for a friend and a home. This *personality* will make for
him many friends and some enemies in the future. The power
of life lies in the heart."

The weather door opened, and little Ben came into the
room and asked for a cooky out of the earthen jar.

"Where's your guinea pig, my boy?" asked Uncle Benjamin. "I only see him now and then."

"Why do you call him a guinea pig, uncle?" asked little
Ben. "He did not come from Guinea, and he is not a pig.
He came from South America, where it is warm, and he is a
covey; he is not a bit of a rabbit, and not a pig."

"Where do you keep him?" asked Uncle Benjamin.

"I keep him where he is warm, uncle. It makes my heart
all shrink up to see the little thing shiver when the wind strikes
him. It is cruel to bring such animals into a climate like
this."

"There are tens of thousands of guinea pigs, or coveys, in
the land where they are found. Yes, millions, I am told. One
guinea pig don't count for much."

"But, uncle, one feels the cold wind as much as another
would—as much as each of all the millions would."

"But, Ben, you have not answered my question. Where
is the little covey now?"

Little Ben colored red, and looked suspiciously toward the
door of the room in which his father was at work. He presently saw his father's paper hat through the light over the
door, and said:

" Let me tell you some other time, uncle. They will laugh at me if I tell you now."

" Benjamin," said his mother, " we are going to have a family gathering this year on the anniversary of the day when your father landed here in 1685. The family are all coming home, and the two Folger girls—the schoolmarms—will be here from Nantucket. You will have to take the guinea-pig box out of your room under the eaves. The Folger girls are very particular. What would your aunts Hannah and Patience Folger, the schoolmarms, say if they were to find your room a sty for a guinea pig? "

" My little covey, mother," said Ben. " I'll put the cage into the shop. No, he would be killed there. I'll put him where he will not offend my aunts, mother."

Abiah Folger began to spin again, and the wheel and the wind united did indeed make a lonely atmosphere. Uncle Benjamin punched the fire, which roared at times lustily under the great shelf where were a row of pewter platters.

Little Ben drew near the fire. Suddenly Uncle Ben started.

" Oh, my eyes! what is that, Ben? "

Ben looked about.

" I don't see anything, uncle."

" Your coat sleeve keeps jumping. I have seen it four or five times. What is the matter there? "

Uncle Ben put the tongs in the chimney nook, and said:

" There is a bunch on your arm, Ben."

" No, no, no, uncle."

" There is, and it moves about."

"I have no wound, or boil, nor anything, uncle."

"There it goes again, or else my head is wrong. There! there! Abiah, stop spinning a minute and come here."

The wheel stopped. Abiah, with a troubled look, came to the hearth and leaned over it with one hand against the shelf.

"What has he been doing now?" she asked in a troubled tone.

"Look at his arm there! It bulges out."

Uncle Ben put out his hand to touch the protrusion. He laid his finger on the place carefully, when suddenly the bunch was gone, and just then appeared a little head outside the sleeve.

"I told you that there was something there! I knew that there was all the time."

There was—it was the little covey or guinea pig.

"What did I tell you before Ben came in?" said Uncle Benjamin.

Little Ben did not know what his uncle had said to his mother before he opened the door; but he heard him say now mysteriously:

"It is a cold day for shelterless things. That little bunch on his arm illustrates what I mean by personality. There are more guinea pigs than one in this cold world."

Abiah went to her wheel in silence, and it began to buzz again.

Little Ben went into the room where his father was at work.

The wheel stopped.

4

"I do love that boy," said Abiah, "notwithstanding all the fault they find with him."

"So do I, Abiah. I'm glad that you made him my god-son. All people are common in this world except those who have personality. He had a great-uncle that was just like him, and, Abiah, he became a friend of Lord Halifax."

"I am afraid that poor little Ben, after all his care of the guinea pig, will never commend himself to Lord Halifax. But we can not tell."

"No, Abiah, we can not tell, but stranger things have happened, and such things begin in that way."

CHAPTER VII.

LITTLE Ben had some reasons to dread the visits of his two stately aunts from Nantucket, the schoolmarms, whom his mother called "the girls."

But one November day, as he came home after the arrival of the stage from Salem, he was met at the door by his uncle with the question:

"Who do you think has come?"

"I don't know, uncle. Josiah?"

"No."

"Brother John from Rhode Island? Esther and Martha from school? Zachary from Annapolis?"

"Not right yet."

"Esther and Martha from school at Nantucket?"

"Yes; and your Aunt Hannah and Aunt Prudence have come with them, with bandboxes, caps, snuffboxes, and all. They came on the sloop. It is a time for little boys to be quiet now, and to keep guinea pigs and such things well out of sight."

"How long are *they* going to stay, uncle?"

By "they" he referred to his aunts.

"A week or more, I guess. This will be your still week."

"But I can not keep still, uncle; I am a boy."

Little Benjamin went into the home room and there met his stately aunts, the school teachers.

There was a great fire in the room, and the pewter platters shone there like silver. His aunts received him kindly, but in a very condescending way. They had not yet discovered any "personality" in the short, little boy of the numerous family.

The aunts delighted in imparting moral instruction, and they saw in little Ben, as they thought, a useful opportunity for such culture.

That night the family, with the aunts from Nantucket, sat down by the great fire under the shining platters to hear Uncle Benjamin relate a marvelous story. Every family has one wonder story, and this was the one wonder story of the Franklin side of the family. Uncle Benjamin wished the two "aunts" to hear this story "on his side of the house."

"There was only one of our family in England who ever became great, and that was my Uncle Thomas," he began.

"Only think of that, little Ben," said Aunt Hannah Folger, "only one."

"Only one," said Aunt Prudence Folger, "and may you become like him."

"He was born a smith, and so he was bred, for it was the custom of our family that the eldest son should be a smith— a Franklin."

"Sit very still, my little boy," said the two aunts, "and you shall be told what happened. He was a smith."

"There was a man in our town," continued Uncle Ben, "whose name was Palmer, and he became an esquire."

"Maybe that *you* will become an esquire," said Aunt Esther to Ben.

"He became an esquire," said Aunt Prudence. "Sit very still, and you shall hear."

"This man liked to encourage people; he used to say good things of them so as to help them grow. If one encourage the good things which one finds in people it helps them. It is a good thing to say good words."

"If you do not say too many," said Josiah Franklin. "I sometimes think we do to little Ben."

"Well, this Esquire Palmer told Uncle Tom one day that he would make a good lawyer. Tom was very much surprised, and said, 'I am poor; if I had any one to help me I would study for the bar.' 'I will help you,' said Esquire Palmer. So Uncle Tom dropped the hammer and went to school."

"And *you* may one day leave the candle shop and go to school," said Aunt Esther, moralizing.

"I hope so," said little Ben humbly.

"Not but that the candle shop is a very useful place," said the other aunt.

"Uncle Tom read law, and began to practice it in the town and county of Northampton. He was public-spirited, and he became a leader in all the enterprises of the county, and people looked up to him as a great man. Everything that he touched improved."

"Just think of that," said Aunt Esther to Ben. "Everything that he touched improved. That is the way to make success for yourself—help others."

"May you profit by his example, Ben," said Aunt Prudence, bobbing her cap border.

"He made everything better—the church, the town, the public ways, the societies, the homes. He was a just man, and he used to say that what the world wanted was *justice*. Everybody found him a friend, except he who was unjust. And at last Lord Halifax saw how useful he had become, and he honored him with his friendship. When he died, which was some fourteen years ago, all the people felt that they had lost a friend."

The two aunts bowed over in reverence for such a character. Aunt Esther did more than this. She put her finger slowly and impressively on little Ben's arm, and said:

"It may be that you will grow up and be like him."

"Or like Father Folger," added Aunt Prudence, who wished to remind Uncle Benjamin that the Folgers too had a family history.

Little Ben was really impressed by the homely story which he now heard a second time. It presented a looking-glass to him, and he saw himself in it. He looked up to his Uncle Ben with an earnest face, and said:

"I would like to help folks, too; why can I not, if Uncle Tom did?"

"A very proper remark," said Aunt Esther.

"Very," said Aunt Prudence.

"Good intentions are all right," said Josiah Franklin. "They do to sail away with, but where will one land if he has not got the steering gear? That is a good story, Brother Ben. Encourage little Ben here all you can; it may be that you might have become a man like Uncle Tom if you had had some esquire to encourage you."

The aunts sat still and thought of this suggestion.

Then Josiah played on his violin, and the two aunts told tales of the work of *their* good father among the Indians of Martha's Vineyard and Nantucket.

A baby lay in Abiah Franklin's arms sleeping while these family stories were related. It was a girl, and they had named her Jane, and called her "Jenny."

Amid the story-telling Jenny awoke, and put out her arms to Ben.

"The baby takes to Ben," said the mother. "The first person that she seemed to notice was Ben, and she can hardly keep her little eyes off of him."

Ben took little Jenny into his arms..

As Uncle Benjamin grew older the library of pamphlets that he had sold and on whose margins he had written the best thoughts of his life haunted him. He would sometimes be heard to exclaim:

"Those pamphlets! those pamphlets!"

"Why do you think so much of the lost pamphlets, uncle?" said little Ben.

"Hoi, Ben, hoi! 'tis on your account, Ben. I want you to have them, Ben, and read them when you are old; and I want my son Samuel to have them, although his mind does not turn to philosophy as yours does. It tore my heart to part with them, but I did it for you. One must save or be a slave. You see what it is to be poor. But it is all right, Ben, as the book of Job tells us; all things that happen to a man with good intentions are for his best good."

It was Uncle Benjamin's purpose to mold the character of his little godson. He had the Froebel ideas, although he lived before the time of the great apostle of soul education.

"The first thing for a boy like you, Ben, is to have a definite purpose, and the next is to have fixed habits to carry forward that purpose, to make life automatic."

"What do you mean by *automatic*, uncle?"

"Your heart beats itself, does it not? You do not make it beat. Your muscles do their work without any thought on your part; so the stomach assimilates its food. The first thing in education, more than cultivation of memory or reason, is to teach one to do right, right all the time, because it is just as the heart beats and the muscles or the stomach do their work. I want so to mold you that justice shall be the law of your life—so that to do right all the time will be a part of your nature. This is the first principle of home education."

Little Ben only in part comprehended this simple philosophy.

"But, uncle," said he, "what should be my purpose in life?"

"You have the nature of your great-uncle Tom—you love to be doing things to help others, just as he did. The purpose of your life should be to improve things. Genius creates things, but benevolence improves things. You will understand what I mean some day, when you shall grow up and go to England and hear the chimes of Northampton ring."

Uncle Benjamin liked to take little Ben out to sea. They journeyed so far that they sometimes lost sight of the State House, the lions and unicorns, and the window from which new kings and royal governors had been proclaimed.

These excursions were the times that Uncle Ben sought to mold the will of little Ben after the purpose that he saw in him. He told him the stories of life that educate the imagination, that help to make fixed habit.

"If I only had those pamphlets," he said on these excursions, "what a help they would be to us! You will never forget those pamphlets, will you, Ben?"

CHAPTER VIII.

LITTLE BEN SHOWS HIS HANDWRITING TO THE FAMILY.

Mr. George Brownell kept a writing school, and little Ben was sent to him to learn to write his name and to "do sums."

Franklin did indeed learn to write his name—very neatly and with the customary flourish. In this respect he greatly pleased the genial old master.

"That handwriting," he said, "is fit to put before a king. Maybe it will be some day, who knows? But, Ben," he added, "I am sorry to say it, although you write your name so well, you are a dunce at doing your sums. Now, if I were in your place I would make up for that."

In picturing these encouraging schooldays in after years, Benjamin Franklin kindly says of the old pedagogue: "He was a skillful master, and successful in his profession, employing the mildest and most encouraging methods. Under him I learned to write a good hand pretty soon, but he could not teach me arithmetic."

One afternoon, toward evening, after good Master Brownell had encouraged him by speaking well of his copy book, he came home with a light heart. He found his Uncle Benjamin, and his cousin, Samuel Franklin, Uncle Benjamin's son, at the candle shop.

"Uncle Benjamin," he said, "I have something to show you; I have brought home my copy book. Master Brownell says it is done pretty well, but that I ought to do my sums better, and that I 'must make up for that.'"

"He is right, little Ben. We have to try to make up for our defects all our lives. Let me look at the book. Now that is what I call right good writing."

"Do you see anything peculiar about it?" asked Ben. "Master Brownell said that it was good enough to' set before a king, and that it might be, some day."

Little Ben's big brothers, who had come in, laughed, and slapped their hands on their knees.

Josiah Franklin left his tallow boiling, and said:

"Let me see it, Ben."

He mounted his spectacles and held up the copy book, turning his eyes upon the boy's signature.

"That flourish to your name does look curious. It is all tied up, and seems to come to a conclusion, as though your mind had carried out its original intention. There is character in the flourish. Ben, you have done well. But you must make up for your sums.—Brother Ben, that is a good hand, but I guess the sun will go around and around the world many times before kings ever set their eyes on it. But it will tell for sure. The good Book says, 'Seest thou a man diligent in his business——' Well, you all know the rest. I repeat that text often, so that my boys can hear."

Samuel Franklin, Uncle Ben's son, examined the copy book.

"Samuel," said Uncle Ben, "I used to write a hand something like that. I wish that I had my pamphlets; I would show you my hand at the time of the Restoration. I used to write political proverbs in my pamphlets in that way.

"I want you," he continued, "to honor that handwriting, and do your master credit. The master has tried to do well by you. I hope that handwriting may be used for the benefit of others; live for influences, not for wealth or fame. My life will not fail if I can live in you and Samuel here. Remember that everything that you do for others will send you up the ladder of life, and I will go with you, even if the daisies do then blow over me.

"Ben, you and Samuel should be friends, and, if you should do well in life, and he should do the same—which Heaven grant that he may!—I want you sometimes to meet by the gate post and think of me.

"If you are ever tempted to step downward, think of me, Ben; think of me, Samuel. Meet sometimes at the gate post, and remember all these things. You will be older some day, and I will be gone."

The old man held up the copy book again.

"'Fit to set before kings,'" he repeated. "That was a great compliment."

Little Jane, the baby, seeing the people all pleased, held out her hands to Ben.

"Jenny shall see it," said Ben. He took the copy book and held it up before her eyes. She laughed with the rest.

That signature was to remap the world. It was to be set
to four documents that changed the history of mankind.
Reader, would you like to see how a copy of it looked? We
may fancy that the curious flourish first saw the light in Mr.
Brownell's school.

CHAPTER IX.

UNCLE BENJAMIN'S SECRET.

Little Ben was fond of making toy boats and ships and sailing them. He sometimes took them to the pond on the Common, and sometimes to wharves at low tide.

One day, as he was going out of the door of the sign of the Blue Ball, boat in hand, Uncle Benjamin followed him.

The old man with white hair watched the boy fondly day by day, and he found in him many new things that made him proud to have him bear his name.

"Ben," he called after him, "may I go too?"

"Yes, yes, Uncle Benjamin. I am going down beside Long Wharf. Let us take Baby Jane, and I will leave the boat behind. The baby likes to go out with us."

The old man's heart was glad to feel the heart that was in the voice.

Little Ben took Baby Jane from his mother's arms, and they went toward the sea, where were small crafts, and sat down on board of one of the safely anchored boats. It was a sunny day, with a light breeze, and the harbor lay before them bright, calm, and fair.

"Ben, let us talk together a little. I am an old man; I do not know how many years or even days more I may have

UNCLE BENJAMIN'S SECRET.

to spend with you. I hope many, for I have always loved to live, and, since I have come to know you and to give my heart to you, life is dearer to me than ever. I have a secret which I wish to tell you.

"Ben, as I have said, I have found in you *personality.* You do not fully know what that means now. Think of it fifty years from now, then you will know. You just now gave up your boat-sailing for me and the baby. You like to help others to be more comfortable and happy, and that is the way to grow. That is the law of life, and the purpose of life is to grow. You may not understand what I mean now; think of what I say fifty years from now.

"Ben, I have faith in you. I want that you should always remember me as one who saw what was in you and believed in you."

"Is that the secret that you wanted to tell me, uncle?" asked little Ben.

"No, no, no, Ben; I am a poor man after a hard life. You do pity me, don't you? Where are my ten children now, except one? Go ask the English graveyard. My wife is gone. I am almost alone in the world. All bright things seemed to be going out in my life when you came into it bearing my name. I like to tell you this again and again. Oh, little Ben, you do not know how I love you! To be with you is to be happy.

"One after one my ten children went away to their long rest where the English violets come and go. Two after one they went, three after two, and four after three. I lost my property, and Samuel went to America, and I was told that Brother Josiah had named you for me and made me your godfather. Then, as there was nothing but graves left for me in old England, I wished to come to America too.

"Ben, Ben, you have heard all this before, but, listen, I must tell you more. I wanted to cross the ocean, but I had little money for such a removal, and I used to walk about London with empty hands and wish for £100, and my wishes brought me nothing but sorrow, and I would go to my poor lodgings and weep. Oh, you can not tell how I used to feel!

"I had a few things left—they were as dear to me as my own heart. I am coming to the secret now, Ben. You are asking in your mind what those things were that I sold; they were the things most precious of all to me, and among them were—were my pamphlets."

The old man bowed over, and his lip quivered.

"What were your pamphlets, uncle? You said that you would explain to me what they were."

"Ben, there are some things that we come to possess that are a part of ourselves. Our heart goes into them—our blood—our life—our hope. It was so with my pamphlets, Ben. This is the secret I have to tell.

"I loved the cause of the Commonwealth—Cromwell's days. In the last days of the Commonwealth, when I had but little money to spare, I used to buy pamphlets on the times. When I had read a pamphlet, thoughts would come to me. I did not seem to think them; they came to me, and I used to note these thoughts down on the margins of the leaves in the pamphlets. Those thoughts were more to me than anything that I ever had in life."

"I would have felt so too, uncle."

"Years passed, and I had a little library of pamphlets, the margins filled with my own thoughts. Poetry is the soul's vision, and I wrote my poetry on those pamphlets. Ben, oh, my pamphlets! my pamphlets! They were my soul; all the best of me went into them.

"Well, Ben, times changed. King Charles returned, and the Commonwealth vanished, but I still added to my pamphlets for years and years. Then I heard of you. I always loved Brother Josiah, and my son was on this side of the water, and the longing grew to sail for America, where my heart then was, as I have told you."

"I see how you felt, uncle."

"I dreamed how to get the money; I prayed for the money. One day a London bookseller said to me: 'You have been collecting pamphlets. Have you one entitled Human Freedom'? I answered that I had, but that it was covered with notes. He asked me to let him come to my lodgings and read it. He came and looked over all my pamphlets, and told me that a part of the collection had become rare and valuable; that they might have a value in legal cases that would arise owing to the change in the times. He offered to buy them. I refused to sell them, on account of what I had written on the margins of the leaves. What I wrote were my revelations.

"He went away. Then my loneliness increased, and my longing to come to America. I could sell my valuables, and among them the pamphlets, and this would give me money wherewith to make the great change."

"You sold them, uncle?"

"When I thought of Brother Josiah, I was tempted to do

it. But I at first said 'No.' When I heard that my son was making a home for himself here, I again was tempted to do it. But I said, 'No.' I could not sell myself.

"Then there came a letter from Brother Josiah. It said: 'I have another son. We have named him Benjamin, after you. We have named you as his godfather.'

"Then I sat down on the side of the bed in my room, and the tears fell.

"'*We have named him Benjamin*'—how those words went to my heart!"

"It was the first time that you ever heard of me, wasn't it, uncle?"

"Yes, yes; it makes me happy to hear you say that. And you will never forget me, will you, Ben?"

"Never, uncle, if I live to be eighty years old! But, uncle, you sold the pamphlets!"

"Yes. When I read your name in Josiah's letter I felt a weight lifted from my mind. I said to myself that I would part with myself—that is, the pamphlets—for you."

"Did you sell them for me, uncle?"

"Yes, I sold them for you, Benjamin."

"What was the man's name that brought them, uncle?"

"I hoped that you would ask me that. His name was Axel. Repeat it, Ben."

"Axel."

"It is a hard name to forget."

"I shall never forget it, uncle."

"Ben, you may go to London sometime."

"We are all poor now."

" But you have *personality,* and people who look out for others are needed by others for many things. Maybe they will sometime send you there."

" Who, uncle? "

" Oh, I don't know. But if ever you should go to London, go to all the old bookstores, and what name will you look for? "

" Axel, uncle."

" Ben, those are not books; they are myself. I sold myself when I sold them—I sold myself for you. Axel, Ben, Axel."

Little Ben repeated " Axel," and wondered if he would ever see London or meet with his uncle in those pamphlets which the latter claimed to be his other self.

" Axel," he repeated, pinching Baby Jane's cheek. Baby Jane laughed in the sunlight on the blue sea when she saw the excitement in Ben's face.

The tide was coming in, the boat was rocking, and Ben said:

" We must go home now, for Jenny's sake."

CHAPTER X.

THE STONE WHARF, AND LADY WIGGLEWORTH, WHO FELL
ASLEEP IN CHURCH.

DID little Ben's trumpet and gun indicate that he would become a statesman whose cause would employ armies? We do not know. The free will of a boy on the playground is likely to present a picture of his leading traits of character. In old New England days there was a custom of testing a child's character in a novel way. A bottle, a coin, and a Bible were laid on the floor at some distance apart to tempt the notice of the little one when he first began to creep. It was supposed that the one of the three objects that he crept toward and seized upon was prophetic of his future character—that the three objects represented worldly pleasure, the seeking for wealth, and the spiritual life.

Franklin's love for public improvements was certainly indicated in his early years. He liked the water and boats, and he saw how convenient a little wharf near his house would be; so he planned to build one, and laid his plans before his companions.

"We will build it of stone," he said. "There are plenty of stones near the wharf."

"But the workmen there would not let us have them," said a companion.

"We will take them after they have gone from their work. We can build the wharf in a single evening. The workmen may scold, but they will not scold the stone landing out of the water again."

One early twilight of a long day the boys assembled at the place chosen by young Franklin for his wharf, and began to work like beavers, and before the deep shadows of night they had removed the stones to the water and builded quite a little wharf or landing.

"We can catch minnows and sail our boats from here now," said young Franklin as he looked with pride on the triumphs of his plan. "All the boys will be free to use this landing," he thought. "Won't it make the people wonder!"

It did.

The next morning the weather door of the thrifty tallow chandler opened with a ring.

"Josiah Franklin, where is that boy of yours?" asked a magistrate.

The paper cap bobbed up, and the man at the molds bent his head forward with wondering eyes.

"Which boy?"

"Ben, the one that is always leading other boys round."

"I dunno. He's making a boat—or was.—Benjamin!" he called; "I say, Benjamin!"

The door of the living room opened, and little Ben appeared.

"Here's a man who has come to see you. What have you been doing now?"

"Boy," said the man—he spoke the word so loudly that the little boy felt that it raised him almost to the dignity of a man.

"What, sir?" gasped Ben, very intelligent as to what would follow.

"Did you put those stones into the water?"

"Yes, sir."

"What did you do that for?"

"To make a wharf, sir."

"'To make a wharf, sir!' Didn't you have the sense to know that those stones were building stones and belonged to the workmen?"

"No, sir; I didn't know that they belonged to any one. I thought that they belonged to everybody."

"You did, you little rascal! Then why did you wait to have the workmen go away before you put them into the water?"

"The workmen would have hindered us, sir. They don't think that improvements can be made by little shavers like us. I wanted to surprise them, sir—to show them what we could do, sir."

"Benjamin Franklin," said Josiah, "come here, and I will show you what I can do.—Stranger, the boy's godfather has come to live with us and to take charge of him, and he does need a godfather, if ever a stripling did."

Josiah Franklin laid his hand on the boy, and the workman went away. The father removed the boy's jacket, and showed him what he could do, the memory of which was not a short one.

"I did not mean any harm, father," young Benjamin said over and over. "It was a mistake."

"My boy," said the tallow chandler, softening, "never make a second mistake. There are some people who learn wisdom from their first mistakes by never making second mistakes. May you be one of them."

"I shall never do anything that I don't think is honest, father. I thought stones and rocks belonged to the people."

"But there are many things that belong to the people in this world that you have no right to use, my son. When you want to make any more public improvements, first come and talk with me about them, or go to your Uncle Ben, into whose charge I am going to put you—and no small job he will have of it, in my thinking!"

Benjamin Franklin said, when he was growing old and was writing his own life, that his father *convinced* him at the time of this event that "that which is not honest could not be useful."

We can see in fancy his father with a primitive switch thus *convincing* him. He never forgot the moral lesson.

Where was Jamie the Scotchman during this convincing episode? When he heard that the little wharf-builder, bursting with desire for public improvement, had fallen into disgrace, he came upon him slyly:

"So you've been building a wharf for the boys of the town. When one begins so soon in life to improve the town, there can be no telling what he will do when he grows up. Perhaps you will become one of the great benefactors of Boston yet. Who knows?"

"We can't tell," said the future projector of Franklin Park, philosophically.

"No, that is a fact, bubby. Take your finger out of your mouth and go to cutting candle wicks. It must make a family proud to have in it such a promising one as you! You'll be apt to set something ablaze some day if you keep on as you've begun."

He did.

Jamie the Scotchman went out, causing the bell on the door to ring. He whistled lustily as he went down the street.

Little Benjamin sat cutting wicks for the candle molds and wondering at the ways of the world. He had not intended to do wrong. He may have thought that the stones, although put aside by the workmen, were common property. He had made a mistake. But how are mistakes to be avoided in life? He would ask his Uncle Benjamin, the poet, when he should meet him. It was well, indeed, never to make a *second* mistake, but better not to make any mistake at all. Uncle Benjamin was wise, and could write poetry. He would ask him.

Besides Jamie the Scotchman, who spent much time at the Blue Ball, little Benjamin's brother James seems to have looked upon him as one whose activities of mind were too obvious, and needed to be suppressed.

The evening that followed the disgrace of little Ben was a serious one in the Franklin family. Uncle Ben had "gone to meeting" in the Old South Church.

The shop, with its molded candles, dipped candles, ingot bars of soap, pewter molds, and kettles, was not an unpleasant place in the evening, and old sea captains used to drop in to talk with Josiah, and sometimes the leading members of the Old South Church came to discuss church affairs, which were really town affairs, for the church governed the town.

On this particular night little Ben sat in the corner of the shop very quietly, holding little Jane as usual. The time had come for a perfect calm in his life, and he himself was well aware how becoming was silence in his case.

Among those who used to come to the shop evenings to talk with Josiah and Uncle Ben, the poet, was one Captain Holmes. He came to-night, stamping his feet at the door, causing the bell to ring very violently and the faces of some of the Franklin children to appear in the window framed over the shop door. How comical they looked!

"Where's Ben to-night?" asked Captain Holmes.

Little Ben's heart thumped. He thought the captain meant *him.*

"He's gone to meetin'," said Josiah. "Come, sit down. Ben will be at home early."

Little Ben's heart did not beat so fast now.

"Where's that boy o' yourn?" asked the captain.

Ben's heart began to beat again.

"There, in the corner," said Josiah, with a doubtful look in his face.

"He'll be given to making public improvements when he grows up," said the captain. "But I hope that he will not take other people's property to do it. If there is any type of man for whom I have no use it is he who does good with what belongs to others."

The door between the shop and the living room opened, and the grieved, patient face of Abiah appeared.

"Good evening, Captain Holmes," said Abiah. "I heard what you said—how could I help it?—and it hurt me. No descendant of Peter Folger will ever desire to use other people's property for his own advantage. Ben won't."

"That's right, my good woman, stand up for your own. Every drop of an English exile's blood is better than its weight in gold."

"Ben is a boy," said Abiah. "If he makes an error, it will be followed by a contrite heart."

Little Ben could hear no more. He flew, as it were, up to the garret chamber and laid down on the trestle bed. A pet squirrel came to comfort him or to get some corn. He folded the squirrel in his bosom.

Ting-a-ling! It was Uncle Ben, the poet, whose name he had disgraced. He could endure no more; he began to sob, and so went to sleep, his little squirrel pitying him, perhaps.

There was another heart that pitied the boy. It was Uncle Ben's. Poor Uncle Ben! He sleeps now at the side of the Franklin monument in the Granary burying ground, and we like to cast a kindly glance that way as we pass the Park Street Church on Tremont Street, on the west side. It is a good thing to have good parents, and also to have a good uncle with a poetic mind and a loving heart.

There was one trait in little Benjamin's character that Josiah Franklin saw with his keen eye to business, and it gave him hope. He was diligent. One of Josiah Franklin's favorite texts of Scripture was, "Seest thou a man diligent in his business? he shall stand before kings; he shall not stand before mean men." This text he used to often repeat, or a part of it, and little Ben must have thought that it applied to him. Hints of hope, not detraction, build a boy.

Jamie the Scotchman had little expectation that puttering Ben would ever "stand before kings." Not he. He had not that kind of vision.

"Ah, boy, I could tell you a whole history of diligent boys who not only came to stand before kings, but who overturned thrones; and he who discrowns a king is greater than a king," said he one day. "Think what you might become."

"Maybe I will."

"Will what?"

"Be some one in the world."

"Sorry a boy you would make to 'stand before kings,' and I don't think you'll ever be likely to take off the crown from anybody. So your poor old father might as well leave that text out of the Scriptures. There are no pebbles in your sling of life. If there were, wonders would never cease. You are just your Uncle Ben over again. I'm sorry for ye, and for all."

Little Ben looked sorry too, and he wondered if there really were in the text something prophetic for him, or if Jamie the Scotchman were the true seer. But many poor boys had come to stand before kings, and some such boys had left tyrants without a crown.

Jamie the Scotchman thought that he had the gift of

"second sight," as a consciousness of future events was called, but he usually saw shadows. He liked to talk to himself, walking with his hands behind him.

After his dire prophecy concerning the future of little Ben he walked down to Long Wharf with Uncle Benjamin, talking to himself for the latter to hear.

"Ye can't always tell," said he; "I didn't speak out of the true inward spirit when I said those things. It hurt the little shaver to tell him there was no future in him; I could see it did. The boy has a curious way of saying wise things; such words fly out of his mouth like swallows from a cave. If I were to take up a dead brand in the blacksmith's shop and he was around, as he commonly is, he would say, 'The more you handle a burned stick the smuttier you become'; or if I were to pick up a horseshoe there, and say, 'For the want of a nail the shoe was lost,' he would answer, 'And for want of a shoe the horse was lost.' Then, after a time, he would add, 'For want of a horse the rider was lost,' and so on. His mind works in that way. Maybe he'll become a philosopher. Philosophers stand before kings. I now have the true inner sight and open vision. I can see a streak of light in that curious gift of his. But blood tells, and his folks on his father's side were blacksmiths over in England, and philosophers don't come from the forge more'n eagles do from the hen yard.

"I said what I did to stimulate him. It cut the little shaver to the quick, didn't it? Now he wouldn't have been so cut if there had been nothing there. The Lord forgive me if I did wrong!"

He walked down the wharf to the end. Beyond lay the blue harbor and the green islands. The town had only some ten thousand inhabitants then, but several great ships lay in the harbor under the three hills, two of which now are gone.

The harbor was girded with oaks and pines. Here and there a giant elm, still the glory of New England, lifted its bowery top like a cathedral amid towns of trees. Sea birds screamed low over the waters, and ospreys wheeled high in the air.

Jamie the Scotchman had not many things to occupy his thoughts, so he sat down to wonder as to what that curious Franklin boy might become.

A new thought struck him.

" He has French blood in him—the old family name used to be Franklein," he said to himself. " Now what does that signify? French blood is gentle; it likes to be free. I don't see that it might not be a good thing to have; the French like to find out things and give away to others what they discover."

A shell fell into the water before him from high in the air. The water spouted up, causing an osprey to swoop down, but to rise again.

Jamie the Scotchman turned his head.

" You, Ben? You follow me 'round everywhere. What makes ye, when I treat ye so? "

" If a boy didn't hope for anything he would never have the heartache."

" True, true, my boy; and what of that? "

"I would rather expect something and have the heart-ache."

"No one ever misses his expectations who looks for the heartache in this world. But what queer turns your mind does take, and what curious questions you do ask! Let us return to the Blue Ball."

They did, through winding streets, one or more of which were said to follow the wanderings of William Blackstone's cow from the Common. Boston still follows the same interesting animal.

There were windmills on the hills and tidemills near the water. There was a ferryboat between Boston and Charlestown, and on the now Chelsea side was the great Rumney Marsh. On the Common, which was a pasture, was a branching elm, a place of executions. Near it was a pond into which had been cast the Wishing Stone around which, it was reported, that if one went three times at night and repeated the Lord's Prayer *backward* at each circuit one might have whatever he wished for. Near the pond and the great tree were the Charles River marshes. Such was Boston in 1715–'20.

Little Ben went to the South Church on Sundays, and the tithingman was there. The latter sat in the gallery among the children with his long rod, called the tithing stick, with which he used to touch or correct any boy or girl who whispered in meeting, who fell asleep, or who misbehaved. Little Ben must have looked from the family pew in awe at the tithingman. The old-time ministers pictured the Lord himself as being a kind of a tithingman, sitting up in heaven and watching out for the unwary. Good Josiah

Franklin governed the conduct of the children in his own pew. You may be sure that none of them whispered there or fell asleep or misbehaved.

The tithingman, who was a church constable, was annually elected to keep peace and order in the church. In England he collected tithes, or a tenth part of the parish income, which the people were supposed, after the Mosaic command, to offer to the church. He sometimes wore a peculiar dress; he was usually a very solemn-looking man, the good man of whom all the children, and some of the old women, stood in terror.

A crafty man was the tithingman in the pursuit of his duties. He was on the watch all the time, and, as suspicion breeds suspicion, so the children were on the watch for him. The sermons were long, the hourglass was sometimes twice turned during the service, and the children often kept themselves awake by looking out for the tithingman, who was watching out for them. This was hardly the modern idea of heart culture and spiritual development, but the old Puritan churches made strong men who faced their age with iron purposes.

We said that the tithingman was sometimes a terror to old women. Why was he so? It was sweet for certain good old people to sleep in church, and his duties extended to all sleepers, young and old. But he did not smite the good old ladies with a stick. In some churches, possibly in this one, he carefully tickled their noses with a feather. This led to a gentle awakening, very charitable and kindly.

It is a warm summer day. Josiah Franklin's pew is crowded, and little Ben has gone to the gallery to sit among the boys. Uncle Ben, the poet, is there, for he sees that the family pew is full.

How can little Ben help whispering now, when the venerable poet is by his side and will not harshly reprove him, and when so many little things are happening that tempt him to share his thoughts with his amiable godfather?

But he restrained himself long and well.

In her high-backed pew, provided with the luxury of the cushion, sat fine old Lady Wiggleworth, all in silks, satins, and plumes. Little Ben, looking over the gallery rail, saw that my lady's plumes nodded, and he gently touched Uncle Ben and pointed down. Suddenly there came a tap of the tithing stick on his head, and he was in disgrace. He looked very solemn now; so did Uncle Ben. It was a solemn time after one had been touched by the tithing rod.

But the tithingman had seen Lady Wiggleworth's nodding plumes. Could it be possible that this woman, who was received at the Province House, had lost her moral and physical control?

If such a thing had happened, he must yet do his duty. He would have done that had the queen been there. The law of Heaven makes no exception, nor did he.

He tiptoed down the stair and stood before the old lady's pew. All her plumes were nodding, something like the picture of a far ship in a rolling sea. My lady was asleep.

The tithingman's heart beat high, but his resolution did not falter. If it had, it would soon have been restored, for my lady began to snore.

Gently, very gently, the tithingman took from his side

pocket a feather. He touched with it gently, very gently, a sensitive part of the oblivious old lady's nose. She partly awoke and brushed her nose with her hand. But her head turned to the other side of her shoulders, and she relapsed into slumber again.

The sermon was still beating the sounding-board, and a more vigorous duty devolved upon the tithingman.

He pushed the feather up my lady's nose, where the membrane was more sensitive and more quickly communicated with the brain. He did this vigorously and more vigorously. It was an obstinate case.

"Scat!"

The tithingman jumped. My lady opened her eyes. The sermon was still beating the sounding-board, but she was not then aware that she, too, had spoken in meeting.

There were some queer church customs in the days of Boston town.

CHAPTER XI.

•

JENNY.

JENNY FRANKLIN, the "pet and beauty of the family," Benjamin's favorite sister, was born in 1712, and was six years younger than he.

"My little Jenny," said Josiah, "has the Franklin heart." Little Ben found that heart in her baby days, and it was true to him to the end.

Uncle Benjamin had entertained such large hopes of the future of little Ben since the boy first sent to him a piece of poetry to England, that he wrote of him:

> "For if the bud bear grain, what will the top?"

and again:

> "When flowers are beautiful before they're blown,
> What rarities will afterward be shown!
> If trees good fruit un'noculated bear,
> You may be sure't will afterward be rare.
> If fruits are sweet before they've time to yellow,
> How luscious will they be when they are mellow!"

He also saw great promise in bright little Jenny, who had heart full of sympathy and affection. Jenny, Ben, and Uncle Benjamin became one in heart and companionship.

Beacon Hill was a lovely spot in summer in old Boston days. Below it was the Common, with great trees and wind-

70

ing ways. It commanded a view of the wide harbor and far blue sea. It looked over a curve of the river Charles, and the bright shallow inlet or pond, where the Boston and Maine depot now stands, that was filled up from the earth of the fine old hillside. The latter place may have been the scene of Ben's bridge, which he built in the night in a forbidden way. The place is not certainly known.

Uncle Benjamin, one Sunday after church, took Ben and little Jenny, who was a girl then, to the top of the hill. It was a showery afternoon in summer—now bright, now overcast—and all the birds were singing on the Common between the showers.

In one of the shining hours between the showers they sat down under an ancient forest tree, and little Jenny rested her arms on one of the knees of Uncle Benjamin, and Ben leaned on the other. The old man looked down on the harbor, which was full of ships, and said:

"I wish I had my sermons that I left behind. I would read one of them to you now."

"I would rather hear you talk," said Ben, with conscientious frankness.

"So would I," said Jenny, who thought that Ben was a philosopher even at this early age, and who echoed nearly everything that he said.

"Look over the harbor," said the old man. "There are more and more ships coming in every year. This is going to be a great city, and America will become a great country. Ben, I hope there will never be any wars on this side of the water. War is sloth's maintainer, and the shield of pride;

it makes many poor and few rich, and fewer wise.* Ben, this is going to be a great country, and I want you to be true to the new country."

"I will always be true to my country," said Ben.

"And I will be true to my home," said little Jenny.

"So you will, so you will, my darling little pet; I can see that," said Uncle Benjamin.

Ben was so pleased at his echo that he put his arm around his sister's neck and kissed her many times.

The old man's heart was touched at the scene. He thought of his lost children, who were sleeping under the cover of the violets now.

"It is going to rain again," he said. "The robins are all singing, and we will have to go home. But, children, I want to leave a lesson in your minds. Listen to Uncle Ben, whose heart is glad to see you so loving toward each other and me.

"*More than wealth, more than fame, more than anything, is the power of the human heart, and that power is developed by seeking the good of others.* Live for influences that multiply, and for the things that live. Now what did I say, Ben?"

"You said that more than wealth, more than fame, more than anything, was the power of the human heart, and that that power was developed in seeking the good of others."

"That's right, my man.—Now, Jenny, what did I say?"

"I couldn't repeat all those big words, uncle."

---

* The old man's own words to Benjamin on war.

" Well, you lovely little *creeter*, you; you do not need to repeat it; you know the lesson already; it was born in you; you have the Franklin heart! "

" Beloved Boston," Franklin used to say when he became old. What wonder, when it was associated with memories like these!

CHAPTER XII.

A CHIME OF BELLS IN NOTTINGHAM.

SOME time after Uncle Benjamin, who became familiarly known as Uncle Ben, had revealed to little Ben his heart's secret, and how that he had for his sake sold his library of pamphlets, which was his other self, the two again went down to the wharves to see the ships that had come in.

They again seated themselves in an anchored boat.

"Ben," said Uncle Benjamin, "I have something more on my mind. I did not tell you all when we talked here before. You will never forget what I told you—will you?"

"Never, uncle, if I live to be old. My heart will always be true to you."

"So it will, so it will, Ben. So it will. I want to tell you something more about your Great-uncle Thomas. You favor him. Did any one ever tell you that the people used to think him to be a wizard?"

"No, no, uncle. You yourself said that once. What is a wizard?"

"It is a man who can do strange things, no one can tell how. They come to him."

"But what made them think him a wizard?"

"Oh, people used to be ignorant and superstitious, like

Reuben of the Mill, your father's old friend and mine. There was an inn called the World's End, at Ecton, near an old farm and forge. The people used to gather there and tell stories about witches and wizards that would have made your flesh creep, and left you afraid to go to bed, even with a guinea pig in your room.

"Your Great-uncle Thomas was always inventing things to benefit the people. At last he invented a way by which it might rain and rain, and there might be freshets and freshets, and yet their meadows would not be overflown. The water would all run off from the meadows like rain from a duck's back. He made a kind of drain that ran sideways. Now the pious Brownites thought that this was flying in the face of Providence, and people began to talk mysteriously about him at the World's End.

"But it was not that which I have heavy on my mind or light on my mind, for it is a happy thought. There are not many romantic things in our family history. The Franklins were men of the farm, forge, and fire. But there was one thing in our history that was poetry. It was this—listen now.

"What was the name of that man to whom I sold the pamphlets?" he asked in an aside.

"Axel."

"That is right—always remember that name—Axel.

"Now listen to that other thing. Your uncle, or great-uncle Thomas, started a subscription for a chime of bells. The family all loved music—that is what makes your father play the violin. Your Great-uncle Thomas loved music in the air. You may be able to buy a spinet for Jenny some day.

"Now your Great-uncle Thomas's soul is, as it were, in those chimes of Nottingham. I pray that you may go to England some day before you die and hear the chimes of Nottingham. You will hear a part of your own family's soul, my boy. It is the things that men do that live. If you ever find the pamphlets, which are myself—myself that is gone—you will read in them my thoughts on the Toleration Act, and on Liberty, and on the soul, and the rights of man. What was the man's name?"

"Axel."

"Right."

Little Jenny, who loved to follow little Ben, had come down to the wharf to hear "Uncle Benjamin talk." She had joined them in the boat on the sunny water. She had become deeply interested in Uncle Tom and the chimes of Nottingham.

"Uncle Ben," she asked, "was Uncle Tom ever laughed at?"

"Yes, yes; the old neighbors who would hang about the smithy used to laugh at him. They thought him visionary. Why did you ask me that?"

"What makes people who come to the shop laugh at Ben? It hurts me. I think Ben is real good. He is good to me, and I am always going to be good to him. I like Ben better than *almost* anybody."

"A beneficent purpose is at first ridiculed," said Uncle Benjamin.

Little Ben seemed to comprehend the meaning of this principle, but the "big words" were lost on Jenny.

"He whose good purpose is laughed at," said Uncle Benjamin, "will be likely to live to laugh at those who laughed at him if he so desired; but, hark! a generous man does not laugh at any one's right intentions. Ben, never stop to answer back when they laugh at you. Life is too short. It robs the future to seek revenge."

Uncle Benjamin was right.

Did little Ben heed the admonition of his uncle on this bright day in Boston, to follow beneficence with a ready step, and not to stop to "answer back"? Was little Jenny's heart comforted in after years in finding Ben, who was so good to her now, *commended?* We are to follow a family history, and we shall see.

As the three went back to the Blue Ball, Ben, holding his uncle by the one hand and Jane by the other, said:

"I do like to hear Jane speak well of me, and stand up for me. I care more for that than *almost* any other thing."

"Well, live that she may always speak well of you," said Uncle Benjamin; "so that she may speak well of you when you two shall meet for the last time."

"Uncle," said Jenny, "why do you always have something solemn to say? Ben isn't solemn, is he?"

"No, my girl, your brother Ben is a very lively boy. You will have to hold him back some day, I fear."

"No, no, uncle, I shall always push him on. He likes to go ahead. I like to see him go—don't you?"

CHAPTER XIII.

THE ELDER FRANKLIN'S STORIES.

Peter Folger, Quaker, the grandfather of Benjamin Franklin, was one of those noblemen of Nature whose heart beat for humanity. He had been associated in the work of Thomas Mayhew, the Indian Apostle, who was the son of Thomas Mayhew, Governor of Martha's Vineyard. The younger Mayhew gathered an Indian church of some hundred or more members, and the Indians so much loved him that they remained true to him and their church during Philip's war.

What stories Abiah Franklin could have told, and doubtless did tell, of her old home at Nantucket!—stories of the true hearts of the pioneers, of people who loved others more than themselves, and not like the sea-rovers who at this time were making material for the Pirate's Own Book.

Josiah, too, had his stories of Old England and the conventicles, heroic tales of the beginning of the long struggle for freedom of opinion. Hard and rough were the stories of the Commonwealth, of Cromwell, Pym, and Sir Henry Vane, the younger.

There was one very pleasing old tale that haunted Boston at this time, of the Hebrew parable order, or after the manner of the German legend. Such stories were rare in those days of pirates, Indians, and ghosts, the latter of whom were supposed to make their homes in their graves and to come forth in their graveclothes, and to set the hearts of unquiet souls to beating, and like feet to flying with electrical swiftness before the days of electricity.

Governor Winthrop—the same who got lost in the Mystic woods, and came at night to an Indian hut in a tree and climbed into it, and was ordered out of it at a later hour when the squaw came home—took a very charitable view of life. He liked to reform wrongdoers by changing their hearts. Out of his large love for every one came this story of old Boston days.

We will listen to it by the Franklin fire in the candle shop. It was an early winter tale, and it will be a good warm place to hear it there.

"It is a cold night," said Josiah, "and Heaven pity those without fuel on a night like this! There are not overmany like Governor Winthrop in the world."

Abiah drew her chair up nearer to the great fire, for it made one chilly to hear the beginning of that story, but the end of it made the heart warm.

"It was in the early days of the colony," said Josiah, "and the woods in the winter were bare, and the fields were cold. There was a lack of wood on the Mystic near the town.

"A poor man lived there on the salt marsh with his family. He had had a hard time to raise enough for their support. A snowstorm came, and his fuel was spent, his hearth was cold, and there was nothing to burn.

" The great house of the Governor rose over the ice-bordered marshes. Near it were long sheds, and under them high piles of wood brought from the hills.

" The poor man had no wood, but after a little time smoke was seen coming out of his chimney.

" There came one day a man to the Governor, and said:

" Pardon me, Governor, I am loath in my heart to accuse any one, but in the interest of justice I have something which I must tell you.'

" ' Speak on, neighbor.'

" ' Some one has been stealing your wood.'

" ' It is a hard winter for the poor. Who has done this?'

" ' The man who lives on the marsh.'

" ' His crop was not large this year.'

" ' No, it failed.'

" ' He has a wife and children.'

" ' True, Governor.'

" ' He has always borne a good reputation.'

" ' True, Governor, and that makes the case more difficult.'

" ' Neighbor, don't speak of this thing to others, but send that man to me.'

" The man on the marsh came to the Governor's. His face was as white as snow. How he had suffered!

" ' Neighbor,' said the Governor, ' this is a cold winter.'

" ' It is, your Honor.'

" ' I hope that your family are comfortable.'

" ' No, your Honor; they have sometimes gone to bed supperless and cold.'

"'It hurts my conscience to know that. Have you any fuel?'

"'None, your Honor. My children have kept their bed for warmth.'

"'But I have a good woodpile. See the shed: there is more wood there than I can burn. I ought not to sit down by a comfortable fire night after night, while my neighbor's family is cold.'

"'I am glad that you are so well provided for, for you are a good man, and have a heart to feel for those in need.'

"'Neighbor, there is my woodpile. It is yours as well as mine. I would not feel warm if I were to sit down by my fire and remember that you and your wife and your children were cold. When you need any fuel, come to my woodpile and take all the wood that you want.'

"The man on the marsh went away, his head hanging down. I believe that there came into his heart the powerful resolution that he would never steal again, and we have no record that he ever did. The Governor's hope for him had made him another man.

"He came for the wood in his necessity one day. The Governor looked at him pleasantly.

"'Why did you not come to me before?'"

Josiah Franklin looked around on the group at the fireside, and opened the family Bible.

"Do you think that the Governor did right, Brother Ben?"

"Well, it isn't altogether clear to me."

"What do you think, Abiah?"

"Father would have done as he did. He hindered no one, but helped every one. He saw life on that side."

"Well, little Ben, what have you to say?"

"The Governor looked upon the heart, didn't he? He felt for the man. Would it not be better for all to look that way? The worth of life depends upon those we help, lift, and make, not in those we destroy. I like the old Governor, I do, and I am sorry that there are not many more like him. That seems like a Luke story, father. Read a story from Luke."

Josiah read a story from Luke.

There followed a long prayer, as usual. Then the children kissed their mother and Jenny and crept up to their chamber. The nine-o'clock bell had rung, and the streets were still. The watchman with his lantern went by, saying, "Nine o'clock, and all is well!" None of the family heard him say, "Ten o'clock, and all is well!" They were in slumberland after their hard, homely toil, and some of them may have been dreaming of the good old Governor, who followed literally the words of the Master who taught on the Mount of Beatitudes.

CHAPTER XIV.

THE TREASURE-FINDER.

LITTLE Benjamin once had the boy fever to go to sea. This fever was a kind of nervous epidemic among the boys of the time, a disease of the imagination as it were. Many boys had it in Boston; they disappeared, and the town crier called out something like this:

" Hear ye!

Hear ye!

Boy lost—lost—lost!

Who returns him will be rewarded."

He rang the bell as he cried. The crier's was the first bell that was rung in Boston.

But why did boys have this peculiar fever in Boston and other New England towns at this time? It was largely owing to the stories that were told them. Few things affect the imagination of a boy like a story. De Foe's Robinson Crusoe was the live story of the times. Sindbad the sailor was not unknown.

Old sailors used to meet by the Town Pump and spin wonderful " yarns," as story-telling of the sea was then described.

But there was one house in Boston that in itself was a story. It was made of brick, and rose over the town, at the

83

North End, in the "Faire Green Lane," now decaying Chatham
Street. In it lived Sir William Phips, or Phipps, the first
provincial Governor under the charter which he himself had
brought from England.

Sir William had been born poor, in Maine, and had made
his great fortune by an adventure on the sea.

The story of Sindbad the Sailor was hardly more than a
match for his, with its realities.

He was one of a family of twenty-six children; he had been
taught to read and write when nearly grown up; had come to
Boston as an adventurer, and had found a friend in a comely
and sympathetic widow, who helped to educate him, and to
whom he used to say:

"All in good time we will come to live in the brick house
in the Faire Green Lane."

A Boston boy like young Franklin, among the pots and
kettles of life, could not help recalling what this poor sailor
lad had done for himself when he saw the brick house loom-
ing over the bowery lane.

The candle shop at the Blue Ball, that general place for
story-telling by winter fires, when it was warm there and
the winds were cold outside, often heard this story, and such
stories as the Winthrop Silver Cup, which may still be seen;
of lively Anne Pollard, who was the first to leap on shore
here from the first boat load of pioneers as it came near the
shore at the North End, when the hills were covered with
blueberries; of old "sea dogs" and wonderful ships, like
Sir Francis Drake and the Golden Hynde, or "Sir Francis
and his shipload of gold," which ship returned to England one

day with chests of gold, but not with Sir Francis, whose body had been left in many fathoms of sea! Ben listened to these tales with wonder, with Jenny by his side, leaning on him.

What was the story of Sir William Phipps, that so haunted the minds of Boston boys and caused their pulses to beat and the sea fever to rise?

It was known in England as well as in America; it was a wonder tale over the sea, for it was associated with titled names. Uncle Ben knew it well, and told it picturesquely, with much moralizing.

Let us suppose it to be a cold winter's night, when the winds are abroad and the clouds fly over the moon. Josiah Franklin has played his violin, the family have sung " Martyrs "; the fire is falling down, and " people are going to meetin'," as a running of sparks among the soot was called, when such a thing happened in the back of the chimney.

Little Ben's imagination is hungry, and he asks for the twice-told tale of Sir William. He would be another Sir William himself some day.

By the dying coals Uncle Ben tells the story. What a story it was! No wonder that it made an inexperienced boy want to go to sea, and especially such boys as led an uneventful life in the ropewalk or in the candle shop!

Uncle Ben first told the incident of Sir William's promise to the widow who took him to her home when he was poor, that she should live in the brick house; and then he pictured the young sailor's wonderful voyages to fulfill this promise. He called the sailor the " Treasure-finder."

Let us snuggle down by the fire on this cold night in Bos-

7

ton town, beside little Ben and Jenny, and listen to the story.

Uncle Ben, mayhap, shakes his snuffbox, and says:

"That boy dreamed dreams in the daytime, but he was an honest man." Uncle Ben rang these words like a bell in his story.

"He was an honest man; but a man in this world must save or be a slave, and young William's mind went sailing far away from the New England coast, and a-sailing went he. What did he find? Wonders! Listen, and I will tell you.

"William Phips, or Phipps, went to the Spanish Main, and he began to hear a very marvelous story there. The sailors loitering in the ports loved to tell the legend of a certain Spanish treasure ship that had gone down in a storm, and they imagined themselves finding it and becoming rich. The legend seized upon the fancy of William the sailor and entered his dreams. It was only a vague fancy at first, but in the twilight of one burning day a cool island of palms appeared, and as it faded away a sailor who stood waching it said to him:

"'There is a sunken reef off this coast somewhere; we are steering for it, and I have been told that it was on that reef that the Spanish treasure ship went down. They say that ship had millions of gold on board. I wonder if anybody will ever find her?'

"William, the sailor, started. Why might not he find her? —William was an honest man.

"It was early evening at sea. The shadows of night fell on the Bahama Islands. The sea and the heavens seemed to mingle. The stars were in the water; the heavens were there. A stranger on the planet could not have told which was the sea and which was the sky.

" The sails were limp. There was a silence around. The ship seemed to move through some region of space. William Phipps sat by himself on the deck and dreamed. Many people dream, but it is of no use to dream unless you *do*.

" He seemed to see her again who had been the good angel of his life; he saw the gabled house in the bowery lane, and two faces looking out of the same window over Boston town.— William was honest.

" He dreamed that he himself was the captain of a ship. He saw himself in England, in the presence of the king. He is master of an expedition now, in his sea dream. He finds the sunken treasure ship. He is made rich by it, and he returns to Boston and buys the gabled house in the cool green lane by the sea. An honest man was Sir William. He was not *Sir* William then.

" He returned to Boston with his dream. William stayed in port for a time, and then prepared for a long voyage; but before he went away he obtained a promise from the widow that if she ever married any one it should be himself. There was nothing wrong in that.

" The ship owners saw that he had honor, and that they could trust him. He was advanced in the service, and he learned how to command a ship. ·

" He returned and married the widow, and went forth again to try to reap the harvest of the sea for her, carrying with him his dreams.—He was an honest man.

"William Phipps, the sailor, heard more and more in regard to the sunken treasure ship, and he went to England and applied to the king for ships and men to go in search of this mine of gold in the sea.

"Gold was then the royal want, and King James's heart was made right glad to hear the bold adventurer's story. The king put at his command ships and men, and young William Phipps—now Commander Phipps—went to the white reef in the blue Bahama Sea and searched the long sea wall for treasures faithfully, but in vain. He was compelled to return to England as empty-handed as when he went out.

"He heard of the great admiral, the Duke of Albemarle, and was introduced to him by William Penn. The duke heard his story, and furnished him with the means to continue the search for the golden ship in the coral reef.

"Ideals change into realities and will is way. Commander William bethought him of a new plan of gaining the needed intelligence. Might not some very old person know the place where the ship was wrecked? The thought was light. He found an old Indian on a near island who remembered the wreck, and who said he could pilot him to the very spot where the ship had gone down.

"Captain William's heart was light again. With the Indian on board he drifted to the rippling waters over the reef.

"Below was a coral world in a sea as clear as the sky. Out of it flying-fish leaped, and through it dolphins swam in pairs, and over it sargasso drifted like cloud shadows.

"Captain William looked down. Was it over these placid

waters that the storm had made wreckage many years ago?
Was it here that the exultant Spanish sailors had felt the shock
that turned joy into terror, and sent the ship reeling down,
with the spoils of Indian caciques, or of Incarial temples, or
of Andean treasures?

"The old Indian pointed to a sunken, ribbed wall in the
clear sea. The hearts of the sailors thrilled as they stood
there under the fiery noonday sky.

"Down went the divers—down!

"Up came one presently with the news—'The wreck is
there; we have found it!'

"'Search!' cried Captain William, with a glad wife and a
gable house in Boston town before his eyes. 'Down!'

"Another diver came up bringing a bag. It looked like a
salt bag.

"An officer took an axe and severed the bag. The salt
flew; the sailors threw up their hands with a cry—out of the
bag poured a glittering stream of gold!

"Captain William reeled. His visions were now taking
solid forms; they had created for him a new world.

"'Down! down!' he commanded.

"They broke open a bag which was like a crystal sack. It
was full of treasure, and in its folds was a goblet of gold.

"They shouted over the treasure and held up the golden cup
to the balmy air. It had doubtless belonged to a Spanish
don.

"More salt bags of gold! The deck was covered with gold!
It is related that one of the officers of the ship went mad at
the sight. But Captain William did not go mad as he sur-

veyed the work of the men in the vanishing twilight. He had been there in spirit before; he had expected something, and he was on familiar ground when he had found it. He had been a prophetic soul.

"He carried home the treasure to England, and, soul of honor that he was, he delivered every dollar's worth of it to the duke. His name filled England; and his honesty was a national surprise, though why it should have been we can not say. But didn't I tell you he was an honest man?

"The duke was made happy, and began to cast about how to bestow upon him a fitting reward.

"'What can I do for you?' asked his Highness.

"I have a wife in Boston town, over the sea. She is a good woman. Her faith in me made me all I am. She is the world to me, for she believed in me when no one else did.'

"'You are a fortunate man. We will send her the goblet of gold, and it shall be called the Albemarle Cup.'

"The imagination of Captain William Phipps must have kindled and glowed as he received the 'dead don's cup,' which in itself was a fortune.

"'And to you, for your honor and honesty, shall be given an ample fortune, and there shall be bestowed upon you the honor of knighthood. You shall be able to present to your good wife, whose faith has been so well bestowed, the Albemarle Cup, in the name of the Duke of Albemarle and of Sir William Phipps!'

"Captain William Phipps returned to Boston a baronet, with the Albemarle Cup. The widow that he had won was

Lady Phipps. New England never had a wonder tale like that.

"The Albemarle Cup! The fame of it filled Boston town. There it stood in massive gold, in Lady Phipps's simple parlor, among humbler decorations. How strange it looked to her as she saw it! Then must have arisen before her the boy from the Maine woods, one of twenty-six school-denied children; the ungainly young sailor with his hot temper and scars; the dreamer of golden dreams; the captain, the fortune-finder, the knight. Another link was soon added to this marvelous chain of events. The house of gables in the green lane was offered for sale. Sir William purchased it, and the Albemarle Cup was taken into it, amid furnishings worthy of a knight and lady.

"The two looked out of the upper window over Boston town.—He was an honest man."

After this many-time repeated declaration that Sir William was an honest man," he added: " A man must get a living somehow—he must get a living somehow; either he must save or be a slave."

Little Ben thought that he would like to earn a living in some such way as that. The brick house in the " Faire Green Lane " meant much to him after stories like those. He surely was almost as poor as Sir William was at his age. Could he turn his own dreams into gold, or into that which is better than gold?

"Jenny," he said, " I would like to be able to give a brick house in the Faire Green Lane to father and mother, and to you. Maybe I will some day. I will be true to my home!"

CHAPTER XV.

"HAVE I A CHANCE?"

BLESSED is he who lends good books to young people. There was such a man in Boston town named Adams, one hundred and ninety years ago. His influence still lives, for he lent such books to young Benjamin Franklin.

The boy was slowly learning what noble minds had done in the world; how they became immortal by leaving their thought and works behind them. His constant question was, What have I the chance or the opportunity to do? What can I do that will benefit others?

It was a November evening. The days were short; the night came on at six o'clock. These were the dark days of the year.

"There is to be a candle-light meeting in the South Church, and I must go," said Uncle Benjamin. "It will be pretty cold there to-night, Ben; you had better get the foot stove."

The foot stove was a tin or brass box in a wooden frame with a handle. It was filled with live coals, and was carried to the church by a handle, as one would carry a dinner pail.

Little Benjamin brought the stove out of a cupboard to the hearth, took out of it a pan, which he filled with hard coals and replaced it.

"Ben," said Uncle Ben, "you had better go along with us and carry the stove."

"I will go, too," said Josiah Franklin. "There is to be a lecture to-night on the book of Job. I always thought that that book is the greatest poem in all the world. Job arrived at a conclusion, and one that will stand. He tells us, since we can not know the first cause and the end, that we must be always ignorant of the deepest things of life, but that we must do just right in everything; and if we do that, everything which happens to us will be for our best good, and the very best thing that could happen whether we gain or lose, have or want. I may be a poor man, with my tallow dips, but I have always been determined to do just right. It may be that I will be blessed in my children—who knows? and then men may say of me, 'There was a man!'"

"'And he dwelt in the land of Uz,'" said Uncle Ben.

"Wait for me a few minutes while I get ready," said Josiah Franklin. "I will have to shave."

The prospect of a lecture in the old South Church on the philosophical patriarch who dwelt in the land of Uz, and led his flocks, and saw the planets come and go in their eternal march, on the open plains or through the branches of pastoral palms, was a very agreeable one to little Ben.

He thought.

"Uncle Benjamin," he said, "a man who writes a book like Job leaves his thoughts behind him. He does not die like other men; his life goes on."

"Yes, that is what some people call an objective life. I

call it a *projective* life. A man who builds men, or things, for the use of men, lives in the things he builds. He has immortality in this world. A man who builds a house leaves his thought in the form of the house he builds. If he make a road, he lives in the road; if he invent a useful thing, he lives in the invention. A man may live in a ship that he has caused to be constructed, or his mind may see the form of a church, a hall, or a temple, and he may so build after what he sees that he makes his thoughts creative, and he lives on in the things that he creates after he dies. It was so with the builders of cities, of the Pyramids. So Romulus—if there were such a man—lives in Rome, and Columbus in the lands that he discovered. The Pilgrim Fathers will always live in New England. Those who do things and make things leave behind them a life outside of themselves. I call such works a man's projected life."

Little Ben sat swinging the foot stove.

"He lives the longest in this world who invents the most useful things for others," continued Uncle Benjamin. "The thoughts of Copernicus, Galileo, and Newton changed the world. Those men can never die."

Little Ben swung the stove in his hand.

Suddenly he looked up, and we fancy him to have said:

"Uncle Benjamin, have *I* a chance?"

Jamie the Scotchman came into the house, jingling the door bell as he shut the door.

"Philosophizing?" said he.

"Little Ben here is inquiring in regard to his chance of doing something in the world—of living so as to leave his thoughts in creative forms behind. What do you think about it, Jamie?"

"Well, I don't know; it is a pretty hard case. Drumsticks will make a noise, so any man may make himself heard if he will. Certain it is Ben has no gifts; at least, I have never discerned any. There are no Attic bees buzzing around him, none that I have seen, unless there be such things up in the attic, which would not be likely in a new house like this."

Uncle Ben pitied the little boy, whose feelings he saw were hurt.

"Jamie, I have read much, and have made some observation, and life tells me that character, industry, and a determined purpose will do much for a man that has no special gifts. The Scriptures do not say that a man of gifts shall stand before kings, but that the man 'diligent in his business' shall do so. Ben here can rise with the best of the world, and if he has thoughts, he can project them. It is thinking that makes men work. He thinks.—Ben, you can do anything that any one else of your opportunities has ever done. There—I hate to see the boy discouraged."

"The fifteenth child among seventeen children would not seem likely to have a very broad outlook," said Jamie, "but it is good to encourage him; it is good to encourage anybody. He is one of the human family, like all the rest of us.—Are you going to the lecture? I will go along with you."

Josiah Franklin was now ready to go, and the party started. Josiah carried a lantern, and little Benjamin the foot stove with the coals. As they walked along they met other people with lanterns and foot stoves.

Uncle Benjamin felt hurt at what Jamie had said, so he proceeded to encourage the boy as they went along.

"If you could invent a stove that would warm the whole church, you would have a *projected* life, for example," said he.

"Have I a chance?" asked again the future inventor of the Franklin stove.

"Or if you could print something original that might live; or found a society to study science—something might come out of that; or could make some scheme for a better government of the people in these parts; but that would be too great for you. There I go!" ·

Uncle Benjamin stumbled. Little Ben helped him up.

They came to the South Church, where many lanterns, foot stoves, and tallow dips were gathered, and shadowy forms were moving to and fro.

Little Ben set down the stove in the pew. The lecture began. He heard the minister read the sublime passage of the ancient poem beginning, "Then the Lord answered Job out of the whirlwind, and said." He heard about the "morning stars singing together," the "sweet influences of Pleiades," and the question, "Canst thou bind the sea?"

The boy asked, "Have I a chance? have I a chance?" The discouraging words of Jamie the Scotchman hung over his mind like a cloud.

The influence of the coals led Josiah Franklin to slumber-land after his hard day's work. Little Ben saw his father nod and nod. But Uncle Benjamin was in the Orient with the minister, having a hard experience for the good of life with the patriarch Job.

"Have I a chance?" The boy shed tears. If he had not gifts, he knew that he had personality, but there was something stirring within him that led his thoughts to seek the good of others.

The nine-o'clock bell rang. The lecture was over.

"Good—wasn't it?" said Jamie the Scotchman as they went out of the church and looked down to the harbor glimmering under the moon and stars, and added:

"Ben, you will be sure to have one thing to spur you on to lead that 'projected life' your Uncle Benjamin tells about."

"What is that, sir?"

"A hard time, like Job—a mighty hard time."

"The true way to knowledge," said Uncle Benjamin encouragingly.

Uncle Benjamin felt a hand in his great mitten. It was little Ben's. The confidence touched his heart.

"Ben, you are as likely to have a projected life as anybody. A man rises by overcoming his defects. Strength comes in that way."

Little Ben went through the jingling door with a heart now heavy, now light. He set down the lantern, and climbed up to his bed under the roof.

He was soon in bed, the question, "Have I a chance?" still haunting him.

In summer there would be the sound of the wings of the swallows or purple swifts in the chimney at night as they became displaced from their nests. He would start up to listen to the whirring wings, then sink into slumber, to awake a blithe, light-hearted boy again.

All was silent now. He could not sleep. His fancy was too wide awake. Was Uncle Benjamin right, or Jamie the Scotchman? Had he a chance?

CHAPTER XVI

"A BOOK THAT INFLUENCED THE CHARACTER OF A MAN WHO LED HIS AGE."

"You must read good books," said Benjamin Franklin's godfather. "How sorry I am that I had to sell my pamphlets!"

Books have stamped their character on young men at the susceptible age and the turning points of life. But their influence for good or evil comes to receptive characters. "He is a genius," says Emerson, "who gives me back my own thoughts." The gospel says, "He that hath ears to hear, let him hear."

Abraham Lincoln would walk twenty miles to borrow a law book, and would sit down on a log by the wayside to study it on his return from such a journey. Horace Greeley says that when he was a boy he would go reading to a woodpile. "I would take a pine knot," he said, "put it on the back log, pile my books around me, and lie down and read all through the long winter evenings." He read the kind of books for which his soul hungered. He read to find in books what he himself wished to be. A true artist sees and hears only what he wishes to see and hear. An active, earnest, resolute soul reads only that which helps him fulfill the haunting purpose of his life. Almost every great man's books that were his companions in early years were pictures of what he most wished to be and to do.

How many men have had their spiritual life quickened by a hymn! How many by a single poem! Homer and Ossian filled the imagination of Napoleon. Plutarch's Lives has helped form the characters of a thousand heroes, and Emerson placed Plutarch next to the Bible in the rank of beneficent influences. We would say to every boy, Read Plutarch; read the best books first.

A few books well read would be an education. Let a boy read the Bible, Josephus, Plutarch's Lives, Rawlinson's, Hallam's, Macaulay's, Bancroft's, and Prescott's histories, Shakespeare, Tennyson, and Longfellow, and he would have a basis of knowledge of such substantial worth and moral and literary standard as to cause his intelligence to be respected everywhere and to become a power. Yet all these books could be purchased for twenty-five dollars, and the time that many waste in unprofitable reading for three years would be sufficient to master them.

"I am a part of all that I have met," says Tennyson, and a man becomes a part of all the books that color his mind and character. Ask a company of people what books they most sought in childhood, and you may have a mental photograph of each.

Benjamin Franklin says that his opinions and character were so greatly influenced by his reading Cotton Mather's Essays to do Good, that he owed to that book his rise in life. A boy, he says, should read that book with pen and note-book in hand.

Benjamin Franklin declared that it was in this book that he found the statements of the purposes in life that met his own views. "To do good," he said, was the true aim of existence, and the resolution became fixed in his soul to seek to make his life as beneficent as possible to all men. How to help somebody and to improve something became the dreams of his days and nights. "A high aim is curative," says Emerson. Franklin had some evil tendencies of nature and habit, but his purpose to live for the welfare of everybody and everything overcame them all in the end, and made him honestly confess his faults and try to make amends for his lapses. To do good was an impelling purpose that led him to the building of the little wharf, where boys might have firm footing whence to sail their boats, and it continued through many wiser experiences up to the magic bottle, in which was stored the revelation of that agent of the earth and skies that would prove the most beneficent of all new discoveries.

The book confirmed all that Uncle Benjamin had said. In it he saw what he should struggle to be: he put his resolution into this vision, and so took the first step on the ladder of life which was to give him a large view of human affairs.

He turned from the candle molds to Cotton Mather's strong pages, which few boys would care to read now, and from them, a little later, to Addison, and from both to talk with Jenny about what he would like to do and to become, and, like William Phips to the widow, he promised Jenny that they, too, should one day live in some "Faire Green Lane in Boston town." He would be true to his home—he and Jenny.

CHAPTER XVII.

BESIDES his instruction from encouraging Mr. Brownell and his Uncle Benjamin, little Benjamin Franklin had spent one year at school and several years of self-instruction under helps. His father needed him in the candle shop, and he could not give him a larger education with so many mouths to feed.

Young Ben did not like his occupation in the candle shop. He worked with his hands while his heart was absent, and his imagination was even farther away.

He had a brother John who had helped his father when a boy, who married and moved to Rhode Island to follow there his father's trade as a candle and soap maker. John's removal doubled the usefulness of little Ben among the candle molds and soap kettles. He saw how this kind of work would increase as he grew older; he longed for a different occupation, something that would satisfy his mental faculties and give him intellectual opportunities, and his dreams went sailing to the seas and lands where his brother Josiah had been. There were palms in his fancy, gayly plumed birds, tropical waters, and a free life under vertical suns—India, the Spanish Main, the ports of the Mediterranean. He talked so much of going to sea that his father saw that his shop was not the place for this large-brained boy with an inventive faculty.

"Ben," said Josiah Franklin one day, "this is no place for you—you are not balanced like other boys; your head is canted the *other* way. You'll be running off to sea some day, just as Josiah did. Come, let us go out into the town, and I will try to find another place for you. You will have to become an apprentice boy."

"Anything, father, but this dull work. I seem here to be giving all my time to nothing. Soap and candles are good and useful things, but people can make them who can do nothing else. I want a place that will give me a chance to work with my head. What is my head for?"

"I don't know, Ben; it will take time to answer that. You do seem to have good faculties, if you *are* my son. I would be glad to have you do the very best that you are capable of doing, and Heaven knows that I would give you an education if I were able. Come, let us go."

They went out into the streets of Boston town. The place then contained something more than two thousand houses, most of them built of timber and covered with cedar shingles; a few of them were stately edifices of brick and tiles. It had seven churches, and they were near the sign of the Blue Ball: King's Chapel, Brattle Street, the Old Quaker, the New North, the New South, the New Brick, and Christ Church. There was a free writing school on Cornhill, a school at the South End, and another writing school on Love Lane. Ben Franklin could not enter these simple school doors for the want of means. To gain the Franklin Medal, provided by legacy of Benjamin Franklin, is now the high ambition of every Boston Latin schoolboy. There were fortifications on Fort Hill and a powder house on the Common. There were inns, taverns, and ordinaries everywhere. Boston was a town of inns with queer names; Long Wharf was the seaway to the ships. Chatham Street now was then a fair green lane; Salem Street was a place of property people or people of "quality."

In King's Chapel was a state pew for the royal Governors. On the pulpit stood an hourglass in a frame of brass. The pillars were hung with escutcheons of the king.

Ben may have passed the old Latin School which at first was established at a place just east of King's Chapel. If so, he must have wished to be entered there as a pupil again. The school has distributed his medals now for several generations. He may have passed the old inns like the Blue Anchor Tavern, or the Royal Exchange, or the fire of 1711 may have wiped out some of these old historic buildings, and new ones to take their places may have been rising or have been but recently completed. The old Corner Bookstore was there, for it was built directly after the fire of 1711. It is the oldest brick building now standing in the city, and one of the few on which little Ben's eyes could have rested. A new town arose after the fire.

Josiah Franklin and little Ben visited the workshops of carpenters, turners, glaziers, and others, but, although they had a good time together in the study, the kind father could not find a place that suited his son. Ben did not like to be apprenticed to any of the tradesmen that he met.

He had a brother James, of a bright mind but of no very

amiable disposition, who was a printer. He had been to London to improve his trade, and on his return he became the one printer in the town.

One evening, between the violin and the Bible, Josiah Franklin suddenly said:

"Ben, you look here!"

"What, father?" asked the boy, starting.

"It all comes to me what you ought to do. You should become a printer."

"That I would like, father."

"Then the way is clear—let me apprentice you to James."

"Would he have me, father? We do not always get on well together. I want to learn the printer's trade; that would help me on to an education."

Josiah Franklin was now a happier man. Ben would have no more desire to go to sea. If he could become anything out of the ordinary, the printer's trade would be the open way.

He went to his son James and presented the matter. As a result, they drew up an indenture.

This indenture, which may be found in Franklin's principal biographies, was a very queer document, but follows the usual form of the times of George I. It was severe—a form by which a lad was practically sold into slavery, and yet it contained the demands that develop right conduct in life. Ben was not constituted to be an apprentice boy under these sharp conditions even to his own brother. But all began well. His mother, who worried lest he should follow the example of his brother Josiah, now had heart content. His father secured an apprentice, and probably had drawn up for him a like form of indenture.

Benjamin, too, was happy now. He saw that his new way of life led to somewhere—where? He would do his best to make it lead to the best in life. He started with a high resolve, which we are sorry he did not always fulfill in the letter, though the spirit of it never was lost.

His successor in the tallow shop does not seem to have been more happy than he. His name was Tinsley. There appeared in the New England Courant of 1722 the following queer advertisement, which we copy because it affords a picture of the times:

Ran away from his Master, Mr. Josiah Franklin, of Boston, Tallow-Chandler, on the first of this instant July, an Irish Man-servant, named William Tinsley, about 20 Years of Age, of a middle Stature, black Hair, lately cut off, somewhat fresh-coloured Countenance, a large lower Lip, of a mean Aspect, large Legs, and heavy in his Going. He had on, when he went away, a felt Hat, a white knit Cap, striped with red and blue, white Shirt, and neck-cloth, a brown coloured Jacket, almost new, a frieze Coat, of a dark Colour, grey yarn Stockings, leather Breeches, trimmed with black, and round to'd Shoes. Whoever shall apprehend the said runaway' Servant, and him safely convey to his above said Master, at the blue Ball, in Union street, Boston, shall have forty Shillings Reward, and all necessary Charges paid.

As this advertisement was continued for three successive weeks, we are at liberty to conclude that William Tinsley was not " apprehended."

Let the reader be glad that he did not live in those days. The best of all ages is now.

"And so you have begun life as a printer?" said Uncle Benjamin. "A printer's trade is one after my own heart. It develops thought. If I could have only kept my pamphlets until now, you would have printed the notes that I made. One of them says that what people want is not favors or patronage of any kind, but *justice*. Remember that, Ben. What the world wants is justice. You may become a printer in your own right some day."

"I want to become one, uncle. That is just what is in my heart. I can see success in my mind."

"But you can do it if you will. Everything goes down before 'I will!' The Alps fell before Hannibal. Have a deaf ear, Ben, toward all who say 'You *can't!*' Such men don't count with those in the march; they are stragglers. Don't you be laughed down by anybody. Hold your head high; there is just as much royal blood in your veins as there is in any king on earth. There is no royal blood but that which springs from true worth. I put that down in my documents years ago.

"Life is too short to stop to quarrel with any one by the way. If a man calls you a fool, you need not come out under your own signature and deny it. Your life should do that. I am quoting from my pamphlets again.

"If you meet old Mr. Calamity in your way, the kind of man who tells you that you have no ground of expectation, and that everything in the world is going to ruin, just whistle, and luck will come to you, my boy. I only wish that I had my documents—my pamphlets, I mean. I would have left them to you in my will. In the present state of society one must save or be a slave—that also I wrote down in my documents. It is a pity that it is so, but it is. Save what you can while you are young, and it will give your mind leisure to work when you are older. *That* was in my pamphlets. I hope that I may live to see you the best printer in the colonies."

The boy absorbed the spirit of these proverbial sayings. They were to his liking and bent of mind. But there came into his young face a shadow.

"Uncle Ben, I know what you say is true. I have listened to you; now I would like you to hear me. You saw the boys going to the Latin School this morning?"

"Yes, Ben."

"I can not go there."

"O Ben! that is hard," said Jenny, who was by his side.

"But you can go to school, Ben," said Uncle Benjamin.

"Where, uncle?"

"To life—and graduate there as well as any of them."

"I would like to study Latin."

"Well, what is to hinder you, Ben? One only needs to learn the alphabet to learn all that can be known through books. You know *that* now."

"I would like to learn French. Other boys can; I can not."

"The time will come when you can. The gates open before a purpose. You can study French later in life, and, it may be, make as good use of French as any of them."

" Why can not I do as other boys? "

" You can, Ben. You can so live that the Boston Latin School to which you can not go now will honor you some day."

" I would be sorry to see another boy feel as I have felt when I have seen the boys going to that school with happy faces to learn the things that I want to know. But father has done the best that he can for me."

" Yes, Ben, he has, and you only need to do the best that you can for yourself to graduate at the head of all in the school of life. I know how to feel for you, Ben. I have stood in shoes like yours many times. When you have done as I have told you, then think of me. The world may soon forget me. I want you so to live that it will not as soon forget you."

The cloud passed from the boy's face. Hope came to him, and he was merry again. He locked Jenny in his arms, whirled her around, and said:

" I am glad to hear the bells ring for other boys, even if I must go to my trade."

" I like the spirit of what you say," said Uncle Benjamin. " You have the blood of Peter Folger and of your Great-uncle Tom in your veins. Peter gave his heart to the needs of the Indians, and to toleration; your Great-uncle Tom started the subscription for the bells of Nottingham, and became a magistrate, and a just one. You may not be able to answer the bell of the Latin School, but if you are only true to the best that is in you, little Ben, you may make bells ring for joy. I can hear them now in my mind's ear. Don't laugh at your old uncle; you can do it, little Ben—can't he Jenny?"

"He just can—I can help him. Ben can do anything—he may make the Latin School bell ring for others yet—like Uncle Tom. He is the boy to do it, and I am the sister to help him to do it—ain't I, Uncle Benjamin?"

CHAPTER XVIII

LITTLE BEN'S ADVENTURES AS A POET.

THAT was a charmed life that little Ben Franklin led in the early days of his apprenticeship. He always thought of provincial Boston as his "beloved city." When he grew old, the Boston of his boyhood was to him a delightful dream.

He and his father were on excellent terms with each other. His father, though a very grave, pious man, whose delight was to go to the Old South Church with his large family, allowed little Ben to crack his jokes on him.

He was accustomed to say long graces at meals, at which the food was not overmuch, and the hungry children many. One day, after he had salted down a large quantity of meat in a barrel, he was surprised to hear Ben ask:

"Father, why don't you say grace over it now?"

"What do you mean, Ben?"

"Wouldn't it be saving of time to say grace now over the whole barrel of provisions, and then you could omit it at meals?"

But the strong member of the Old South Church had no such ideas of religious economy as revealed his son's mathematical mind.

The Franklin family must have presented a lively appearance at church in old Dr. Joseph Sewell's day. They heard some sound preaching there, and Dr. Sewell lived as he preached. He was offered the presidency of Harvard College, but honors were as bubbles to him, and he refused it for a position of less money and fame, but of more direct spiritual influence, and better in accord with the modest views of his ability. He began to preach in the Old South Church when Ben was seven years of age; he preached a sermon there on his eightieth birthday.

These were fine old times in Boston town. Some linen spinners came over from Londonderry, in Ireland, and they established a spinning school. They also brought with them the potato, which soon became a great luxury.

Josiah Franklin probably pastured his cows on the Common, and little Ben may often have sat down under the old elm by the frog pond and looked over the Charles River marshes, which were then where the Public Garden now is.

But the delight of the boy's life was still Uncle Benjamin, the poet. The two read and roamed together. Now Ben had a poetic vein in him, a small one probably inherited from his grandfather Folger, and it began to be active at this time.

There were terrible stories of pirates in the air. They kindled the boy's lively imagination; they represented the large subject of retributive justice, and he resolved to devote his poetic sense to one of these alarming characters.

There was a dreadful pirate by the name of Edward Teach, but commonly called " Blackbeard." He was born in Bristol, England. He became the terror of the Atlantic coast, and had many adventures off the Carolinas. He was at length captured and executed.

One day little Ben came to his brother James with a paper.

"James, I have been writing something, and I have come to read it to you."

"What?"

"Poetry."

"Like Uncle Ben's?"

"No; it is on Blackbeard."

James thought that a very interesting subject, and prepared to listen to his poet brother.

Little Ben unfolded the paper and began to read his lines, which were indeed heroic.

> "Come, all you jolly sailors,
>   You all so stout and brave!"

"Good!" said James.   "That starts off fine."
Ben continued:

> "Come, hearken and I'll tell you
>   What happened on the wave."

"Better yet—I like that.   Why, Uncle Ben could not excel that.   What next?"

> "Oh, 'tis of that bloody Blackbeard
>   I'm going now to tell,
> And as how, by gallant Maynard,
>   He soon was sent to *hell*,
> With a down, down, down, derry down!"

James lifted his hands at this refrain after the old English ballad style.

"Ben, I'll tell you what we'll do.   I'll print the verses for you, and you shall sell them on the street."

The poet Arion at his coronation at Corinth could not have

felt prouder than little Ben at that hour. He would be both a poet and bookseller, and his brother would be his publisher.

He may have cried on Boston street:

"Blackboard—broadside!" or something like that. It would have been honorable advertising.

His success as a poet was instantaneous. His poem sold well. Compliments fell upon him like a sun shower. He wrote another poem of like value, and it sold "prodigiously." He thought indeed he was a great poet, and had started out on Shakespeare's primrose way to fame and glory. Alas! how many under like circumstances have been deceived. He lived to call his ballads "wretched stuff." How many who thought they were poets have lived to take the same view of their work!

His second poem was called the Light-House Tragedy. It related to a recent event, and set the whole town to talking, and the admiration for the young poet was doubled.

In the midst of the great sale of his poems by himself, and of all the flatteries of the town, he went for approval to his father. The result was unexpected; the rain of sunshine changed into a winter storm indeed.

"Father, you have heard that I have become a poet?"

"Ha! ha! ha!" laughed Josiah, in his paper cap and leather breeches. "Like your Uncle Ben, my boy, and he amounted to nothing at all as a poet. A poet—my stars!"

"I thought that you looked upon Uncle Ben as the best man in all the world. The people love him. When he enters the Old South Church there is silence."

"That is all very true, my boy, but he lives between the

heavens and the earth, and can not get up to the one or down to the other. Poets are beggars, in some way or other. They live in garrets among the mice and bats. Their country is the imagination, and that is the next door to nowhere. You a poet! What puckers my face up—*so?*"

" But my poetry sells, father," looking into his father's droll face, his heart sinking.

" Your poetry! It sells, my boy, because you are a little shaver and appear to be smart, and also because your rhymes refer to events in which everybody is interested. But, my son, your poetry, as you call it, has no merit in itself. It is full of all kinds of errors. It is style that makes a poem live; yours has no style."

" But, father, many people do not think so."

" But they will. You will think so some day."

" But isn't there something good in it?"

" Nothing, Ben. You never was born to be a poet. You have the ability to earn a living, same as I have done. Poets don't have that kind of ability; they beg. There are not many men who can earn a living by selling their fancies, which is mostly moonshine."

This was unsympathetic. Ben looked at the soap kettles and candle molds and wondered if these things had not blinded his father's poetic perceptions. There was no Vale of Tempe here.

But Josiah Franklin had hard common sense. Little Ben's dreams of poetic fame came down from the skies at one arrow. That was a bitter hour.

" If I can not be a poet," he thought, " I can still be useful," and he reverted from heroic ballads to stern old Cotton Mather's Essays to do Good. The fated poet is always left a like resource.

Yet many people who have not become poets, but who have risen to be eminent men, have had poetic dreams in early life; they have had the poetic mind. A little poetry in one's composition is no common gift; it is a stamp of superiority in some direction. Josiah Franklin was a wise man, but his views of poetry as such were of a low standard. Poetry is the highest expression of life, the noblest exercise of the spiritual faculties.

So poor little Ben had soared to be laughed at again. But there was something out of the common stirring in him, and he would fly again some day. The victories of the vanquished are the brightest of all.

Franklin, after having been thus given over to the waste barrel by his father, now resolved to acquire a strong, correct, and impressive prose style of writing. He found Addison's Spectator one of the best of all examples of literary style, and he began to make it a study. In works of the imagination he read De Foe and Bunyan.

This good resolution was his second step up on the ladder of life.

Others were contributing to his brother James's paper, why should not he? But James, after the going out of the poetic meteor, might not be willing to consider his plain prose.

Benjamin Franklin has now written an article in plain prose, which he wishes to appear in his brother's paper. If it were accepted, he would have to put it into type himself, and probably to deliver the paper to its patrons. He is sixteen years old. He has become a vegetarian, and lives by himself, and seeks pleasure chiefly in books.

It is night. There are but few lamps in the Boston streets. With a manuscript hidden in his pocket Benjamin walks slyly toward the office of James Franklin, Printer, where all is dark and still. He looks around, tucks his manuscript suddenly under the office door, turns and runs. Oh, how he does glide away! Is he a genius or a fool? He wonders what his brother will say of the manuscript, when he reads it in the morning.

In the morning he went to his work.

Some friends of James came into the office.

"I have found something here this morning," said James, "that I think is good. It was tucked under the door. It seems to me uncommonly good. You must read it."

He handed it to one of his friends.

"That is the best article I have read for a long time," said one of the callers. "There is force in it. It goes like a song that whistles. It carries you. I advise you to use it. Everybody would read that and like it. I wonder who wrote it? You should find out. A person who can write like that should never be idle. He was born to write."

James handed it to another caller.

"There are brains in that ink. The piece flows out of life. Who do you think wrote it?"

"I have no idea," said James.—"Here, Ben, set it up. Here's nuts for you. If I knew who wrote it I would ask the writer to send in other articles."

Benjamin Franklin's Autobiography and Charles Dickens's
9

novels have had a sale equaled by a few books in the world. The two authors began their literary life in a like manner, by tucking their manuscripts under the editor's door at night and running away. They both came to wonder at themselves at finding themselves suddenly people of interest. Still, we could hardly say to the literary candidate, " Fling your article into the editor's room at night and run," though modesty, silence, and prudence are commendable in a beginner, and qualities that win.

What pen name did Ben Franklin sign to this interesting article? It was one that implies his purpose in life; you may read his biography in it—SILENCE DOGOOD.

The day after the name of Silence Dogood had attracted the attention of Boston town, Benjamin said to Jane, his sympathetic little sister:

" Jenny, let's go to walk this evening upon Beacon Hill. I have something to tell you."

They went out in the early twilight together, up the brow of the hill which the early settlers seem to have found a blackberry pasture, to the tree where they had gone with Uncle Benjamin on the showery, shining midsummer Sunday.

" Can you repeat what Uncle Benjamin said to us here, two years ago? " asked Ben.

" No; it was too long. You repeat it to me again and I will learn it."

" He said, ' More than wealth, or fame. or anything, is the power of the human heart, and that that power is developed in seeking the good of others.' Jenny. what did father say when he read the piece by Silence Dogood in the Courant? "

" He clapped his hand on his leather breeches so that they rattled; he did, Ben, and he exclaimed, ' That is a good one!' and he read the piece to mother, and she asked him who he supposed wrote it, and she shook her head, and he said, ' I wish that I knew.' "

" Would you like to know who wrote it, Jenny? "

" Yes. Do you know? "

" *I* wrote it. Jenny, you must not tell. I am writing another piece. James does not know. I tucked the manuscript under the door. I am going to put another one under the door at night."

" O Ben, Ben. you will be a great man yet, and I hope that I will live to see it. But why did you take the name of *Silence Dogood* " ?

" That carries out Uncle Ben's idea. It stands for seeking the good of others quietly. That name is what I would like to be."

" It is what you will be, Ben. Uncle would say that the Franklin heart is in that name. If you should ever become a big man, Ben, and I should come to see you when we are old, I will say, ' Silence Dogood, more than wealth, more than fame, and more than anything else, is the power of the human heart.' There, I have quoted it correctly now. Maybe the day will come. Maybe we will live to be old, and you will write things that everybody will read, and I will take care of father and mother while you go out into the world."

" Wherever I may go, and whatever I may become or fail to be, my heart will always be true to you, Jenny."

" And I will do all I can for father and mother; I will be

your heart to them, so that you may give your time to your pen. Every one in a family should seek to do for the family what others lack or are not able to do. You can write; I can not, but, Ben, I can love."

She walked about the wild rose bushes, where the red-winged blackbirds were singing.

"O Ben," she continued, "I am so glad that you wrote that piece, and that father liked it so well! I would not have been more glad had you received a present from a king. Maybe you will receive a present from a king some day, if you write as well as that."

"You will keep the secret, Jenny?"

"Yes, Ben, I will look for the paper to-morrow. How glad Uncle Ben would be if he knew it. Why, Ben, that name, Silence Dogood, is a piece in itself. It is a picture of your heart. You are just like Uncle Ben, Silence Dogood."

The name of Silence Dogood became famous in Boston town. Jenny obtained Ben's permission to tell Uncle Benjamin the great secret, and Uncle Benjamin's heart was so delighted that he went to his room and told the secret "to the Lord."

The three hearts were now very, very happy for a time. Jenny was growing up a beautiful girl, and her thoughts were much given to her hard-working parents and to laughed-at, laughing little Ben.

When Uncle Benjamin had heard of Ben's failure as a poet and success as Silence Dogood, he took him down to Long Wharf again.

"I am an old man," he said. "But here I have a lesson

for you. If you are conscious that you have any gift, even in small degree, never let the world laugh it away. See ' that no man take thy crown,' the Scripture says. Every one who has contributed anything to the progress of the world has been laughed at. Stick a pin in thee, Ben.

"Now, Ben, you may not have the poet's imagination or art, but if you have the poetical mind do not be laughed out of an attempt to express it. You may not become a poet; I do not think that you ever will. Perhaps you will write proverbs, and proverbs are a kind of poems. I am going to reprove Brother Josiah for what he has said. He has given over your education to me, and it is my duty to develop you after your own gifts.

"Let us go back to the shop. I want to have a talk with Josiah; but, before we leave, I have a short word to say to you.

"Hoi, Ben, hoi!—I don't know what makes me repeat these words; they are not swear words, Ben, but they come to me when my feelings are awakened.

"It is hard, hard for one to see what he wants to be and to be kept back. I wanted to be a philosopher and a poet. Don't you laugh, Ben. I did; I wanted to be both, and I was so poor that I was obliged to write my thoughts on the margin of the leaves of my pamphlets, which I sold to come to teach you. Ben, Ben, listen: I can never be a philosopher or a poet, but you may. Don't laugh, Ben. Don't let any one laugh you out of your best ideas, Ben. You may. The world will never read what I wrote. They may read what you will write, and if you follow my ideas and they are read, you will be content. Hoi, Ben, hoi!"

They went to the candle shop.

"Josiah, you do wrong to try to suppress Ben's gift at rhyme. A man without poetry in his soul amounts to no more than a chopping block. The world just hammers itself on him, and that is all. You would not make Ben a dunce!"

"No, brother, no; but a goose is not a nightingale, and the world will not stop to listen if she mounts a tree and attempts to sing."

"No, Brother Josiah, but a goose that would like to sing like a nightingale would be no common goose; she would find better pasture than other geese. Small gifts are to be prized. 'A little diamond is worth a mountain of glass,' as the proverb says."

"Well, if you must write poetry, don't publish it until it is called for."

"Well, Brother Josiah, your advice will do for me, for I am an old man; but I must teach Ben never to be laughed out of any good idea that may come to him. Is not that right, brother?"

"Yes, Uncle Ben. But you can't make a hen soar to the skies like an eagle. If you are not a poet, you have a perfect character, and that is why I leave the training of Ben to you. If you can make a man of him, the world will be better for him; and if you can make something else of him besides a poet out of his poetical gift, I shall be very glad. Your poetry has not helped you in life, has it, Benjamin?"

"I don't know. You think it is that that has made me a burden to you."

Josiah looked his brother in the face.

"A burden? No, brother. One of the greatest joys of my life

was to have you come here, and it will be the greatest blessing to my life if you can make the life of little Ben a blessing to the world. I am not much of a musician, but I like to sound the fiddle, and if you have any poetic light, let it shine—but as a tallow dip, like my fiddling. You are right, brother, in teaching little Ben never to be laughed down. I don't blame any one for crying his goods if he has anything to sell. But if he has not, he had better be content to warm his hands by his own fire."

"Brother Josiah, listen to me. Little Ben here has something to sell.—Hoi, Ben, hoi! you listen.—There have thoughts come to me that I know did not rise out of the dust. I have been too poor to publish them. You may laugh at me, and call me a poor philosopher and say that my philosophy has kept me poor. But Benjamin here is going to give my thoughts to the world, and the things that I put into my pamphlets are going to live. It was not you that gave Ben to me: it was Heaven. A veil hangs over us in this world, and if a man does good in his heart, the hand behind that veil moves all the events of his life for good.

"Don't laugh at us, Josiah; we are weaving together thoughts that will feed the world. That we are.—Hoi, Ben, hoi!"

"Well, Brother, your faith makes you a happy old man. I hope that you will be able to make something of Ben, and that he may do credit to your good name. It may be so. Faith sees.

"I love to see you go into the South Church, Brother. As soon as your face appears all the people look very happy, and sit still. The children all sit still. The tithingman stands still; he has nothing to do for a time.

"It is something, Brother Ben, to be able to cast such an influence as that—something that money can not buy. I am sorry if I have hurt your feelings. Heaven be praised for such men as you are, Brother Ben! I hope that I may live to see all that you see by faith. I think I may, Brother Ben. 'Men do not gather grapes of thorns, or figs of thistles,' but they do gather grapes of grapes and figs of figs. I hope that Ben will be the book of your life, and make up for the pamphlets. It would be a good book for men to read."

"Hoi, Ben, hoi!" said the old man, "I can see that it will."

One Sunday, after church, in summer, Uncle Ben the poet and Silence Dogood went down on Long Wharf to enjoy the breezes from the sea. Uncle Ben was glad to learn more of the literary successes of Silence Dogood.

"To fail in poetry is to succeed in prose," said the fine old man. "But much that we call prose is poetry: rhymes are only childish jingles. The greatest poetry in the world is written without rhyme. It is the magic spirit and the magic words that make true poetry. The book of Job, in my opinion, is the greatest poetry ever written. Poetry is not made, it exists; and one who is prepared to receive it catches it as it flows. Ben, you are going to succeed in prose. You are going to become a ready writer. Study Addison more and more."

"Uncle Ben, do you not think that it is the hardest thing in life for one to be told that he can not do what he most wants to do?"

" Yes, Ben, that is the hardest thing in life. It is a cruel thing to crush any one in his highest hope and expectation."

" Was Solomon a poet?   Are the Proverbs poetry?"

" Yes, yes.   The book of Proverbs is a thousand poems."

" Then, Uncle Ben, I may be a poet yet.   That kind of little poems come to me."

" Ha! ha! ha!"

A voice rang out behind them.

It was Jamie the Scotchman.

" Well, Ben, it is good to fly high. I infer that you expect to become a proverb poet, after the manner of Solomon. The people here will all be quoting you some day. It may be that you will be quoted in England and France. Ha! ha! ha! What good times," he added, " you two have together— dreaming! Well, it costs nothing to dream. There is no toll demanded of him who travels in the clouds. Move along, young Solomon, and let me sit down on the sea wall beside you. When you write a book of proverb poetry I hope I'll be living to read it. One don't make a silk purse out of a sow's ear— there's a proverb for you!—nor gather wisdom except by experi- ence—there's another; and some folks do not get wisdom even from experience." He looked suspiciously toward Uncle Ben.

" Experience keeps a dear school," said Uncle Ben in a kindly way.

" And some people can learn of no other," added Silence Dogood.

" And some folks not even there," said Jamie the Scotch- man.

The loons came semicircling along the sea wall, their necks aslant, and uttering cries in a mocking tone.

" Well, I declare, it makes the loons laugh—and no wonder! " said Jamie the Scotchman. He lighted his pipe, whose bowl was a piece of corncob, and whiffed away in silence for a time, holding up one knee in his clasped hands.

Silence Dogood surveyed his surroundings, which were ship cargoes.

" The empty bags do not stand up," he said.

" Well, what do you infer from that? " asked Jamie.

Silence Dogood did not answer, but the thought in his mind was evident. It was simply this: that, come what would in life, he would not fail. He put his hand on Uncle Benjamin's shoulder, for who does not long to reach out his hand toward the fire in the cold, and to touch the form that entemples the most sympathetic heart? He dreamed there on the sea wall, where the loons seemed to laugh, and his dreams came true. Every attainment in life is first a dream.

Silence Dogood, dream on! Add intelligence to intelligence, virtue to virtue, benevolence to benevolence, faith to faith, for so ascends the ladder of life.

Uncle Benjamin was right. Let no man be laughed out of ideals that are true, because they do not reach their development at once.

Many young people stand in the situation in which we find young Franklin now. Many older people do in their early work. England laughed at Boswell, but he came to be held as the prince of biographers, and his methods as the true manner of picturing life and making the past live in letters.

People with a purpose who have been laughed at are many in the history of the world. From Romulus and the builders of the walls of Jerusalem to Columbus, ridicule makes a long record, and the world does not seem to grow wiser by its mistakes. Even Edison, in our own day, was ridiculed, when a youth, for his abstractions, and his efforts were ignored by scientists.

Two generations ago a jeering company of people, uttering comical jests under the cover of their hands, went down to a place on the banks of the Hudson to see, as they said, "a crazy man attempt to move a boat by steam." They returned with large eyes and free lips. *That boat moved.*

In the early part of the century a young Scotchman named Carlyle laid before the greatest of English scholars and critics a manuscript entitled Sartor Resartus. The great critic read the manuscript and pronounced it "the stupidest stuff that he ever set eyes on." He laughed at a manuscript that became one of the literary masterpieces of the century. A like experience had Milton, when he once said that he would write a poem that should be the glory of his country.

A young graduate named Longfellow wrote poems that came to him amid the woods and fields, and published them in newspapers and magazines, and gathered them into a book. The book fell into the hands of one then held to be supreme as a literary judge—Edgar Allen Poe. It was laughed at in ink that made the literary world laugh. The poet Longfellow's bust now holds an ideal place in Westminster Abbey, between the memorials of Dryden and Chaucer, and at the foot of the tombs of England's kings.

Keats was laughed at; Wordsworth was deemed a fool.

A number of disdainful doctors met on October 16, 1846, in the amphitheater of the Massachusetts General Hospital in Boston, to see a young medical student try to demonstrate that a patient upon whom a surgical operation was to be performed could be rendered insensible to pain. The sufferer was brought into the clear light. The young student touched his face with an unknown liquid whose strange odor filled the room. He was in oblivion. The knives cut and the blood flowed, and he knew it not. Pain was thus banished from the room of surgery. That young medical student and dentist was Dr. W. T. G. Morton, whose monument may be seen in the Boston Public Garden, and in whose honor the semicentennial of the discovery of anæsthesia has but recently been celebrated.

"So, with a few romantic boys and crazy girls you expect to see the world converted," said a wise New York journal less than a century ago, as the first missionaries began to sail away. But the song still arose over the sea—

> "In the desert let me labor,
> On the mountain let me till"—

until there came a missionary jubilee, whose anthems were repeated from land to land until they encircled the earth.

When Browning first published Sordello, the poem met with common ridicule. Even Alfred Tennyson is said to have remarked that "there were but two lines in it that he could understand, and they were both untrue." The first line of the poem was, "Who will, *may* hear Sordello's story told"; and the last line of the poem was, "Who would, *has* heard Sordello's story told." Yet the poem is ranked now among the intellectual achievements of the century in the analysis of one of the deeper problems of life.

Samuel F. B. Morse was laughed at. McCormick, whose invention reaps the fields of the world, was ridiculed by the London Times, "the Thunderer." "If that crazy Wheelwright calls again, do not admit him," said a British consul to his servant, of one who wished to make new ports and a new commerce for South America, and whose plans are about to harness the Andes with railways. William Wheelwright's memory lives in grateful statues now.

Columbus was not only laughed at by the Council of Salamanca, but was jeered at by the children in the streets, as he journeyed from town to town holding his orphan boy by the hand. He wandered in the visions of God and the stars, and he came to say, after the shouts of homage that greeted him as the viceroy of isles, "God made me the messenger of the new heavens and new earth, and told me where to find them!"

Burton, in his Anatomy of Melancholy, presents a picture of the unfortunate condition of many lives of whom the world expected nothing, and for whom it had only the smile of incredulity when in them the Godlike purpose appeared. He says:

"Hannibal had but one eye; Appius Claudius and Timoleon were blind, as were John, King of Bohemia, and Tiresais the prophet. Homer was blind; yet who, saith Tully, made more accurate, lively, or better descriptions with both his eyes! Democritus was blind, yet, as Laertius writes of him, he saw more than all Greece besides. . . . Æsop was crooked, Socrates purblind, Democritus withered, Seneca lean and harsh, ugly to behold; yet show me so many flourishing wits, such divine spirits. Horace, a little, blear-eyed, contemptible fellow, yet who so sententious and wise? Marcilius Ficinus, Faber Stapulensis, a couple of dwarfs; Melanchthon, a short, hard-favored man, yet of incomparable parts of all three; Galba the emperor was crook-backed; Epictetus, lame; the great Alexander a little man of stature; Augustus Cæsar, of the same pitch; Agesilaus, *despicabili forma,* one of the most deformed princes that Egypt ever had, was yet, in wisdom and knowledge, far beyond his predecessors."

Why do I call your attention to these struggles in this place in association of an incident of a failure in life that was ridiculed?

It has been my lot, in a somewhat active life in the city of Boston for twenty-five years, to meet every day an inspiring name that all the world knows, and that stands for what right resolution, the overcoming of besetting sins in youth, and persevering energy may accomplish against the ridicule of the world. There have been many books written having that name as a title—FRANKLIN.

I have almost daily passed the solemn, pyramidal monument in the old Granary Burying Ground, between the Tremont Building and Park Street Church, that bears the names of the Franklin family, in which the parents have found eternal honor by the achievements of their son.

As I pass the Boston City Hall there appears the Franklin statue.

As I face the Old South Church and its ancient neighborhood I am in the place of the traditions of the birth of Benjamin Franklin and of his baptism. It may be that I will return by the way of Franklin Street, or visit the Franklin School, or go to the Mechanics' Building, where I may see the primitive printing press at which Franklin worked, and which was buried in the earth at Newport, Rhode Island, at the time of the Revolutionary War.

If I go to the Public Library, I may find there two original portraits of Franklin and a Franklin gallery, and a picture of him once owned by Thomas Jefferson.

If I go to the Memorial Hall at Harvard College, I will there see another portrait of the philosopher in the grand gallery of noble men. Or I may go to Boston's wide pleasure ground, the Franklin Park, by an electric car made possible by the discoveries of Franklin.

Nearly all of Franklin's early efforts were laughed at, but he would not be laughed down. Time is the friend of every true purpose.

Boys with a purpose, face the future, do good in silence, and trust. You will find some Uncle Benjamin and sister Jenny to hold you by the hand. Be in dead earnest, and face the future, and forward march! The captains of industry and the leaders of every achievement say, " Guide right! Turn to the right, and advance! "

CHAPTER XIX.

THESE were fine old times, but they were English times; English ideas ruled Boston town. There was little liberty of opinion or of the press in those days. The Franklins belonged to a few families who hoped to find in the province freedom of thought. James Franklin was a testy man, but he breathed free air, and one day in his paper, the Courant, he published the following simple sentences, the like of which any one might print anywhere in the civilized world to-day: "If Almighty God will have Canada subdued without the assistance of those miserable Savages, in whom we have too much confidence, we shall be glad that there will be no sacrifices offered up to the Devil upon the occasion; God alone will have all the glory."

What had he done? He had protested against the use of Indians in the war then being waged against Canada.

He was arrested on a charge that the article in which this paragraph appeared, and some like articles, "contained reflections of a very high nature." He was sentenced to a month's imprisonment and forbidden to publish the paper. So James went to jail, and he left the management of the paper to Benjamin.

This incident gives us a remarkable view of the times. But Boston was only following the English law and custom.

The printing office was now carried on in Benjamin's name. Little Ben grew and flourished, until his popularity excited the envy of his brother. One day they quarreled, and James, almost in the spirit of Cain, struck his bright, enterprising apprentice. Benjamin had a proud heart. He would not stand a blow from James without a protest. What was he to do?

He resolved to leave the office of his brother James forever. He did so, and tried to secure work elsewhere. His brother's influence prevented him from doing this. His resentment against his brother grew more bitter, and blinded him to all besides. This was conduct unworthy of a young philosopher. In his resentment he does not seem to have regarded the feelings of his good father, or the heart of his mother that would ache and find relief in tears at night, nor even of Jenny, whom he loved. He took a sloop for New York, and bade good-by to no one. The sail dipped down the harbor, and the three hills of Boston faded from his view.

He was now on the ocean, and out in the world alone. We are sorry to say that he faced life with such a deep resentment toward his brother in his heart. He afterward came to regard his going away in this manner as one of the mistakes of his life which he would wish to correct. His better heart came back again, true to his home.

He was not popular in Boston in his last days there. New influences had come into his life. He had loved argument and disputation, and there is a subtile manner of discussion called the " Socratic method," which he had found in Xenophon,

10

in which one confuses an opponent by asking questions and never making direct assertions himself, but using the subjunctive mood. It is an art of entanglement. The boy had delighted in "twisting people all up," and making them contradict themselves after a perversion of the manner described by Xenophon in his Life of Socrates.

As religion and politics formed the principal subjects of these discussions, and he liked to take the unpopular view in order to throw his mental antagonist, he had fallen into disfavor, to which disesteem his brother's charges against him had added. These things made Jenny's heart ache, but she never ceased to believe in Ben.

Few boys ever left the city in provincial times with less promise of any great future, so far as public opinion is concerned. But, notwithstanding these errors of judgment, he still carried with him a purpose of being a benefactor, and his dream was to help the world. The star of this purpose ever shone before him in the deserts of his wanderings.

But how was he to succeed, after thus following his own personal feeling in matters like these? By correcting his own errors as soon as he saw them, and never repeating them again. This he did; he openly acknowledged his faults, and tried to make amends for them. He who confesses his errors, and seeks to retrieve them, has a heart and purpose that the public will love. But it is a higher and nobler life not to fall into such errors.

This was about the year 1723. A curious incident happened on the voyage to New York. Young Franklin had become a vegetarian—that is, he had been convinced that it was wrong to kill animals for food, and wrong to eat flesh of any kind.

The ship became becalmed, and the sailors betook themselves to fishing. Franklin loved to argue still, notwithstanding his unhappy experiences.

" Fishing is murder," said he. " Why should these inhabitants of the sea be deprived of their lives and opportunities of enjoyment? They have never done any one harm, and they live the lives for which Nature made them. They have the same right to liberty that they have to life."

This indicated a true heart. But when the steward began to cook the fish that the sailors had caught, the frying of them did have a savory smell.

Young Franklin now began to be tempted from theory by appetite. How could he get over his principles and share the meal with the sailors? The cook seized a large fish to prepare it for the frying-pan. As he cut off its head and opened him he found in him a little fish.

" So you eat fish," said Franklin, addressing the prize; " then why may I not eat *you?* " He did so, and from this time left off his vegetarian habits, which habits, like his aspiration to be a poet, did credit to his heart.

His argument in this case had no force. The fish had not a moral nature, and because an animal or reptile without such a nature should eat other animals or reptiles would furnish no reason why a being governed by laws outside of himself should do the same.

October found him in New York, a Dutch town of less than ten thousand inhabitants. He was about eighteen years of age. New York then had little in common with the city of to-day. Its streets were marked by gable ends and cobble stones. Franklin applied for work to a printer there, and the latter commended him to go to Philadelphia. He followed the advice, going by sea, friendless and forlorn, with only a few shillings in his pocket.

He helped row the boat across the Delaware. He offered the boatman his fare.

"No," said the boatman, "I ought to take nothing; you helped row."

Franklin had just one silver dollar and a shilling in copper coin. He insisted that the ferryman should take the coin. He said of this liberal sense of honor afterward that one is "sometimes more generous when he has little money than when he has plenty."

Philadelphia, the city of Penn, now rose before him, and he entered it a friendless lad, whom none knew and few could have noticed. Would any one then have dreamed that he would one day become the governor of the province?

Benjamin Franklin had now found the world indeed, and his brother James had lost the greatest apprentice that the world ever had. Both were blind. Each had needed that early training that develops the spiritual powers, and makes it a delight to say "No" to all the lower passions of human nature.

Josiah and Abiah Franklin had had great hopes of little Ben. The boy had a large brain and a tender heart. From their point of view they had trained him well. They had sent him to the Old South Church and had made him the subject of their daily prayers. In fact, these good people had done their best to make him a " steady boy," according to their light. The education of the inner life was like a sealed book to them. But they were yet people upon whom a larger light was breaking. The poor old soap and candle maker went on with his business at the Blue Ball with a heavy heart.

" Gone, gone," said Jamie the Scotchman. " He'll find proverbs enough on his way of life. This is a hard world, but he has a heart to return to the right. I pity good Abiah Franklin, but we often have to trust where we can not see."

CHAPTER XX.

LAUGHED AT AGAIN.

Franklin's first day in Philadelphia is well known to the world. He has related it in Addisonian English, and it has been read almost as widely as the adventures of Robinson Crusoe or Bunyan's Pilgrim's Progress.

We must give a part of the narrative here in his own language, for a merry girl is about to laugh at the Boston boy as she sees him pass, and he will cause this lovely girl to laugh with him many times in his rising career and in different spirit from that on the occasion when she first beheld him, the awkward and comical-looking boy wandering he knew not where on the street.

Let us follow him through his own narrative until he meets the eyes of Deborah Read, a fair lass of eighteen.

On his arrival at Philadelphia, he tells us, he was in his working dress; his best clothes were to come by sea. He was covered with dirt; his pockets were filled with shirts and stockings. He was unacquainted with a single soul in the place, and knew not where to seek for a lodging. Fatigued with walking, rowing, and having passed the night without sleep, he was extremely hungry, and all his money consisted of a Dutch dollar and about a shilling's worth of coppers, which latter he gave to the boatman for his passage.

He walked toward the top of the street, looking eagerly on both sides, till he came to Market Street, where he met with a child with a loaf of bread. Often he had made his dinner on dry bread. He inquired of the child where he had bought the bread, and went straight to the baker's shop which the latter pointed out to him. He asked for some biscuits, expecting to find such as they had in Boston; but they made, it seems, none of that sort in Philadelphia. He then asked for a threepenny loaf. They made no loaves of that price. Finding himself ignorant of the prices as well as of the different kinds of bread, he desired the baker to let him have threepenny worth of bread of some kind or other. The baker gave him three large rolls. He was surprised at receiving so much; he took them, however, and having no room in his pockets, he walked on with a roll under each arm, eating the third. In this manner he went through Market Street to Fourth Street, and passed the house of Mr. Read, the father of his future wife. The girl was standing at the door, observed him, and thought with reason that he made a very singular and grotesque appearance, and laughed merrily. We repeat the many-times-told tale in nearly his own words.

So here we find our young adventurer laughed at again. We can fancy the young girl standing on her father's doorsteps on that mellow autumn day. There comes up the street a lad with two rolls of bread under his arm, and eating a third roll, his pockets full of the simpler necessities of clothing, which must have made him look like a ragman; everything about him was queer and seemingly wrong. She may have seen that he was just from the boat, and a traveler, but when did ever a traveler look so entirely out of his senses as this one did?

Never mind, Ben Franklin. You will one day stand in Versailles in the velvet robes of state, and the French king will give you his portrait framed in four hundred and eight diamonds.

"I then turned the corner," he continues, "and went through Chestnut Street, eating my roll all the way; and having made this round, I found myself again on Market Street Wharf, near the boat in which I arrived. I stepped into it to take a draught of river water, and finding myself satisfied with my first roll, I gave the other two to a woman and her child who had come down the river with us in the boat and was waiting to continue her journey. Thus refreshed, I regained the street, which was now full of well-dressed people, all going the same way. I joined them, and was thus led to a large Quakers' meeting-house near the market-place. I sat down with the rest, and, after looking round me for some time, hearing nothing said, and being drowsy from my last night's labor and want of rest, I fell into a sound sleep. In this state I continued till the assembly dispersed, when one of the congregation had the goodness to wake me. This was consequently the first house I entered or in which I slept at Philadelphia.

"I began again to walk along the streets by the riverside, and, looking attentively in the face of every one I met with, I at length perceived a young Quaker whose countenance pleased me. I accosted him, and begged him to inform me where a stranger might find a lodging. We were then near the sign of the Three Mariners. 'They receive travelers here,' said he, 'but it is not a house that bears a good character. If you will go with me I will show you a better one.' He conducted me to the Crooked Billet, in Water Street. There I ordered something for dinner, and during my meal a number of curious questions were put to me, my youth and appearance exciting the suspicion of my being a young runaway. After dinner my drowsiness returned, and I threw myself upon a bed without taking off my clothes, and slept till six o'clock in the evening, when I was called to supper. I afterward went to bed at a very early hour, and did not awake till the next morning.

"As soon as I got up I put myself in as decent a trim as I could, and went to the house of Andrew Bradford, the printer. I found his father in the shop, whom I had seen at New York. Having traveled on horseback, he had arrived at Philadelphia before me. He introduced me to his son, who received me with civility and gave me some breakfast, but told me he had no occasion at present for a journeyman, having lately procured one. He added that there was another printer newly settled in the town, of the name of Keimer, who might perhaps employ me, and that in case of refusal I should be welcome to lodge at his house. He would give me a little work now and then till something better should be found.

" The old man offered to introduce me to the new printer. When we were at his house, 'Neighbor,' said he, 'I bring you a young man in the printing business; perhaps you may have need of his services.'

" Keimer asked me some questions, put a composing stick

in my hand to see how I could work, and then said that at present he had nothing for me to do, but that he should soon be able to employ me. At the same time taking old Bradford for an inhabitant of the town well disposed toward him, he communicated his project to him and the prospect he had of success. Bradford was careful not to discover that he was the father of the other printer; and from what Keimer had said, that he hoped shortly to be in possession of the greater part of the business of the town, led him, by artful questions and by starting some difficulties, to disclose all his views, what his hopes were founded upon, and how he intended to proceed. I was present and heard it all. I instantly saw that one of the two was a cunning old fox and the other a perfect novice. Bradford left me with Keimer, who was strangely surprised when I informed him who the old man was.

"I found Keimer's printing materials to consist of an old, damaged press and a small font of worn-out English letters, with which he himself was at work upon an elegy upon Aquilla Rose, an ingenious young man and of excellent character, highly esteemed in the town, Secretary to the Assembly and a very tolerable poet. Keimer also made verses, but they were indifferent ones. He could not be said to write in verse, for his method was to set the lines as they followed from his muse; and as he worked without copy, had but one set of letter cases, and as the elegy would occupy all his types, it was impossible for any one to assist him. I endeavored to put his press in order, which he had not yet used, and of which indeed he understood nothing: and, having promised to come and work off his elegy as soon as it should be ready,

I returned to the house of Bradford, who gave me some trifles to do for the present, for which I had my board and lodging.

"In a few days Keimer sent for me to print off his elegy. He had now procured another set of letter cases, and had a pamphlet to reprint, upon which he set me to work.

"The two Philadelphia printers appeared destitute of every qualification necessary in their profession. Bradford had not been brought up to it, and was very illiterate. Keimer, though he understood a little of the business, was merely a compositor, and wholly incapable of working at press. He had been one of the French prophets, and knew how to imitate their supernatural agitations. At the time of our first acquaintance he professed no particular religion, but a little of all upon occasion. He was totally ignorant of the world, and a great knave at heart, as I had afterward an opportunity of experiencing.

"Keimer could not endure that, working with him, I should lodge at Bradford's. He had indeed a house, but it was unfurnished, so that he could not take me in. He procured me a lodging at Mr. Read's, his landlord, whom I have already mentioned. My trunk and effects being now arrived, I thought of making, in the eyes of Miss Read, a more respectable appearance than when chance exhibited me to her view, eating my roll and wandering in the streets.

"From this period I began to contract acquaintance with such young people as were fond of reading, and spent my evenings with them agreeably, while at the same time I gained money by my industry, and, thanks to my frugality, lived contentedly. I thus forgot Boston as much as possible, and wished every one to be ignorant of the place of my residence, except my friend Collins, to whom I wrote, and who kept my secret.

" An accident, however, happened which sent me home much sooner than I proposed. I had a brother-in-law, of the name of Robert Holmes, master of a trading sloop from Boston to Delaware. Being at Newcastle, forty miles below Philadelphia, he heard of me, and wrote to inform me of the chagrin which my sudden departure from Boston had occasioned my parents, and of the affection which they still entertained for me, assuring me that, if I would return, everything should be adjusted to my satisfaction; and he was very pressing in his entreaties. I answered his letter, thanked him for his advice, and explained the reasons which had induced me to quit Boston with such force and clearness that he was convinced I had been less to blame than he had imagined.

" Sir William Keith, Governor of the province, was at Newcastle at the time. Captain Holmes, being by chance in his company when he received my letter, took occasion to speak of me and showed it to him. The Governor read it, and appeared surprised when he learned of my age. He thought me, he said, a young man of very promising talents, and that of consequence I ought to be encouraged; that there were at Philadelphia none but very ignorant printers, and that if I were to set up for myself he had no doubt of my success; that, for his own part, he would procure me all the public business, and would render me every other service in his power. My brother-in-law related all this to me afterward at Boston, but I knew nothing of it at the time. When, one day, Keimer and I being at work together near the window, we saw the Governor and another gentleman, Colonel French, of Newcastle, handsomely dressed, cross the street and make directly for our house. We heard them at the door, and Keimer, believing it to be a visit to himself, went immediately down; but the Governor inquired for me, came upstairs, and, with a condescension and politeness to which I had not at all been accustomed, paid me many compliments, desired to be acquainted with me, obligingly reproached me for not having made myself known to him on my arrival in the town, and wished me to accompany him to a tavern, where he and Colonel French were going to have some excellent Madeira wine.

"I was, I confess, somewhat surprised, and Keimer appeared thunderstruck. I went, however, with the Governor and the colonel to a tavern at the corner of Third Street, where he proposed to me to establish a printing house. He set forth the probabilities of success, and himself and Colonel French assured me that I should have their protection and influence in obtaining the printing of the public papers of both governments; and as I appeared to doubt whether my father would assist me in this enterprise, Sir William said that he would give me a letter to him, in which he would represent the advantages of the scheme in a light which he had no doubt would determine him. It was thus concluded that I should return to Boston by the first vessel with the letter of recommendation from the Governor to my father. Meanwhile the project was to be kept secret, and I continued to work for Keimer as before.

"The Governor sent every now and then to invite me to

dine with him. I considered this a very great honor, and I was the more sensible of it as he conversed with me in the most affable, familiar, and friendly manner imaginable.

"Toward the end of April, 1724, a small vessel was ready to sail for Boston. I took leave of Keimer upon the pretext of going to see my parents. The Governor gave me a long letter, in which he said many flattering things of me to my father, and strongly recommended the project of my settling at Philadelphia as a thing which could not fail to make my fortune."

What is there prophetic of a great life in this homely narrative? Read over again the incident of the three rolls, one of which he ate, and two of which he gave to the poor woman and her child who needed them more than he. All his money on that day was one silver dollar. In that incident we see the heart and the persistent purpose to do good. He had made mistakes, but the resolution that he had made on reading Cotton Mather's meaty book was unshaken. He would correct his errors and yield to his better nature, and this purpose to help others would grow, and so he would overcome evil with good.

He who helps one helps two. The poor woman may never have been heard of in public, except in this story, but that act of sharing the rolls, with one for the little child, made Ben Franklin a larger man. "The purpose of life is to grow."

Benjamin Franklin is now a seed in the wind, but he is a good seed in the wind—good at heart, with a right purpose. The stream of life is turned aside, but it will flow true again toward the great ocean of that which is broadest and best.

For this little Jenny at home is hoping, and Abiah Franklin praying, and Josiah Franklin keeping silence in regard to his family affairs.

These were hard days for Uncle Benjamin and his philosophy, and for Jenny and her human faith.

LONDON AND A LONG SWIM.

WHAT kind of a man was Governor Sir William Keith? There are not many such, but one such may be found in almost every large community. He desired popularity, and he loved to please every one. He was constantly promising what he was not able to fulfill. He had a lively imagination, and he liked to think what he would do if he could for every bright person he met; and these things which he would like to do he promised, and his promises often ended in disapponitment. It delighted him to see faces light up with hope. Did he intend to deceive? No. He had a heart to bless the whole world. He was for a time a very popular Governor, but he who had given away expectations that but disappointed so many hearts was at last disappointed in all his expectations. He was greatly pleased with young Benjamin Franklin when he first met him, just as he had been with many other promising young men. He liked a young man who had the hope of the future in his face. This young printer who had entertained Boston under the name of Silence Dogood won his heart on a further acquaintance, and so he used to invite him to his home. He there showed him how essential a good printer would be to the province; how such a young man as he would make a fortune;

and he urged him to go back to his father in Boston and borrow money for such an enterprise. He gave him a long letter of commendation to his father, a droll missive indeed to carry to clear-sighted, long-headed Josiah Franklin.

With this grand letter and twenty-five pounds in silver in his pocket and a gold watch besides, and his vision full of rainbows, he returned to the Puritan town. He went to the printing office, which was again under the charge of his brother James. He was finely dressed, and as he had come back with such flattering prospects he had a grain of vanity.

He entered James's office. The latter looked at him with wide eyes, then turned from him coldly.

But Silence Dogood was not to be chilled. The printers flocked around him with wonder, as though he had been a returning Sindbad, and he began to relate to them his adventures in Philadelphia. James heard him with envy, doubtful of the land "where rocs flew away with elephants." But when Benjamin showed the men his watch, and finally shared with them a silver dollar in hospitalities, he fancied that his brother had come there to insult him, and he felt more bitterly toward him than ever before. Benjamin had much to learn in life. He and his brother, notwithstanding their good Quaker-born mother, had not learned the secret of the harmony of Abraham and Lot.

But one of these lessons of life our elated printer was to learn, and at once.

He returned to his home at the Blue Ball. His parents had not heard from him since he went away some seven months before, and they, though grieved at his conduct, received him joyfully. There was always an open door in Abiah Folger's heart.

11

The Quaker blood of good Peter Folger never ceased to course warm in her veins.

Ben told his marvelous story. After the literary adventures of Silence Dogood in Boston, his parents could believe much, but when he came to tell of his intimacy with Sir William Keith, Governor of the Province of Pennsylvania, successor to the great William Penn, they knew not what to think. Either Sir William must be a singular man, or they must have underrated the ability of young Silence Dogood.

"This is great news indeed. But what proof do you bring of your good fortune, my son?" asked the level-headed Josiah, lifting his spectacles upon his forehead and giving his son a searching look.

Young Benjamin took from his pocket the letter of Sir William and laid it before his father. It indeed had the viceroyal seal of the province.

His father put down his spectacles from his forehead, and his wife Abiah drew up her chair beside him, and he read the letter to himself and then reviewed it aloud.

The letter told him what a wonderfully promising young man Benjamin was; how well he was adapted to become the printer of the province, and how he only needed a loan wherewith to begin business to make a fortune.

Josiah Franklin could not doubt the genuineness of the letter. He sat thinking, drumming on a soap shelf.

"But why, my boy, if you are so able and so much needed does not Governor Keith lend you the money himself?"

Ben sat silent. Not all the arts of the Socratic method could suggest any answer to this question.

"I am glad that you have an influential patron," said Josiah, "but to a man of hard sense it would seem very strange that he should not advance the money himself to help one so likely to become so useful to the province to begin business. People are seldom offered something for nothing in this world, and why this man has made himself your patron I can not see, even through my spectacles."

"He wishes, father, to make me a printer for the advancement of the province."

"Then why, my son, should not a governor of a rich province himself provide you with means to become a printer for the advancement of the province?"

Socrates himself could not have answered this question.

"Did you tell him that your father was an honest, hard-working soap boiler and candle maker?"

"No," said the young man.

"Benjamin, I have a large family, and I am unable to lend you the money that the Governor requests. But even if I had the money I should hesitate to let you have it for such a purpose. You are too young to start in business, and your character is not settled. That troubles me, Ben. Your character is not settled. You have made some bad mistakes already. You went away without bidding your mother good-by, and now return to me with a letter from the Governor of Pennsylvania who asks me to loan you money to set you up in business, because you are so agreeable and promising. O Ben, Ben, did you not think that I had more sense than that?"

Josiah lifted his spectacles up to his forehead, and looked

his finely dressed son fully in the face. The pride of the latter began to shrink. He saw himself as he was.

But Abiah pleaded for her large-brained boy—Abiah, whose heart was always open, in whom lived Peter Folger still. Jenny had but one thing to say. It was, " Ben, don't go back, don't go back."

" I will tell you what I will do," said Josiah. " I will write a letter to Governor Keith, telling him the plain truth of my circumstances. That is just right. If when you are twenty years of age you will have saved a part of the money to begin business, I will do what I can for you."

With this letter Silence Dogood returned to Philadelphia in humiliation. We think it was this Silence Dogood who wrote the oft-quoted proverb, " A good kick out of doors is worth all the rich uncles in the world."

Young Franklin presented his father's letter to Governor Keith.

" Your father is too prudent," said the latter. " He says that you are too young and unsettled for business. Some people are thirty years old at eighteen. It is not years that are to be considered in this case, but fitness for work. I will start you in business myself."

Silence Dogood rejoiced. Here was a man who was " better than a father "—the " best man in all the world," he thought.

" Make out an inventory of the things that you need to begin the business of a printer, and I will send to London for them."

Benjamin did so, an inventory to the amount of one hundred pounds. He brought it to the Governor, who greatly surprised him by a suggestion.

"Perhaps," said Sir William, "you would like to go to London and get the machinery yourself. I would give you a letter of credit."

Was it raining gold?

"I would like to go to London," answered the young printer.

"Then I will provide for your journey. You shall go with Captain Annis." This captain sailed yearly from Philadelphia to London.

Waiting the sailing of the ship months passed away. Governor Keith entertained the young printer at his home. The sailing time came. Franklin went to the office of the Governor to receive the letter of credit and promised letters of introduction.

"All in good time, my boy," said the Governor's clerk, "but the Governor is busy and can not see you now. If you will call on Wednesday you will receive the letters."

Young Franklin called at the office on the day appointed.

"All in good time, my boy," said the clerk. "The Governor has not had time to fix them up and get them ready. They will be sent to you on board the ship with the Governor's mail."

So Franklin went on board the ship. As the Governor's mail came on board he asked the captain to let him see the letters, but the latter told him that he must wait until the ship got under way.

Out at sea the Governor's letters were shown to him. There

were several directed to people "in the care of Benjamin Franklin." He supposed these contained notes of introduction and the letter of credit, so he passed happily over the sea.

He reached London December 24, 1724. He rushed into the grand old city bearing the letters directed in his care. He took the one deemed most important to the office of the gentleman to whom it was directed. "This letter is from Governor Keith, of the Province of Pennsylvania," said Franklin.

"I know of no such person," said the man. The latter opened the letter. "Oh, I see," said he, "it is from one Riddleson. I have found him out to be a rascal, an exile, and refuse to entertain any communication from him."

Franklin's face fell. His heart turned heavy. He went out wondering. "Was his father's advice sound, after all?"

The rest of the letters that had been directed in his care were not written by Governor Keith, but by people in the province to their friends, of which he had been made a postboy. There were in the mail no letters of introduction from Governor Keith to any one, and no letter of credit.

He found himself alone in London, that great wilderness of homes. Of Keith's conduct he thus speaks in his autobiography :

"What shall we think of a Governor playing such pitiful tricks, and imposing so grossly upon a poor ignorant boy? It was a habit he had acquired; he wished to please everybody, and having little to give, he gave expectations. He was otherwise an ingenuous, sensible man, a pretty good writer, and a good Governor for the people, though not for his constituents, the Proprietaries, whose instructions he sometimes disregarded.

Several of our best laws were of his planning, and passed during his administration."

He found work as a journeyman printer in London, and we are sorry to say lived like most journeymen printers there. But Silence Dogood had to make himself useful even among these unsettled people. He instituted new ways of business and life of advantage to journeymen printers, and so kept the chain of his purpose lengthening.

There was a series of curious incidents that happened during the last part of this year of residence in London that came near changing his career. It was in 1726; he was about twenty years old. He had always loved the water, to be on it and in it, and he became an expert swimmer when he was a lad in Boston town.

He had led a temperate life among the London apprentices, and had kept his physical strength unimpaired. He drank water while they drank beer. They laughed at him, but he was able to carry up stairs a heavier case of type than any of them. They called him the " American water-drinker," but there came a day when he performed a feat that became the admiration of the young London printers. He loved companionship, and had many intimate friends, and among them there was one Wygate, who went swimming with him, probably in the Thames, and whom he taught to swim in two lessons.

One day Wygate invited him to go into the country with him and some of his friends. They had a merry time and returned by water. After they had embarked from Chelsea, a suburb which was then some four and a half miles from St. Paul's Cathedral, Wygate said to him:

"Franklin, you are a water boy; let us see how well you can swim."

Franklin knew his strength and skill. He took off his clothing and leaped into the river, and probably performed all the old feats that one can do in the water.

His dexterity delighted the party, but it soon won their applause.

He swam a mile.

"Come on board!" shouted they. "Are you going to swim back to London?"

"Yes," came a voice as if from a fish in the bright, sunny water:

He swam two miles.

The wonder of the party grew.

Three miles.

They cheered.

Four miles to Blackfriars Bridge. Such a thing had never been known among the apprentice lads. The swim brought young Franklin immediate fame among these apprentices, and it spread and filled London.

Sir William Wyndham, once Chancellor of the Exchequer, heard of this exploit, and desired to see him. He had two sons who were about to travel, to whom he wished Franklin to teach swimming. But the two boys were detained in another place, and Franklin never met them. It was proposed to Franklin that he open a swimming school.

But while he was favorable to such agreeable employment, there occurred one of those incidents that seem providential.

He met one day at this shifting period Mr. Denham, the up-

"ARE YOU GOING TO SWIM BACK TO LONDON?"

right merchant, whose integrity came to honor his profession
and Philadelphia. This man had failed in business at Bristol,
and had left England under a cloud. But he had an honest
soul and purpose, and he resolved to pay every dollar that he
owed. To this end he put all the energies of his life into
his business. He went to America to make a fortune, and he
made it. He then returned to Bristol, which he had left in
sorrow and humiliation.

He gave a banquet, and invited to it all the merchants and
people whom he owed. They responded to the unexpected in-
vitation, and wondered what would happen. When they had
seated themselves at the table, and the time to serve the meal
came, the dinner plates were lifted, and each one found before
him the full amount of the money due to him. The banquet of
honor made the name of the merchant famous.

Mr. Denham was a friend to men in need of good influences.
He saw Franklin's need of advice, and he said to him:

"My young friend, you should return to Philadelphia. It
is the place of opportunity."

"But I have not the means."

"I have the means for you. I am about to return to America with a cargo of merchandise. You must go back with me.
Your place in life is there."

Should he go?

It was early summer. He went out on London Bridge one
night. It grew dark late. But at last there gleamed in the
dark water the lights of London like stars. Many voices filled
the air as the boats passed by. The nine o'clock bells rang.
It may be that he heard the Bow bells ring, the bells that said,

"Come back! come back! come back!" to young Dick Whittington when he was running away from his place in life. If so, he must have been reminded of all that this man accomplished by heeding the voice of the bells, and of how King Henry had said, after all his benefactions, "Did ever a prince have such a subject?"

He must have thought of Uncle Tom and the bells of Nottingham on this clear night of lovely airs and out-of-door merriments. Over the great city towered St. Paul's under the rising moon. Afar was the Abbey, with the dust of kings.

Then he thought of Uncle Benjamin's pamphlets. It seemed useless for one to look for books in this great city of London.

Franklin never saw ghosts, except such as arise out of conscience into the eye of the mind. But the old man's form and his counsels now came into the view of the imagination. His old Boston home came back to his dreams; Jenny came back to him, and the face of the young woman whom he had learned to love in Philadelphia.

He resolved to return. America was his land, and he must build with her builders. He sailed for America with his good adviser, the honest merchant, July 21, 1726, and left noblemen's sons to learn to swim in the manner that he himself had mastered the water.

Did he ever see Governor Keith again? Yes. After his return to Philadelphia he met there upon the street one who was becoming a discredited man. The latter recognized him, but his face turned into confusion. He did not bow; nor did Franklin. It was Governor Keith. This Governor Please-Everybody died in London after years of poverty, at the age of eighty.

Silence Dogood may have thought of his father's raised spectacles when he met Sir William that day on the street, and when they did not wish to recognize each other, or of Jenny's words, " Ben, don't go back."

He had learned some hard lessons from the book of life, and he would henceforth be true to the most unselfish counsels on earth—the heart and voice of home.

CHAPTER XXII

A PENNY ROLL WITH HONOR.—JENNY'S SPINNING-WHEEL.

BENJAMIN became a printer again. By the influence of friends he opened in Philadelphia an office in part his own.

Benjamin Franklin had no Froebel education. The great apostle of the education of the spiritual faculties had not yet appeared, and even Pestalozzi, the founder of common schools for character education, could not have been known to him. But when a boy he had grasped the idea that was to be evolved by these two philosophers, that the end of education is character, and that right habits become fixed or automatic, thus virtue must be added to virtue, intelligence to intelligence, benevolence to benevolence, faith to faith.

One day, when he was very poor, there came into his printing office a bustling man.

"See here, my boy, I have a piece for you; there's ginger in it, and it will make a stir. You will get well paid for giving it to the public; all Philadelphia will read it."

"I am glad to get something to give the paper life," said Franklin. "I will read the article as soon as I have time to spare."

"I will call to-morrow," said the man. "It is running water that makes things grow. That article will prove very interesting reading to many people, and it will do them good. It is a needed rebuke. You'll say so when you read it."

Franklin at this time did a great part of the work in the office himself, and he was very busy that day. At last he found time to take up the article. He hoped to find it one that would add to the circulation of the paper. He found that it was written in a revengeful spirit, that it was full of detraction and ridicule, that it would answer no good purpose, that it would awaken animosities and engender bitter feelings and strife. But if used it would be read, laughed at, increase the sale of the paper, and secure him the reputation of publishing a *smart* paper.

Should he publish an article whose influence would be harmful to the public for the sake of money and notoriety?

He here began in himself as an editor that process of moral education which tends to make fixed habits of thought, judgment, and life. He resolved *not* to print the article.

But the author of it would laugh at him—might call him puritanic; would probably say that he did not know when he was " well off "; that he stood in his own light; that he had not the courage to rebuke private evils.

The young printer had the courage to rebuke wrong, but this article was a sting—a revengeful attempt to make one a laughing stock. It had no good motive. But it haunted him. He turned the question of his duty over and over in his mind.

Night came, and he had not the money to purchase a supper or to secure a bed. Should he not print the lively article, and make for himself better fare on the morrow?

No. Manhood is more than money, worth more than

wealth. He went to the baker's and bought a twopenny roll; he ate it in his office, and then lay down on the floor of his office and went to sleep.

The boy's sleep was sweet. He had decided the matter in his own heart, and had given himself a first lesson in what we would to-day call the new education. In this case it was an editorial education.

It was a lovely winter morning. There was joy in all Nature; the air was clear and keen; the Schuylkill rippled bright in the glory of the sun. He rose before the sun, and went to his work with a clear conscience, but probably dreading the anger of the patron when he should give him his decision.

When the baker's shop opened he may have bought another twopenny roll. He certainly sat down and ate one, with a dipper of water.

In the later hours of the morning the door opened, and the patron came in with a beaming face.

" Have you read it? "

" Yes, I have read the article, sir."

" Won't that be a good one? What did you think of it? "

" That I ought not to use it."

" Why? " asked the man, greatly astonished.

" I can not be sure that it would not do injustice to the person whom you have attacked. There are always two sides to a case. I myself would not like to be publicly ridiculed in that manner. Detraction leads to detraction, and hatred begets hate."

" But you must have money, my Boston lad. Have you thought of that? " was the suggestion.

Franklin drew himself up in the strength and resolution of young manhood, and made the following answer, which we give, as we think, almost in his very words:

"I am sorry to say, sir, that I think the article is scurrilous and defamatory. But I have been at a loss, on account of my poverty, whether to reject it or not. I therefore put it to this issue. At night, when my work was done, I bought a two-penny loaf, on which I supped heartily, and then wrapping myself in my greatcoat slept very soundly on the floor until morning, when another loaf and a mug of water afforded a pleasant breakfast. Now, sir, since I can live very comfortably in this manner, why should I prostitute my press to personal hatred or party passion for a more luxurious living?"

This experience may be regarded as temporizing, but it was inward education in the right direction, a step that led upward. It shows the trend of the way, the end of which is the "path of the just, that leads more and more unto the perfect day."

A young man who was willing to eat a twopenny roll and to sleep on the floor of his pressroom for a principle, had in him the power that lifts life, and that sustains it when lifted. He who puts self under himself for the sake of justice has in him the gravitation of the skies. Uncle Ben's counsels were beginning to live in him. Jenny's girl's faith was budding in his heart, and it would one day bloom. He was turning to the right now, and he would advance. There are periods in some people's lives when they do not write often to their best friends; such a one had just passed with Ben. During the Governor Keith misadventures he had not written home often, as the reader may well imagine. But now that he had come back to Philadelphia and was prosperous, the memory of loving Jenny began to steal back into his heart.

He had heard that Jenny, now at sweet sixteen, was famous for her beauty. He may have been jealous of her, we do not know; but he was apprehensive that she might become vain, and he regarded modesty, even at his early age of twenty-one or twenty-two, as a thing very becoming a blooming girl.

One day he wrote to her, "Jenny, I am going to send you a present by the next ship to Boston town."

The promise filled the girl's heart with delight. Her faith in him had never failed, nor had her love for him changed.

What would the present be?

She went to her mother to help her solve this riddle.

"Perhaps it will be a ring," she said. "I would rather have that from Ben than any other thing."

"But he would not send a ring by ship," said her mother, "but by the post chaise."

"True, mother; it can not be that. It may be a spinet. I think it is a spinet. He knows how we have delighted in father's violin. He might like to send me a harp, but what is a spinet but a harp in a box?"

"I think it may be that, Jenny. He would send a spinet by ship, and he knows how much we all love music."

"Yes, and he must see how many girls are adding the music of the spinet to their accomplishments."

"Wouldn't a spinet be rather out of place in a candle shop?" asked the mother.

"Not out of place in the parlor of a candle shop," said Jenny with dignity.

"Do you think that you could learn to play the spinet, Jenny?"

"I would, if Ben were to send me one. I have been true to Ben all along. I have never given him up. He may get out of place in life, but he is sure to get back again. A true heart always does. I am sure that it is a spinet that he will send. I dreamed," she added, "that I heard a humming sound in the air something like a harp. I dreamed it in the morning, and morning dreams come true."

"A humming sound," said Josiah Franklin, who had come within hearing; "there are some things besides spinets that make humming sounds, and Ben must know how poor we are. I am glad that his heart is turning home again, after his *scattering* adventures with the Governor. It is not every one who goes to sea without a rudder that gets back to port again."

Jenny dreamed daily of the coming ship and present. The ship came in, and one evening at dark an old sailor knocked at the door. He presently came in and announced that they had a "boxed-up" thing for one Jane Franklin on board the ship. Should he send it by the cartman to the house?

"Yes, yes!" cried Jenny. "Now I know it is a spinet I heard humming—I told you about it, mother."

The girl awaited the arrival of the gift with a flushed cheek and a beating heart. It came at last, and was brought in by candlelight.

It was indeed a "boxed-up" thing.

The family gathered around it—the father and mother, the boys and the girls.

12

Josiah Franklin broke open the box with his great claw hammer, which might have pleased an Ajax.

"O Jenny!" he exclaimed, "that will make a humming indeed. Ben has not lost his wits yet—or he has found them again."

"What is it? What is it, father?"

"The most sensible thing in all the world. See there, it is a spinning-wheel!"

Jane's heart sank within her. Her dreams vanished into the air—the delights of the return of Sindbad the Sailor were not to be hers yet. The boys giggled. She covered her face with her hands to hide her confusion and to gain heart.

"I don't care," she said at last, choking. "I think Ben is real good, and I will *forgive him*. I can spin. The wheel is a beauty."

The gift was accompanied by a letter. In it Benjamin told her that he had heard that she had been much praised for her beauty, but that it was industry and modesty that most merited commendation in a young girl. The counsel was as homely as much of that that Uncle Benjamin used to give little Benjamin, but she choked down her feelings.

"Benjamin was thinking of you as well as of me when he sent me that present," she said to her mother. "I will make music with the wheel, and the humming will make us all happy. I think that Ben is real good—and a spinet would have been out of place here. I will write him a beautiful letter in return, and will not tell him how I had hoped for a spinet. It is all better as it is. That is best which will do the most good."

If Franklin sent a practical spinning-wheel to Jenny when she was a girl, with much advice in which there was no poetry, such a sense of homely duties soon passed away. He came to send her beautiful presents of fabrics, " black and purple gowns," wearing apparel of elegant texture, and ribbons. When he became rich it was his delight to make happy the home of Jane Mecom—his poetic, true-hearted sister " Jenny," whose heart had beat to his in every step of his advancing life.

She became the mother of a large family of children, and when one of them ran away and went to sea she took all the blame of it to herself, and thought that if she had made his home pleasanter for him he would not have left it. In her self-blame she wrote to her brother to confess how she had failed in her duty toward the boy. Franklin read her heart, and wrote to her that the boy was wholly to blame, which could hardly have been comforting. Jenny would rather have been to blame herself. There was but little wrong in this world in her eyes, except herself.

She saw the world through her own heart.

CHAPTER XXIII

MR. CALAMITY.

THERE was a fine, busy old gentleman that young Franklin met about the time that he opened his printing office, whose course it will be interesting to follow. Almost every young man sometimes meets a man of this type and character. He is certain to be found, as are any of the deterrent people in the Pilgrim's Progress. He is the man in whose eyes there is ruin lurking in every form of prosperity, who sees only the dark side of things—to whom, as we now say, everything "is going to the dogs."

We will call him Mr. Calamity, for that name represents what he had come to be as a prophet.*

One day young Franklin heard behind him the tap, tap, tap of a cane. It was a time when Philadelphia was beginning to rise, and promised unparalleled prosperity. The cane stopped with a heavy sound.

"What—what is this I hear?" said Mr. Calamity. "You are starting a printing office, they say. I am sorry, sorry."

"Why are you sorry, sir?" asked the young printer.

---

* The old gentleman who suggests this character was named Mickle or Mikle.

"Oh, you are a smart, capable young man, one who in the right place would succeed in life. I hate to see you throw yourself away."

"But is not this the right place?"

"What, Philadelphia?"

"Yes, it is growing."

"That shows how people are deceived. Haven't you any eyes?"

"Yes, yes."

"But what were they made for? Can't you see what is coming?"

"A great prosperity, sir."

"Oh, my young man, how you are deceived, and how feather-headed people have deceived you! Don't you know that this show of prosperity is all delusion; that people of level heads are calling in their bills, and that this is a hard time for creditors? The age of finery has gone, and the age of rags has come. Rags, sir, rags!"

"No, sir, no. I thought the people were getting out of debt. See how many people are building."

"They are building to be ready for the crash—they do not know what else to do with their money; calamity is coming."

"But how do you know, sir?"

"Know? It requires but little wit to know. I can feel it in my head. The times are not what they used to be. William Penn is dead, and none of his descendants are equal to him. Look at the Quakers, see how worldly they are becoming! Most people are living beyond their means! Property," he added, "is all on the decline. In a few years you will see people moving away from here. You will hear that the Proprietors have failed. Young man, don't go into business here. Let me tell you a secret, though I hate to do it, as your heart is bent upon setting up the printing business here; listen to me now—the whole province is going to fail. Before us is bankruptcy. Do you hear it—that awful, awful word *bankruptcy?* The Governor himself, in my opinion, is on the way to bankruptcy now. The town will have to all go out of business, and then there will be bats and owls in the garrets, and the wharves will rot. I sometimes think that I will have to quit my country."

"Do other folks think as you do?"

"Ay, ay, don't they? All that have any heads with eyes. Some folks have eyes for the present, some for the past, and some for the future. I am one of those that have eyes for the future. I expect to see grass growing in the streets before I die, and I shall not have to live long to pluck buttercups under the King's Arms. I pity young chickens like you that will have no place to run to."

"But, sir," said young Franklin, "suppose things do take another turn. The young settlers are all building; the old people are enlarging their estates. It is easy to borrow money, and it looks to me that we will have here twice as many people in another generation as we have now. If the city should grow, what an opening there is for a printer! I shall take the risk."

"Risk—risk? Jump off a ship on the high sea with an iron ball on your feet! Go down, and stick there. Business, I tell you, is going to die here, and who would want to read what a stripling like you would write outside of business? You would print that this one had failed, that that one had failed, and one don't collect bills handy from people who have failed. I tell you that the whole province is about to fail, and Philadelphia is going to ruin, and I advise you to turn right about and pack up, and go to some other place. There will never be any chance for you here."

Tap, tap, tap, went his cane, and he moved away.

Young Franklin started to go to his work with a heavy heart. The cane stopped. Old Mr. Calamity looked around.

" I've warned you," said he with a flourish of the cane. " I tell you, I tell you everything is going back to the wilderness, and I pity you, but not half so much as you will pity yourself if you embark in the printing business, and print failures for nothing, to fail yourself some day. This is the age of rags, rags! "

Tap, tap, tap, went on the cane, and the old gentleman chuckled.

Young Franklin went on in his business. What was he to do? He saw everything with hopeful eyes. But he was young. His heart told him to go on in his undertaking, and he went on.

He had been laughed at in Boston, and old Mr. Calamity had risen up here to laugh at him again.

He knew not how it was, but it was in him to become a printer. As the young waterfowl knows the water as soon as it toddles from his nest, so young Franklin from his boyhood saw his life in this new element; the press was to be the source of America's rise, power, and glory, the throne of the republic; it was to make and mold and fulfill by its influence public opinion; the same public opinion was to rule America, and the young printer of Philadelphia was to lead the way now, and to reap the fruits of his spiritual resolution after he was seventy years of age. He saw it, he felt it, he knew his own mind. So he left behind old Mr. Calamity for the present, but he was soon to meet him again.

He had now taken a third step on the ladder of life. His business should be built upon honor.

The next time that he met Mr. Calamity, the old gentleman gave him a view of the prospects of a printer.

"If you think that you are going to get your foot on the ladder of life by becoming a printer, you will find that you have mistaken your calling. None of the great men of old were printers, were they? Homer was no printer, was he?"

"I have never heard that he was."

"Nor did you hear of any one who ever printed the Iliad or the Odyssey. No printer was ever heard of among the immortals. A printer just prints—that is all. Solomon never printed anything, did he?"

"I never read that he did, sir."

"Nor Shakespeare?"

"I never heard that he did, sir."

"A printer has no chance to rise; he just builds the ark for Noah to sail in, and is left behind himself."

"I hope to print some of my own thoughts, sir."

"You do? Ha! ha! ha! Who do you think is going to read them?. Your own thoughts—that does give me a stitch in the side, and makes me laugh so loud and swing my cane so high that it sets the cats and dogs to running. See them go over the garden fence! I shall watch your course, and when you begin to scatter your ideas about in the world, I hope I will be living to gather some of them up. I hope they will never lead a revolution!"

Franklin's "Ça Ira" were the words that led the French Revolution.

CHAPTER XXIV.

FRANKLIN'S STRUGGLES WITH FRANKLIN.

AT the age of fifteen Franklin had avowed himself a deist,
or theist, which must have grieved his parents, who were people of positive Christian faith. He loved to argue, and when
he had learned the Socratic art of asking questions so as to
lead one to confuse himself, and of answering questions in the
subjunctive mood, he sought nothing more than disputations
in the stanch Puritan town. His intimate friends were de-
ists, but they came to early failure through want of faith or any
positive moral conviction. Governor Keith was a deist.

The reader may ask what we mean by a deist here. A
deist or theist in Franklin's time was one who believed in a
God, but questioned the Christian faith and system. He was
not an atheist. He held that a personal governing power
directed all things after his own will and purpose. Under the
providence of this Being things came and went, and man could
not know how or why, but could simply believe that all that
was was for the good of all.

At the age of twenty-two young Franklin began to see that
life without faith had no meaning, but was failure. In the
omnipotence of spiritual life and power the soul must share or

die. Negations or denials did not satisfy him. This was a positive world, governed by spiritual law. To disobey these laws was loss and death.

He had been doing wrong. He had done wrong in yielding to his personal feelings in leaving home in the manner which he did. He had committed acts of social wrong. He had followed at times the law of the lower nature instead of the higher. He had become intimate with two friends who had led him into unworthy conduct, and over whom his own influence had not been good. He saw that the true value of life lies in its influence. There were things in his life that tended to ruin influence. There were no harvests to be expected from the barren rocks of negation and denials of faith in the highest good. Sin gives one nothing that one can keep. He must change his life, he must obey perfectly the spiritual laws of his being. He saw it, and resolved to begin.

Now began a struggle between Benjamin Franklin the natural man and Benjamin Franklin the spiritual man that lasted for life. It became his purpose to gain the spiritual mastery, and to obey the laws of regeneration and eternal life.

Here are his first resolutions:

" Those who write of the art of poetry teach us that, if we would write what may be worth reading, we ought always, before we begin to form a regular plan and design of our piece; otherwise we shall be in danger of incongruity. I am apt to think it is the same as to life. I have never fixed a regular design in life, by which means it has been a confused variety of different scenes. I am now entering upon a new life; let me, therefore, make some resolutions, and form some scheme of action, that henceforth I may live in all respects like a rational creature.

"1. It is necessary for me to be extremely frugal for some time, till I have paid what I owe.

"2. To endeavor to speak truth in every instance, to give nobody expectations that are not likely to be answered, but aim at sincerity in every word and action; the most amiable excellence in a rational being.

"3. To apply myself industriously to whatever business I take in hand, and not divert my mind from my business by any foolish project of growing suddenly rich; for industry and patience are the surest means of plenty.

"4. I resolve to speak ill of no man whatever, not even in a matter of truth; but rather by some means excuse the faults I hear charged upon others, and, upon proper occasions, speak all the good I know of everybody."

But there must be a personal God, since he himself had personality, and he must seek a union of soul with his will beyond these mere moral resolutions.

At the age of twenty-two he composed a litany after the manner of the Episcopal Church, but adapted to his own conditions. In this he prays for help in the points where he had found himself to be morally and spiritually weak.

These petitions and resolutions show his inward struggles. They reveal his ideals, and to fulfill these ideals became the end of his life. For the acts of wrong which he had done in his period of adventures, and the unworthy life that he had then led, he tried to make reparation. The spiritual purpose of Benjamin Franklin had obtained the mastery over the natural man.

Honor was his star, and more spiritual light was his desire and quest.

He married Miss Read, the young woman who had laughed at him when he had entered Philadelphia eating his penny roll, with two rolls of bread under his arm, and his superfluous clothing sticking out of his pocket. He had neglected her during his adventures abroad, but she forgave him, and he had become in high moral resolution another man now.

As a printer in Philadelphia his paper voiced the public mind and heart on all which were then most worthy. To publish a paper that advocates the best sentiments of a virtuous people is the shortest way to influence in the world. Franklin found it so. The people sought in him the representative, and from the printing office he was passed by natural and easy stages to the halls of legislation.

So these resolutions to master himself may be regarded as another step on the ladder of life. To benefit the world by inventions is a good thing, but to lift it by an example of self-control and an unselfish life is a nobler thing, and on this plane we find young Franklin standing now. Franklin is the master of Franklin, and the influence of Silence Dogood through the press is filling the province of Pennsylvania. The paper which he established in Philadelphia was called the Pennsylvania Gazette. In connection with this he began to publish a very popular annual called Poor Richard's Almanac, about which we will tell you in another chapter.

Right doing is the way to advancement—Franklin had this resolution; a newspaper that voices the people is a way to advancement—such a one Franklin had founded; and good humor is a way to advancement, and of this Franklin found an expression in Poor Richard's Almanac which has not yet ceased to be quoted in the world. It was the means of conveying Silence Dogood's special messages to every one. It made the whole world happier. Franklin, on account of the wise sayings in the almanac, himself came to be called " Poor Richard."

CHAPTER XXV.

THE MAGICAL BOTTLE.

Franklin is now a man of character, benevolence, wisdom, and humor. He is a printer, a publisher, a man whose thoughts are influencing public opinion. He is a very prosperous man; he is making money and reputation, but it is not the gaining of either of these that is true success, but of right influence. It is not the answer to the question, What are you worth? or What is your popularity? but What is your influence? that determines the value of a man.

He had founded life on right principles, and he had well learned the trade in his youth that leads a poor young man of right principles and nobility to success. He took the right guideboard, and the " Please-everybody " Governor did him a good service when he showed him that to become a printer in Philadelphia would bring him influence, fame, and fortune. People who are well meaning, beyond the ability to fulfill their intentions, sometimes reveal to others what may be of most use to them. It was not altogether an unfortunate day when the wandering printer boy met Governor Keith.

In the midst of his prosperity Silence Dogood was constantly seeking out inventions to help people. When he was about thirty-four years of age, in the Poor Richard days,

he saw that the forests were disappearing, and that there would
be a need for the people to practice economy in the use of
fuel.   The fireplaces in the chimneys were great consumers of
wood, and in many of them, to use the housewife's phrase,
"the heat all went up the chimney."   But that was not all;
many of the chimneys of the good people smoked, and in making a fire rooms would be filled with smoke, or, to use again the
housewife's term, "the smoke would all come out into the
room."

When this was so the people would all flee to cold rooms
with smarting eyes.   New houses in which chimneys smoked
were sometimes taken down or altered to make room for new
chimneys that would draw.   Franklin sought to bring relief
to this sorry condition of affairs.

He invented the Franklin stove, from which the heat would
go out into the room, and not "up the chimbly," to use a
provincial word.   This cheerful stove became a great comfort
to the province, and to foreign countries as well.   It saved fuel,
and brought the heat of the fire into the room.

He long afterward began to study chimneys, and after much
experiment found that those that smoked need not be taken
down, but that only a draught was needed to cause the smoke
to rise in rarefied air.   The name of the Franklin stove added
very greatly to Poor Richard's wisdom, in making for Franklin an American reputation, which also extended to Europe.
His fame arose along original ways.   Surely no one ever walked
in such ways before.

He formed a club called the Junto, which became very prosperous, and gave strength to his local reputation. He also began

a society for the study of universal knowledge, which was called the Philosophical Society.

A man can do the most when he is doing the most. One thing leads to another; one thing feeds another, and one does not suffer in health or nerves from the many things that one loves to do. It is disinclination or friction that wears one down. People who have been very busy in what they most loved to do have usually lived to be old, and come down to old age in the full exercise of their powers.

While Franklin was thus seeking how he could make himself useful to every one in many ways—for a purpose of usefulness finds many paths—his attention was called to a very curious discovery that had been made in the Dutch city of Leyden, in November, 1745. It was an electrical bottle called the Leyden jar.

Nature herself had been discharging on a stupendous scale her own Leyden jars through all generations, but no one seems to have understood these phenomena until this memorable year brought forth the magical little bottle which was a flashlight in the long darkness of time.

The Greeks had found that amber when rubbed would attract certain light substances, and the ancient philosophers and doctors had discovered the value of an electric shock from a torpedo in rheumatic complaints; that sparks would follow the rubbing of the fur of animals in cold air had also been noticed, but of magnetism, and of electricity, which is a current of magnetism, the world was ignorant, except as to some of its more common and obvious effects.

In 1600 Dr. Gilbert, of England, discovered that many other
13

substances besides amber could be made to develop an attractive power. He also discovered that there are many substances that can not be electrically excited.

In 1650 Otto von Guericke, the inventor of the air-pump, made a machine which looked like a little grindstone—a wheel of sulphur mounted on a turning axle, which being used with friction produced powerful electrical sparks and lights. He found by experiments with this machine that bodies thus exerted by friction may impart electricity to other bodies, and that bodies so electrified may repel as well as attract.

Sir Isaac Newton made an electrical machine of glass, and Stephen Gray, in 1720, said that if a large amount of electricity could be *stored*, great results might be expected from it.

Charles François Dufay detected that there were two kinds of electricity, which he called "vitreous" and "resinous."

A great discovery was coming. The first beams of a new planet were rising. How did there come into existence the "magical bottle" known as the Leyden jar?

At Leyden three philosophers were experimenting in electricity. "We can produce electrical effects," said one. "If we could accumulate and retain electricity we would have power."

They electrified a cannon suspended by silk cords. A few minutes after ceasing to turn the handle of the electrical machine which supplied the cannon with fluid, the charge was gone.

"If we could surround an electrified body with a nonconducting substance," said Professor Musschenbroek, "we could imprison it; we could accumulate and store it." He added:

" Glass is a nonconductor of electricity, and water is a good conductor. If I could charge with electricity water in a bottle, I could possess it and control it like other natural powers."

He attempted to do this. He suspended a wire from a charged cannon to the water in a bottle, but for a time no result followed.

One day, however, Mr. Cuneus, one of the scientists, while engaged in this experiment, chanced to touch the conductor with one hand and the electrified bottle with the other. It was a mere accident. He leaped in terror. What had happened? He had received an electric shock. What did it mean? A revolution in the use of one of the greatest of the occult forces of Nature.

Terror was followed by amazement. Mr. Cuneus told Professor Musschenbroek what had happened.

The professor repeated the experiment, with the same result.

If electricity could be secured, accumulated, and discharged, what might not follow as the results of further experiments?

It was several days before the professor recovered from the shock. " I would not take a second shock," he said, " for the kingdom of France! "

Thus the Leyden jar came into use. The news of the experiment flew over Germany and Europe. Scientific people everywhere went to making Leyden jars and imprisoning electricity.

Society took up the invention as a wonder toy. Gunpowder was discharged from the point of the finger by persons charged on an insulating stool. Electrical kisses passed from bold lips to lips in social circles. Even timid people mounted up on cakes of resin that their friends might see their hair stand on end. Sir William Watson, of London, completed the electrical fountain by coating the bottle in and out with tinfoil.

The great news reached America. Franklin heard of it; no ears were more alert than his to profit by suggestions like this.

Mr. Peter Collinson, of London, sent to him an account of Professor Musschenbroeck's magical bottle.

He told his friends of the Junto Club of the invention, and set them all to rubbing electric substances for sparks.

He had invented many useful things. A new force had fallen under the control of man. He must investigate it; he must experiment with it; he too must have a magical bottle.

"I never," he wrote in 1747, "was before engaged in any study that so totally engrossed my attention and time as this has lately done; for what with making experiments when I can be alone, and repeating them to my friends and acquaintances who from the novelty of the thing come continually in crowds to see them, I have during some months past had little leisure for anything else."

What was magnetism? What was electricity? What secrets of Nature might the magical bottle reveal? To what use might the new power which might be stored and imprisoned be put? Silence Dogood, ponder night and day over the curious toy. The world waits for you to speak, for Nature is about to reveal one of her greatest secrets to you—you who gave two penny rolls to the poor woman and child on the street, after Deborah Read, your wife now, had had her good laugh. Your good wife will laugh again some day, when you have further poked around among electrical tubes and bottles, and have brought your benevolent mind to bear upon some of the secrets contained in the magical bottle. You have added virtue to virtue; you are adding intelligence to intelligence; such things grow. Discoveries come to those who are prepared to receive them.

CHAPTER XXVI.

THE ELECTRIFIED VIAL AND THE QUESTIONS IT RAISED.

THERE came from Europe to America at this time some electrical tubes, which being rubbed produced surprising results. To the curious they were toys, but to Franklin they were prophecies. There were three Philadelphians who joined with Franklin in the study of the effects that could be produced by these tubes and the Leyden vial.

Franklin's son William was verging on manhood. He was beyond the years that we find him experimenting with his father in the old pictures. He became the last royal Governor of New Jersey some years afterward, and a Tory, and his politics at that period was a sore grief to his father's heart. But he was a bright, free-hearted boy now, nearly twenty, and his father loved him, and the two were harmonious and were companions for each other.

Franklin, we may suppose, interested the boy in the bristling tubes and the magical bottle. The stored electricity in the latter was like the imprisoned genii of the Arabian Nights. Let the fairy loose, he suddenly mingled with native elements, and one could not gather him again. But another could be gathered.

186

The Philadelphia philosophers wondered greatly at the new effects that Franklin was able to produce from the tubes and the bottle. Did not the genii in the vial hold the secret of the earth, and might not the earth itself be a magnet, and might not magnetism fill interstellar space?

The wonder grew, and its suggestions. One of the Philadelphia philosophers, Philip Sing, invented an electrical machine. A like machine had been made in Europe, but of this Mr. Sing did not know.

The Philadelphia philosophers discovered the power of metallic points to draw off electricity.

" Electricity is not created by friction," observed one of these men. " It is only collected by it."

" And all our experiments show," argued Franklin, " that electricity is positive and negative."

. During the winter of 1746–'47 these men devoted as much of their time as they could spare to electrical experiments.

" William," said one of the philosophers to the son of Franklin one day, " you have brought your friends here to see the vial genii; he is a lively imp. Let me show you some new things which I found he can do."

He brought out a bottle of spirits and poured the liquid into a plate. " Stand up on the insulating stool, my boy, and let me electrify you, and see if the imp loves liquor."

The lively lad obeyed. He pointed his finger down to the liquor in the plate. It burst into flame, startling the audience.

" Now," said another of the philosophers, " let me ask you to give me a magic torch."

He presented to his finger a candle with an alcoholic wick. The candle was at once lighted, emitting sparks as it began to burn.

"Hoi, hoi!" said the philosopher to the young visitors, "what do you think of a young man whose touch is fire? We have a Faust among us, sure!"

"Now, girls, which of you would like to try an experiment?" we may suppose Father Franklin to say, in the spirit of Poor Richard.

William stepped down, and an adventurous girl took his place on the experimental stool.

"You have all heard of the electric kiss," said Poor Richard. "Let this young lady give you one. I will prepare her for it."

He did.

Another girl stepped up to receive it. She expected to receive a spark from her friend's lips; but instead of a spark she received a shock that caused her to leap and to bend double, and to utter a piercing cry.

"I don't think that the kissing of young men and young women in public is altogether in good taste," said the philosophers, "but if any of you young men want to salute this lively young lady in that way, there will be in this case no objections."

But none of the young men cared to be thrown into convulsions by the innocent-looking lass, who seemed to feel no discomfort.

Experiments like these filled the city and province with amazement. The philosopher made a spider of burned cork that would *run*, and cause other people to run who had not learned the wherefore of the curious experiment.

The wonderful Leyden vial became Franklin's companion. He liked ever to be experimenting in what the new force would do. What next? what next? How like lightning was this electricity! How could he increase electrical force?

He says at the end of a long narrative:

"We made what we called an *electrical battery*, consisting of eleven panes of large sash-glass, armed with thin leaden plates pasted on each side, placed vertically, and supported at two inches distance on silk cords, with thick hooks of leaden wire, one from each side, standing upright, distant from each other, and convenient communications of wire and chain, from the giving side of one pane to the receiving side of the other, that so the whole might be charged together."

Franklin at this time was a stanch royalist. He made a figure of George II, with a crown, and so arranged it that the powerful electrical force might be stored in the *crown*.

"God bless him!" said the philosopher.

A young man seeing that the crown was very attractive, attempted to remove it. It was a thing that the philosopher had expected.

The youth touched the crown. He reeled, and started back with a stroke that filled him with amazement.

"So be it with all of King George's enemies!" said the philosophers. "Never attempt to discrown the king."

"God bless him!" said Franklin. His son always continued to say this, but Franklin himself came to see that he who discrowns kings may be greater than kings, and that it became the duty of a people to discrown tyrannical kings, and to make a king of the popular will.

Franklin now resolved to give up his business affairs to others, to refuse political office, and to devote himself to science. The latter resolution he did not keep. He went to live on a retired spot on the Delaware, where he had a large garden, and could be left to his experiments and thoughts upon them. With him went the magical bottle and his interesting son William.

The power of metallic points to draw off lightning now filled his mind. "Could the lightning be controlled?" he began to ask. "Could the power of the thunderbolt be disarmed?"

Every element can be made to obey its own laws. Water will bear up iron if the iron be hollow. But deeply and more deeply must the thoughts engage the mind of the philosopher. "Is lightning electricity? Does electricity fill all space?" He wrote two philosophical papers at this critical period of his life, when he sought to give up money-making and political life for the study of that science which would be most useful to man. He who gives up gains. He who is willing to deny himself the most shall have the most. He that loseth his life shall save it. He who seeketh the good of others shall find it in himself.

One of these papers was entitled "Opinions and Conjectures concerning the Properties and Effects of the Electrical Matter, and the Means of preserving Ships and Buildings from Lightning, arising from Experiments and Observations at Philadelphia in 1749."

In this treatise, which at last made his fame, he shows the similarity of electricity to lightning, and gives a description of an experiment in which a little lightning-rod had drawn away electricity from an artificial storm cloud. He says:

" If these things are so, may not the knowledge of this power of points be of use to mankind in preserving houses, churches, ships, etc., from the stroke of lightning, by directing us to fix on the highest part of those edifices upright rods of iron made sharp as a needle, and gilt to prevent rusting, and from the foot of those rods a wire down the outside of the building into the ground, or down round one of the shrouds of a ship, and down her side till it reaches the water? Would not these pointed rods probably draw the electrical fire silently out of a cloud before it came nigh enough to strike, and thereby secure us from that most sudden and terrible mischief? "

A great discovery was at hand.

CHAPTER XXVII.

THE GREAT DISCOVERY.

It was a June day, 1752—one of the longest days of the year. Benjamin Franklin was then forty-six years of age.

The house garden was full of bloom; the trees were in leafage, and there was the music of blooms in the hives of the bees.

Beyond the orchards and great trees the majestic Delaware rolled in purple splendor, dotted with slanting sails.

Nature was at the full tide of the year. The river winds swept over the meadows in green waves, where the bobolinks toppled in the joy of their songs.

It had been a hot morning, and billowy clouds began to rise in the still heat on the verge of the sky.

Benjamin Franklin sat amid the vines and roses of his door.

" William," he said to his son, " I am expecting a shower to-day. I have long been looking for one. I want you to remain with me and witness an experiment that I am about to make."

Silence Dogood, or Father Franklin, then brought a kite out to the green lawn. The kite had a very long hempen string, and to the end of it, which he held in his hand, he began to attach some silk and a key.

"When I was a boy," said Franklin, "and lived in the town of Boston by the marshes, I made a curious experiment with a kite. I let it tow me along the water where I went swimming. I have always liked flying kites. I hope that this one will bring me good luck should a shower come."

"What do you expect to do with it, father?"

"If the cloud comes up with thunder, and lightning be electricity, I am going to try to secure a spark from the sky."

The air was still. The cloud was growing into mountain-like peaks. The robins and thrushes were singing lustily in the trees, as before a shower. The men in the cornfields and gardens paused in their work.

Presently a low sound of thunder rolled along the sky. The cloud now loomed high and darkened in the still, hot air.

"It is coming," said Franklin, "and the cloud will be a thunder gust. It is early in the season for such a cloud as that. See how black it grows!"

The kite was made of a large silk handkerchief fastened to a perpendicular stick, on the top of which was a piece of sharpened iron wire. The philosopher examined it carefully.

"What if you should receive a spark from the cloud, father?" asked the young man.

"I would then say lightning was electricity, and that it could be controlled, and that human life might be protected from the thunderbolt."

"But would not that thwart the providence of God?"

"No, it would merely cause a force of Nature to obey its own laws so as to protect life instead of destroying it."

The sky darkened. The sun went out. The sea birds flew inland and screamed. The field birds stood panting on the shrubs with drooping wings.

A rattling thunder peal crossed the sky. The wind began to rise, and to cause the early blasted young fruit to fall in the orchards. The waves on the Delaware curled white.

"Let us go to the cattle-shed," said Father Franklin. "I have been laughed at all my life, and do not care to have my neighbors tell the story of my experiment to others if I should fail."

The two went together to the cattle-shed on the green meadow.

The wind was roaring in the distance. The poultry were running home, and the cattle were seeking the shelter of the trees.

The cloud was now overhead. Dark sheets of rain in the horizon looked like walls of carbon reared against the sky. The lightning was sharp and frequent. There came a vivid flash followed by a peal of thunder that shook the hills.

"The cloud is overhead now," said Franklin.

He ran out into the green meadow and threw the kite against the wind.

It rose rapidly and was soon in the sky, drifting in the clouds that seemed full of the vengeful fluid.

At the termination of the hempen cord dangled the key, and the silk end was wound around the philosopher's hand.

The young man took charge of a Leyden jar which he had

brought to the shed, in which to collect electricity from the clouds, should the experiment prove successful.

The cloud came on in its fury. The rain began to fall. Franklin and his son stood under the shed.

The air seemed electrified, but no electricity appeared in the hempen string. Franklin presented his knuckle to the key, but received no spark.

What was that?

The hempen string began to bristle like the hair of one electrified. Was it the wind? Was it electricity?

Benjamin Franklin now touched the key with thrilling emotion, while his son looked on with an excited face. It was a moment of destiny not only to the two experimenters in the dashing rain, but to the world. If Franklin should receive a spark from the key, it would change the currents of the world's events.

Flash!

It came clear and sharp. The heavens had responded to law—to the command of the human will guided by law.

Again, another spark.

The boy touches the key. He, too, is given the evidence that has been given to his father.

The two looked at each other.

"Lightning is electricity," said Silence Dogood. "It can be drawn away from points of danger; no one need be struck by lightning if he will protect himself."

"God himself," once said a writer, "could not strike one by lightning if one were insulated, without violating his own laws."

And now came the consummation of one of the grandest experiments of time. He charged the Leyden jar from the clouds.

"Stand back!"

He touched his hand boldly to the magical bottle. A shock thrilled him. His dreams had come true. He had conquered one of the most potent elements on earth.

The storm passed, the clouds broke, the wind swept by, and the birds sang again over the bending clover. Night serene with stars came on. That was probably the happiest day in all Franklin's eventful life. Like the patriarch of old, "his children were about him." He shared his triumph with the son whom he loved.

But—he sent a paper on the results of his observation in electricity to the Royal Society at London, in which he announced his discovery that lightning was electricity. The society did not deem it worth publishing: it was a neglected manuscript, and as for his theory in regard to the electric fluid and universality, that, we are told by Franklin's biographers, "was laughed at."

But his views had set all Europe to experimenting. Scientists everywhere were proving that his theories were true. France had become very much excited over the discovery, and was already hailing the philosopher's name with shouts of admiration. Franklin's fame filled Europe, and the greatest of British societies began to honor him. It was Doctor Franklin now!—The honorary degree came to him from many institutions.—Doctor from England, Doctor from France, Doctor from American colleges.

The boy who had shared his penny rolls with the poor woman and her child sat down to hear the world praising him.

The facts that lightning was electricity or electricity was lightning, that it was positive and negative, that it could be controlled, that life could be made safe in the thunder gust, were but the beginning of a series of triumphs that have come to make messengers of the lightning, and brought the nations of the world in daily communication with each other. But the wizardlike Edison has shown that the influences direct and indirect of that June day of 1752 may have yet only begun. What magnetism and its currents are to reveal in another century we can not tell; it fills us with silence and awe to read the prophecies of the scientists of to-day. The electrical mystery is not only moving us and all things; we are burning it, we are making it medicine, health, life. What may it not some day reveal in regard to a spiritual body or the human soul?

The centuries to come can only reveal what will be the end of Franklin's discovery that lightning might be controlled to become the protector and the servant of man. Even his imagination could hardly have forecast the achievements which the imp of the magical bottle would one day accomplish in this blind world. It is not that lightning is electricity, but that electricity is subject to laws, that has made the fiery substance the wonder-worker of the age.

If Uncle Ben, the poet, could have seen this day, how would his heart have rejoiced!

Jane Mecom—Jenny—heard of the fame of her brother by every paper brought by the post. She delighted to tell her

14

old mother the weekly news about Benjamin. One day, when he had received honors from one of the great scientific societies, Abiah said to her daughter:

"You helped Ben in his early days—I can see now that you did."

"How, mother?"

"By believing in him when hardly any one else did. We build up people by believing in them. My dim eyes see it all now. I love to think of the past," she continued, "when you and Ben were so happy together—the days of Uncle Benjamin. I love to think of the old family Thanksgivings. What wonderful days were those when the old clock-cleaner came! How he took the dumb, dusty clock to pieces, and laid it out on the table! How Ben would say, 'you can never make that clock tick again!' and you, Jenny, whose faith never failed, would answer, 'Yes, Ben, he can!' How the old man would break open a walnut and extract the oil from the meat, and apply it with a feather to the little axles of the wheels, and then put the works together, and the clock would go better than before! Do you remember it, Jane? How, then, your wondering eyes would look upon the clock miracle and delight in your faith, and say, 'I told you so, Ben.' How he would kiss you in your happiness that your prophecy had come true. He had said 'No' that you might say 'Yes.'"

"Do you think that his thoughts turn home, mother?"

There was a whir of wings in the chimney.

"More to a true nature than a noisy applause of the crowd is the simple faith of one honest heart," said Abiah Folger in return. "In the silence and desolation of life, which may come to all, such sympathy is the only fountain to which one can turn. Our best thoughts fly homeward like swallows to old chimneys, where they last year brooded over their young, and center in the true hearts left at the fireside. Every true heart is true to his home, and to the graves of those with whom it shared the years when life lay fair before it. Yes, Jane, he thinks of you."

She was right. Jenny had helped her brother by believing in him when he most needed such faith.

There is some good angel, some Jenny, who comes into every one's life. Happy is he who feels the heart touch of such an one, and yields to such unselfish spiritual visions. To do this is to be led by a gentle hand into the best that there is in life.

In sacred hours the voices of these home angels come back to the silent chambers of the heart. We then see that our best hopes were in them, and wish that we could retune the broken chords of the past. The home voice is always true, and we find it so at last.

Franklin had little of his sister's sentiment, but when he thought of the old days, and of the simple hearts that were true to him there, he would say, " Beloved Boston." His heart was in the words. Boston was the town of Jenny.

CHAPTER XXVIII.

HOME-COMING IN DISGUISE.

THERE is a very delightful fiction, which may have blossomed from fact, which used to be found in schoolbooks, under the title of "The Story of Franklin's Return to his Mother after a Long Absence."

It would have been quite like him to have returned to Boston in the guise of a stranger. Some one has said that he had a joke for everything, and that he would have put one into the Declaration of Independence had he been able.

The tendency to make proverbs that Franklin showed in his early years grew, and if he were not indeed as wise as King Solomon, no one since the days of that Oriental monarch has made and "sought out" so many proverbs and given them to the world.

The maxims of Poor Richard, which were at first given to the world through an almanac, spread everywhere. They were current in most Boston homes; they came back to the ears of Jamie the Scotchman—back, we say, for some of them were the echoes of Silence Dogood's life in the Puritan province.

Poor Richard's Almanac was a lively and curious miscellany, and its coming was an event in America. Franklin put the wisdom that he gained by experience into it. In the following resolution was the purpose of his life at this time: "I wished to live," he says, "without committing any fault at any time, and to conquer all that either natural inclination, custom, or company might lead me into."

"But—but," he says," I was surprised to find myself so much fuller of faults than I had imagined; but I had the satisfaction of seeing them diminish." In the spirit of this effort to correct life and to learn wisdom from experience, he gave Poor Richard's Almanac annually to the world. Like some of the proverbs of Solomon, it taught the people life as he himself learned it. For years Franklin lived in Poor Richard, and it was his pulse beat, his open heart, that gave the annual its power. All the sayings of Poor Richard were not original with Franklin. When a critical proverb, or a line from one of the poets, would express his idea or conviction better than he could himself, he used it. For example, he borrowed some beautiful lines from Pope, who in turn had received the leading thought from a satire of Horace.

While Franklin was learning wisdom from life, and expressing it through Poor Richard, he was studying French, Italian, and Spanish, and making himself the master of philosophy. "He who would thrive must rise at five," he makes Poor Richard say. He himself rose at five in the morning, and began the day with a bath and a prayer. Intelligence to intelligence!

Such was his life when Poor Richard was evolved.

Who was Poor Richard, whose influence came to lead the thought of the time?

Poor Richard was a comic almanac, or a character assumed

by Benjamin Franklin, for the purpose of expressing his views of life. Having established a paper, Franklin saw the need of an annual and of an almanac, and he chose to combine the two, and to make the pamphlet a medium of hard sense in a rough, keen, droll way.

He introduces himself in this curious annual as "Richard Saunders," "Poor Richard." He has an industrious wife named Bridget. He publishes his almanac to earn a little money to meet his pressing wants. "The plain truth of the matter is," says this pretended almanac maker, "I am excessive poor, and my wife, good woman, is, I tell her, excessive proud; she cannot bear, she says, to sit spinning in her gown of tow, while I do nothing but gaze at the stars; and has threatened more than once to burn all my books and rattling-traps (as she calls my instruments) if I do not make some profitable use of them for the good of my family. The printer has offer'd me some considerable share of the profits, and I have thus began to comply with my dame's desire."

This Titian Leeds was a pen name for his rival publisher, who also issued an almanac. The two had begun life in Philadelphia together as printers.

The way in which he refers to his rival in his new almanac, as a man about to die to fulfill the predictions of astrology, was so comical as to excite a lively interest. Would he die? If not, what would the *next* almanac say of him? Mr. Leeds (Keimer) had a reputation of a knowledge of astronomy and astrology. In what way could Franklin have introduced a character to the public in the spirit of good-natured rivalry that would have awakened a more genuine curiosity?

The next year Poor Richard announced that his almanac had proved a success, and told the public the news that they were waiting for and much desired to hear: his wife Bridget had profited by it. She was now able to have a dinner-pot of her own, and something to put into it.

But how about Titian Leeds, who was to die after the astrological prediction? The people awaited the news of the fate of this poor man, as we await the tidings of the end of a piece of statesmanship. He thus answers, "I can not say positively whether he is dead or alive," but as the author of the rival almanac had spoken very disrespectfully of him, and as Mr. Leeds when living was a gentleman, he concludes that Mr. Leeds must be dead.

In these comic annuals there is not only the almanacs and the play upon Titian Leeds, but a large amount of rude wisdom in the form of proverbs, aphorisms, and verses, most of which is original, but a part of which, as we have said, is apt quotation. The proverbs were everywhere quoted, and became a part of the national education. They became popular in France, and filled nearly all Europe. They are still quoted. Let us give you some of them:

"Who has deceived thee so oft as thyself?"

"Fly pleasures, and they will follow thee."

"Let thy child's first lesson be obedience, and the second will be what thou wilt."

"Industry need not wish."

> "In things of moment, on thyself depend,
> Nor trust too far thy servant or thy friend;
> With private views, thy friend may promise fair,
> And servants very seldom prove sincere."

Besides these quaint sayings, which became a part of the proverbial wisdom of the world, Franklin had a comical remark for every occasion, as, when a boy, he advised his father to say grace over the whole pork barrel, and so save time at the table. He once admonished Jenny in regard to her spelling, and that after she was advanced in life, by telling her that the true way to spell wife was *yf*. After the treaty of peace with England, he thought it only a courtesy that America should return deported people to their native shores. Once in Paris, on receiving a cake labeled *Le digne Franklin*, which excited the jealousy of Lee and Dean, he said that the present was meant for Lee-Dean-Franklin, that being the pronunciation of the French label. Every event had a comical side for him.

Let us bring prosperous Benjamin Franklin back to Boston to see his widowed mother again, after the old story-book manner. She is nearly blind now, and we may suppose Jamie the Scotchman to be halting and old.

He comes into the town in the stagecoach at night. Boston has grown. The grand old Province House rises above it, the Indian vane turning hither and thither in the wind. The old town pump gleams under a lantern, as does the spring in Spring Lane, which fountain may have led to the settlement of the town. On a hill a beacon gleams over the sea. He passes the stocks and the whipping-post in the shadows.

There is a light in the window of the Blue Ball. He sees it. It is very bright. Is his mother at work now that she is nearly blind?

He dismounts. He passes close to the old window. His

father is not in the room; he never will be there again. But an aged man is there. Who is he?

The man is reading—what? The most popular pamphlet or little book that ever appeared in the colonies; a droll story.

He knocks at the door. The old man rises and opens the door; the bell is gone.

" Abiah, there's a stranger here."

" Ask him who he is."

" Say that he used to work here many years ago, and that he knew Josiah Franklin well, and was acquainted with Ben."

" Tell him to come in," said the bent old woman with white hair.

The stranger entered, and avoided questions by asking them.

" What are you reading to-night, my good friend? " he asked.

" The Old Auctioneer," answered the aged man. " Have you read it? "

" Yes; it is on the taxes."

" So it is—I've read it twice over. I'm now reading it to Abiah. Let me tell you a secret—her son wrote it. My opinion is that it is the smartest piece of work that ever saw the light on this side of the water. What's yourn? "

" There's sense in it."

" What did he say his name was? " asked Abiah.

" Have you ever read any of Poor Richard's maxims? " asked the stranger quickly.

" Yes, yes; we have taken the Almanac for years. Ben publishes it."

"What did he say?" asked Abiah. "I can not hear as well as I once could.—Stranger, I heard you when you spoke loud at the door."

"Repeat some of 'Poor Richard's' sayings," said the stranger.

"You may well say 'repeat,'" said the old man. "I used to hear Ben Franklin say things like that when he was a 'prentice lad."

"Like what, my friend?"

"Like 'The noblest question in the world is what good may I do in it?' There! Like 'None preaches better than the ant, and she says nothing.' There!"

"I see, I see, my good friend, you seem to have confidence in Poor Richard?"

"Sir, I taught him much of his wisdom—he and I used to be great friends. I always knew that he had a star in his soul that would shine—I foresaw it all. I have the gift of second sight. I am a Scotchman."

"And you prophesied good things to him when he was a boy?"

"Yes, yes, or, if I did not, I only spoke in a discouraging way to encourage him. He and I were chums; we used to sit on Long Wharf together and *prognosticate* together. That was a kind of Harvard College to us. Uncle Ben was living then."

"Maybe the stranger would like you to read The Old Auctioneer," said Abiah to the Scotchman. "My boy wrote that—he told you. My boy has good sense—Jamie here will tell you so. I'm older now than I was."

" Yes, yes, read, and let me rest. When the bell rings for nine I will go to the inn."

" Maybe we can keep you here. We'll talk it over later. I want to hear Ben's piece. I'm his mother, and they tell me it is interesting to people who are no relation to him.—Jamie, you read the piece, and then we will talk over the past. It seems like meeting Ben again to hear his pieces read."

Jamie the Scotchman read, and while he did so Abiah, wrinkled and old, looked often toward the stranger out of her dim eyes, while she listened to her son's always popular story of The Old Auctioneer.

" That is a very good piece," said Abiah Franklin; " and now, stranger, let me say that your voice sounds familiar, and I want you to tell me in a good strong tone who you be. I didn't hear you give any name."

" Is it almost nine? " asked the stranger.

Jamie opened the door.

A bell smote the still air, a silverlike bell. It spoke nine times.

" I never heard that bell before," said the stranger.

Suddenly music flooded the air; it seemed descending; there were many bells—and they were singing.

" The Old North chimes," said the Scotchman; " they have just been put up. I wish Ben could hear them; I sort of carry him in my heart."

" Don't speak! It is beautiful," said the stranger. " Hear what they are saying."

" O Jamie, Jamie, *father* used to play that tune on his violin."

"*Father!*" The old woman started.

"Ben, Ben, how could you! Come here; my eyes are failing me, Ben, but my heart will never fail me.—Jamie, prepare for him his old room, and leave us to talk together!"

"I will go out to Mrs. Mecom's, and tell her that Benjamin has come home."

"Yes, yes, go and call Jenny."

They talked together long: of Josiah, now gone; of Uncle Benjamin, long dead; and of Parson Sewell, and the deacons of the South Church, who had passed away.

The door opened. Jenny again stood before him. She led on a boy by the hand, and said to her portly brother:

"This, Benjamin, is Benjamin."

They talked together until the tears came.

He heard the whir of the swallows' wings in the chimney.

"The swallows come back," he said, "but *they* will never come again. It fills my heart with tenderness to hear these old home sounds."

"No, *they* will never come back from the mosses and ferns under the elms," said his mother. "The orioles come, the orchards bloom, and summer lights up the hills, and the leaves fall, but they will know no more changes or seasons. And I am going after their feet into the silence, Ben; I have almost got through. You have been a true son in the main, and Jenny has never stepped aside from the way. Always be good to Jenny."

"Jenny, always be true to mother, and I will be as true to you."

"Brother, I shall always be true to my home."

CHAPTER XXIX.

"THOSE PAMPHLETS."

BENJAMIN FRANKLIN loved to meet Samuel Franklin, Uncle Benjamin's son, who also had caught the gentle philosopher's spirit, and was making good his father's intention. Samuel was a thrifty man in a growing town.

"It is the joy of my life to find you so prosperous," said Franklin, "for it would have made your father's heart happy could he have known that one day I would find you so. Samuel, your father was a good man. I shall never cease to be grateful for his influence over me when I was a boy. He was my schoolmaster."

"Yes, my father was a good man, and I never saw it as I do now. I was not all to him that I ought to have been. He was a poor man; he lived as it were on ideas, and people were accustomed to look upon him as a man who had failed in life."

"He will never fail while you are a man of right influence," said Franklin. "He lives in you."

"I feel his influence more and more every day," said Samuel.

"Samuel Franklin, I do. Success does not consist in popularity or money-making. Right influence is success in life. I have been an unworthy godson of your father, but I am more than ever determined to carry out the principles that he taught me; they are the only things that will stand in life; as for the rest, the grave swallows all. Your father's life shall never be a failure if my life can bring to it honor.

"Samuel, I have not always done my best, but .I resolve more and more to be worthy of the love of all men when I think of what a character your father developed. He thought of himself last. He did not die poor. His hands were empty, but not his heart, and there sleeps no richer man in the Granary burying ground than he.

"Samuel, he parted with his library containing the notes of his best thoughts in life in his efforts to come to America to give me the true lessons in life because I bore his name. It was a brotherly thought indeed that led my father who loved him to name me for him."

"You speak of his library—his collection of religious books and pamphlets, which he wrote over with his own ideas; you have touched a tender spot in my heart. He wanted that I should have those pamphlets, and that I should try to recover them through some London agent. You are going to London. Do you think that they could be recovered after so many years?"

"Samuel, there is a strange thing that I have observed. It is this: When a man looks earnestly for a thing that some one has desired him to have, his mind is curiously influenced and has strange directions. It is like blindfolded children playing hot and cold. There is some strange instinct in one who seeks a hidden object for his own or others' good that leads his feet into mysterious ways. I have much faith in that hidden law. Samuel, I may be able to find those pamphlets; I thought of them when I was in London. If I do, I will buy them at whatever cost, and will bring them to you, and may both of us try to honor the name of that loving, forgiving, noble man until we see each other again. It may be that when I shall come here another time, if I do, I will bring with me the pamphlets."

" If you were to find them, I would indeed believe in a special Providence."

The two parted. Poor Uncle Benjamin had sold his books for money, but was his life a failure, or was he never living more nobly than now?

Franklin went to the Granary burying ground, where the old man slept. Great elms stood before the place. He thought of what his parents had been, how they had struggled and toiled, and how glad they were that Uncle Benjamin had come to them for his sake. He resolved to erect a monument there.

He recalled Uncle Benjamin's teaching, that a man rises by overcoming his defects, and so gains strength.

He had tried to profit by the old man's lesson in answer to his own question, " Have I a chance? "

He had not only struggled to make strong his conscious weaknesses of character, but those of his mental power as well.

His old pedagogue, Mr. Brownell, had been unable to teach him mathematics. In this branch of elementary studies he had proved a failure and a dunce. But he had struggled against this defect of Nature, as against all others, with success.

He was going to London as the agent of the colonies. He

would carry back to England those principles that the old man
had taught him, and would live them there. His Uncle Benjamin had written those principles in his " pamphlets," and
again in his own life. Would he ever see these documents
which had in fact been his schoolbooks, but which had come
to him without the letter, because the old man had been too
poor to keep the books?

CHAPTER XXX.

FRANKLIN went to London.

Franklin loved old bookstores. There were many in London, moldy and musty, in obscure corners, some of them in cellars and in narrow passageways, just off thronging streets.

One day, when he was sixty years of age, just fifty years after his association with Uncle Benjamin, he wandered out into the byways of the old London bookstores.

It was early spring; the winter fogs of London had disappeared, the squares were turning green, the hedgerows blooming, the birds were singing on the thorns. Such a sunny, blue morning might have called him into the country, but he turned instead into the flowerless ways of the book stalls. He wandered about for a time and found nothing. Then he thought of old Humphrey, of whom he had bought books perhaps out of pity. There was something about this man that held him; he seemed somehow like a link of the unknown past. He compelled him to buy books that he did not want or need.

"This is a fine spring morning," said old Humphrey, as he saw the portly form of Franklin enter the door. "I have been thinking of you much of late. I do not seem to be able to have put you out of my mind; and why should I, a fine gentleman

15   213

like you, and uncommonly civil. I have something that I have been allotting on showing you. It is very curious; it is a library of thirty-six volumes of pamphlets, and it minds me that a more interesting collection of pamphlets was never made. I read them myself in lonesome days when there is no trade. Let me show you one of the volumes."

"No, never mind, my friend. I could not buy the whole library, however interesting it might be. I will look for something smaller. This is a very old bookstore."

"Ay, it is that. It has been kept here ever since the times of the Restoration, and before. My wife's father used to keep it when he was an old man and I was a boy. And now I am an old man. I must show you one of those books or pamphlets. They are all written over."

Benjamin Franklin sat down on a stool in the light, and took up an odd volume of the Canterbury Tales.

Old Humphrey lighted a candle and went into a dark recess. He presently returned, bringing one of the thirty-six volumes of pamphlets.

"My American friend, if one liked old things, and the comments of one dead and gone, this library of pamphlets would be food for thought. Just look at this volume!"

He struck the book against a shelf to remove the dust, and handed it to Franklin.

The latter adjusted his spectacles to the light, and turned over the volume.

"As you say," he said to old Humphrey, "it is all written over."

"And uncommonly interesting comments they are. That

A STRANGE DISCOVERY.

library of pamphlets and comments, in my opinion, is as valuable as Pepys's Diary.

Old Humphrey had struck the right chord. In Pepys's Diary, which was kept for nine years during the gay and exciting period of the reign of Charles II, one lives, as it were, amid the old court scenes.

Franklin turned over the leaves of the volume. "It is a curious book," said he.

The light was poor, and he took the book to the door. Above the tall houses of the narrow street was a rift of sunny blue sky.

"There is something in the handwriting that looks familiar," said he. "It seems as though I had seen that writing somewhere before. Where did you find these books?"

"They came to me from my wife's father, who kept the storeway until he was nigh upon ninety years old. He set great store by these books, which led me to read them.

"When Pepys's Diary was printed I was reminded of them, and read them over again, the comments and all. The person who made those notes had a very interesting mind. I think him to have been a philosopher."

The ink on the margin of the volume was fading, and Franklin strained his eyes to read the comments. Suddenly he turned and came into the store and sat down.

"Father Humphrey, bring me another volume."

Father Humphrey lighted the candle again and went into the same dark and tomblike recess, and brought out two more volumes, striking them against the corners of shelves to remove from them the dust and mold.

He noticed that his patron seemed overcome. Franklin was not an emotional man, but his lip quivered.

"You think that the book is interesting?"

He lifted his face and seemed lost in thought.

"Ecton—Ecton—Ecton," he said. "Uncle Tom lived there—Uncle Tom, who started the subscription for the chime of bells."

He had found the word "Ecton" in the pamphlets, and he again began to turn the leaves.

"Squire Isted," he said, "Squire Isted." He had found the name of Squire Isted on one of the leaves. He had heard the name in his youth.

"The World's End," he said. He stood up and turned round and round.

"How queer he acts!" thought Father Humphrey. "I thought him a very calm man. What is it about the World's End?" he asked.

"Oh, it is the name of an old tavern that I have found here. I had some great-uncles that used to have a farm and forge near an inn of that name. That was very long ago, before I was born. Old names seem to me like voices of the past."

He put his spectacles to his eyes and held the book again up to the light.

He presently said: "Luke Fuller—that is an old English name; there was such a one who was ousted for nonconformity in the days of the Conventicles."

He turned round and lifted his face and stood still, like a statue.

Was he going mad? Poor old Father Humphrey began to

look toward the door to see if there were clear way of escape for him should the strange man become violent.

Presently he said:

" Earls—Barton," and lifted his brows.

Then he said:

" Mears—Ashby," and lifted his brows higher.

" What, sir, is it about Earls—Barton, and Mears—Ashby? " asked the timid Father Humphrey.

" Oh, you are _here_. I've heard of these places before—it was many years ago. Some folks came over to America from there."

He turned to the book again. " An Essay on the Toleration Act," said he. " Banbury," he continued. He dropped the book by his side, and lifted his brows again.

Poor Father Humphrey now thought that his customer had indeed gone daft, and was beginning to repeat an old nursery rhyme that that name suggested.

The book went up to the light again. Old Humphrey, frightened, passed him and went to the door, so that he might run if his strange visitor should be incited to do him harm.

Suddenly a very alarming expression came over the book-finder's face. What would he do next, this calm, grand old man, who was going out of his senses in this unfortunate place?

He dropped the book by his side again, and said, as in the voice of another, a long-gone voice:

" Reuben of the Mill—Reuben of the Mill! "

Poor Father Humphrey thought he was summoning the ghost of some strange being from the recesses of the cellar. He began to walk away, when the supposed mind-shattered American seemed to be returning to himself, and said in a very calm and dignified manner:

"Father Humphrey, you must think that I have been acting strangely. There are some notes here that recall old names and places. They carried my thoughts away back to the past."

The timid man came into the shop hopeful of a bargain.

"It is a useful book, I should think," said Franklin, as if holding himself in restraint.

He took the two other volumes that Father Humphrey had brought him and began to look them over.

"Father Humphrey, what do you want for the whole library of the pamphlets?"

"I do not exactly know what price to fix upon them. They might be valuable to an antiquarian some day, perhaps to some solicitor, or to a library. I would be glad to sell them to you, for somehow—and I speak out of my heart, and use no trade language—somehow I want you to buy them. Would five pounds be too much for the thirty volumes?"

"No, no. There are but few that would want them or give them room. I will pay you five pounds for them. I will take one volume away, but for the present you shall keep the others for me."

He left the store. It was a bright day. Happy faces passed him, but he saw them not. He walked, indeed, the streets of London, but it was the Boston of his childhood that was with him now. He wondered at what he had found—he wondered if there were mysterious influences behind life; for he was certain that these pamphlets were those that his god-father Uncle Benjamin had so valued as a part of himself, and that the notes on the margin of the leaves were in the hand-writing of the same kind-hearted man whose influence had so molded his young life.

He went to his apartments, and sat down at his table and read the pamphlet and the notes. He found in the notes the very thoughts and the same expressions of thought that he had received from Uncle Benjamin in his childhood.

What a life had been his, and how much he owed to this honest, pure-minded old man!

He started up.

"I must go back to Father Humphrey," he said, "and find of whom he obtained these books. If these are Uncle Benjamin's pamphlets, this is the strangest incident in all my life; it would look as though there was a finger of Providence in it. I must go back—I must go back."

CHAPTER XXXI.

IN his usual serene manner—for he very rarely became excited, notwithstanding that his conduct and his absentmindedness had surprised old Humphrey—Mr. Franklin made his way again to the bookstore in the alley.

Old Humphrey welcomed him with—

"Well, I am glad to see you again, my American patron. Did you find the volume interesting?"

"Yes, Father Humphrey, that was an interesting book, and there were some very curious comments in it. The notes on the Conventicles and the Toleration Act greatly interested me. The man who was the compiler of that book of pamphlets seems to have been a poet, and to have had relatives who were advocates of justice. I was struck by many wise comments that I found in it written in a peculiar hand. Father Humphrey, who do you suppose made those notes? Where did you find those pamphlets? How did they come to you?"

"Well, that would be hard to say. Those volumes of pamphlets have been in the store many years, and I have often tried to find a purchaser for them. They must have come down from the times of the Restoration. I wouldn't wonder if they were as old as Cromwell's day. There is much about Banbury in them, and old Lord Halifax."

"Old Lord Halifax!" said Franklin in surprise, walking about with a far-away look in his face again and his hands behind him. "I did not find that name in the volume that I took home. I had an uncle who received favors from old Lord Halifax."

"You did, hey? Where did he live?"

"In Ecton, or in Nottingham."

"Now, that is curious. It may be that he made the library of pamphlets."

"No, no; if he had, he would never have sold them. He was a well-to-do man. But you have not answered my questions as to how the library of pamphlets came to you."

"I can't. I found them here when I took charge of the store. My wife's father, as I said, used to keep the store. He died suddenly in old age, and left the store to my wife. He had made a better living than I out of my business. So I took the store. I found the books here. I do not know where my father-in-law obtained them. It was his business to buy rare books, and then find a way to some antiquarian of means who might want them. The owner's name was not left in these books. I have looked for it many times. But there are names of Nottingham people there, and when old Lord Halifax used to visit London I tried to interest him in them, but he did not care to buy them."

"Father Humphrey, what was your wife's father's name?"

"His name was Axel, sir. He was a good man, sir. He

attended the conventicles, sir, and became a Brownite, sir, and——"

Was the American gentleman going daft again?

He stopped at the name of *Axel*, and lifted his brows. He turned around, and bowed over with a look of intense interest.

"Did you say Axel, Father Humphrey?"

"Axel, your honor. Axel. I once heard him say that several of these pamphlets were suppressed after the Restoration, and that they were rare and valuable. I heard him say that they would be useful to a historian, sir."

"I will pay you for the books, and you may hold them in trust for me. They will be sent for some day, or it may be that I will call for them myself. My uncle owned those books. It would have been the dearest thing of his life could the old man have seen what has now happened. Father Humphrey, one's heart's desires bring about strange things. They shape events after a man is dead. It seems to me as though I had been directed here. Father Humphrey, what do you think of such things?"

"Well, I don't know. From the time that I first saw you my mind was turned to the pamphlets. I don't know why. Perhaps the owner's thought, or desires, or prayers led me. It is all very strange."

"Yes, it is very strange," said Franklin, again walking to and fro with his hands behind him. "I wish that all good men's works could be fulfilled in this way."

"How do you know that they are not?"

"Let us hope that they are."

"This is all very strange."

"Very strange, very strange. It is the greatest of blessings in life to have had good ancestors. Uncle Ben was a good old man. I owe much to him, and now I seem to have met with him again—Uncle Benjamin, my father's favorite brother, who used to carry me sailing and made the boat a schoolroom for me in the harbor of Boston town."

He added to himself in an absent way: "Samuel Franklin and I have promised to live so as to honor the character of this old man. I have a great task before me, and I can not tell what the issue will be, but I will hold these pamphlets and keep them until I can look into Samuel's face and say, 'England has done justice to America, and your father's influence has advanced the cause of human rights in the world.'"

Would that day ever come?

He went to Ecton, in Nottinghamshire, with his son, and there heard the chimes in the steeple that had been placed there by Thomas Franklin's influence. He visited the graves of his ancestors and the homes of many poor people who bore the Franklin name. He found three letters that his Uncle Benjamin had written home. He read in them the names of himself and Jenny. How his heart must have turned home on that visit! A biographer of Franklin tells his story in a beautiful simplicity that leaves no call for fictitious enlargement. He says: "Franklin discovered a cousin, a happy and venerable old maid; 'a good, clever woman,' he wrote, 'but poor, though vastly contented with her situation, and very cheerful'—a genuine Franklin, evidently. She gave him some of his Uncle Benjamin's old letters to read, with their pious rhymings and acrostics, in which occurred allusions to himself and his sister Jane when they were children. Continuing their journey, father and son reached Ecton, where so many successive Franklins had plied the blacksmith's hammer. They found that the farm of thirty acres had been sold to strangers. The old stone cottage of their ancestors was used for a school, but was still called the Franklin House. Many relations and connections they hunted up, most of them old and poor, but endowed with the inestimable Franklinian gift of making the best of their lot. They copied tombstones; they examined the parish register; they heard the chime of bells play which Uncle Thomas had caused to be purchased for the quaint old Ecton church seventy years before; and examined other evidences of his worth and public spirit."

CHAPTER XXXII.

WHEN Dr. Franklin was abroad the first time after the misadventure with Governor Keith, and was an agent of the colonies, his fame as a scientist gave him a place in the highest intellectual circles of England, and among his friends were several clergymen of the English Church and certain noblemen of eminent force and character.

When in 1775, while he was again the colonial agent, the events in America became exciting, his position as the representative American in England compelled him to face the rising tide against his country. He was now sixty-nine years of age. He was personally popular, although the king came to regard him with disfavor, and once called him that " insidious man." But he never failed, at any cost of personal reputation, to defend the American cause.

His good humor never forsook him, and the droll, quaint wisdom that had appeared in Poor Richard was turned to good account in the advocacy of the rights of the American colonies.

One evening he dined at the house of a nobleman. It was in the year of the Concord fight, when political events in America were hurrying and were exciting all minds in both countries.

They talked of literature at the party, but the political situation was uppermost in the minds of all.

A gentleman was present whose literary mind made him very interesting to such circles.

"The art of the illustration of the principles of life in fable," he said, "is exhausted. Æsop, La Fontaine, Gay, and others have left nothing further to be produced in parable teaching."

The view was entertaining. He added:

"There is not left a bird, animal, or fish that could be made the subject of any original fable."

Dr. Franklin seemed to be very thoughtful for a time.

"What is your opinion, doctor?" asked the literary gentleman.

"You are wrong, sir. The opportunity to produce fables is limitless. Almost every event offers the fabric of a fable."

"Could you write a fable on any of the events of the present time?" asked the lord curiously.

"If you will order pen and ink and paper, I will give you a picture of the times in fable. A fable comes to me now."

The lord ordered the writing material.

What new animals or birds had taken possession of Franklin's fancy? No new animals or birds, but old ones in new relations.

Franklin wrote out his fable and proceeded to read it. It was a short one, but the effect was direct and surprising. The lord's face must have changed when he listened to it, for it was a time when such things struck to the heart.

The fable not only showed Dr. Franklin's invention, but his courage. It was as follows: " Once upon a time an eagle, scaling round a farmer's barn and espying a hare, darted down upon him like a sunbeam, seized him in his claws, and remounted with him to the air. He soon found that he had a creature of more courage and strength than a hare, for which, notwithstanding the keenness of his eyesight, he had mistaken a cat.

" The snarling and scrambling of his prey were very inconvenient, and, what was worse, she had disengaged herself from his talons, grasped his body with her four limbs, so as to stop his breath, and seized fast hold of his throat with her teeth.

" ' Pray,' said the eagle, ' let go your hold, and I will release you.'

" ' Very fine,' said the cat; ' I have no fancy to fall from this height and be crushed to death. You have taken me up, and you shall stoop and let me down.' The eagle thought it necessary to stoop accordingly."

The eagle, of course, represented England, and the cat America.

Dr. Franklin was a lover of little children and animals— among pet animals, of the American squirrel.

When he returned to England the second time as an agent of the colonies, he wished to make some presents to his English friends who had families.

He liked not only to please children, but to give them those things which would delight them. So he took over to England for presents a cage full of pranky little squirrels.

Among the families of children whom he loved was Dr. Shipley's, the bishop, who had a delightful little daughter, and to her the great Dr. Franklin, who was believed to command the visible heavens, made a present of a cunning American squirrel.

The girl came to love the pet. It was a truly American squirrel; it sought liberty. Franklin called it Mungo.

The girl seems to have given the little creature his will, and let him sometimes go free among the oaks and hedgerows of the fair, green land. But one day it was caught by a dog or cat, or some other animal, and killed. His liberty proved his ruin. Poor Mungo!

There was sorrow in the bishop's home over the loss of the pet, and the poor little girl sought consolation from the philosopher.

But, philosopher that he was, he could not recall to life the little martyr to liberty. So he did about all that can be done in like cases: he wrote for her an epitaph for her pet, setting forth its misfortunes, and giving it a charitable history, which must have been very consoling. He did not indulge in any frivolous rhymes, but used the stately rhythms that befit a very solemn event.

There is a perfect picture of the mother heart of Franklin in this little story. The world has ever asked why this man was so liked. The answer may be read here: A sympathy, guided by principle, that often found expression in humor.

As in the case of good old Sam Adams, the children followed

him. Blessed are those whom mothers and children love. It is the heart that has power. A touch of sympathy outlives tales of achievements of power, as in the story of Ulysses's dog. It is he who sympathizes the most with mankind that longest lives in human affections.

A man's character may be known by the poet that the man seeks as his interpreter. Franklin's favorite poet as he grew old was Cowper. In all his duties of life he never lost that heart charm, the *grandfather* charm; it was active now when children still made his old age happy.

How queerly he must have looked in England with his cage of little squirrels and the children following him in some good bishop's garden!

OLD MR. CALAMITY AGAIN.

FRANKLIN's paper, the Pennsylvania Gazette, which appeared in the year 1729, at first published by Franklin and Meredith, and always very neatly printed, had grown, and its income became large. It did much of the thinking for the province. But Franklin made it what it was by his energy, perseverance, and faith. He returned to America, and the paper voiced his opinions.

In the period of his early struggle, he was wheeling some printing paper in a wheelbarrow along the streets toward his office when he heard the tap, tap, tap of an old man's cane.

He looked around. It was the cane of old Mr. Calamity. This man had advised him not to begin publishing.

"Young man——"

"Good morning, sir. I hope it finds you well."

"It must be hard times when an editor has to carry his printing paper in a wheelbarrow."

"The oracle said, 'Leave no stone unturned if you would find success.'"

"Well, my young friend, if there is anybody that obeys the oracle in Pennsylvania it is you. You dress plainly; you do not indulge in many luxuries; you attend the societies and clubs that seek information; you ought to succeed, but you won't."

The old man lifted his cane and brought it down on the flagging stones with a pump.

" You won't, *now!* "

He stood still for a moment to add to the impression of his words.

" What is this I hear? The province is about to issue paper money? What did I tell you long ago? This is an age of rags. Paper money is rags. Governor Keith's affairs have all gone to ruin; it is unfortunate that he went away. And you are going to print the paper money for the province, are you? Listen to me: in a few years it will not be worth the paper it is printed on, and you will be glad to follow the example of Governor Keith, and get out of Philadelphia. The times are hard, but they are going to be harder. What hope is there for such a man as you? "

Franklin set down his wheelbarrow.

" My good sir, I am doing honest work. It will tell—I have confidence that it will tell."

" Tell! Tell who? "

" The world."

" The world! The owls have not yet ceased to hoot in woods around Philadelphia, and he has a small world that is bounded by the hoot of an owl."

" My father used to say that he who is diligent in his business shall stand before kings," quoting the Scripture.

" Well, you may be as honest and as diligent in your business as you will, it is a small chance that you will ever have of standing before kings. What are you standing before now?—a wheelbarrow. That is as far as you have got. A promising young man it must be to stand before a wheelbarrow and talk about standing before kings!"

"But, sir, I ought not to be standing before a wheelbarrow. I ought to be going on and coining time."

"Well, go right along; you are on the way to Poverty Corner, and you will not need any guide post to find it; take up the handles of the wheelbarrow and go right on. Maybe the king will send a coach for you some day."

He did—more than one king did.

Franklin took the handles of the wheelbarrow, wondering which was the true prophet, his father's Scripture or cautious old Mr. Calamity. As he went on he heard the tap, tap, tap of the cane behind him, and a low laugh at times and the word "kings."

He came to the office, and taking a huge bundle of printing paper on his shoulder went in. The cane passed, tap, tap, tapping. It had an ominous sound. But after the tap, tap, tap of the cane had gone, Franklin could still hear his old father's words in his spiritual memory, and he believed that they were true.

We must continue the story of Mr. Calamity, so as to picture events from a Tory point of view. The incident of the wheelbarrow would long cause him to reproach the name of Franklin.

The Pennsylvania Gazette not only grew and became a source of large revenue, so that Franklin had no more need to wheel to his office printing paper with his own hands, but it crowned with honor the work of which he was never ashamed. The printing of the paper money of the province added to his name, the success that multiplies success began its rounds with the years, and middle life found him a rich man, and his late return from England a man with the lever of power that molds opinion.

Poor old Mr. Calamity must have viewed this growth and prosperity with eyes askance. His cane tapped more rapidly yearly as it passed the great newspaper office, notwithstanding that it bore more and more the weight of years.

Benjamin Franklin was a magnanimous man. He never wasted time in seeking the injury of any who ridiculed and belittled him. He had the largest charity for the mistakes in judgment that men make, and the opportunities of life were too precious for him to waste any time in beating the air where nothing was to be gained. Help the man who some time sought to injure you, and the day may come when he will help you, and such Peter-like experiences are among life's richest harvests. The true friendship gained by forgiveness has a breadth and depth of life that bring one of the highest joys of heaven to the soul.

"I will study many things, for I must be proficient in something," said the poet Longfellow when young. Franklin studied everything—languages, literature, science, and art. His middle life was filled with studies; all life to him was a schoolroom. His studies in middle life bore fruit after he was threescore and ten years of age. They helped to make his paper powerful.

Franklin's success greatly troubled poor old Mr. Calamity.

After the printer made the great discovery that electricity was lightning, the old man opposed the use of lightning-rods.

"What will that man Franklin do next?" he said. "He would oppose the Lord of the heavens from thundering and lightning—he would defy Providence and Omnipotent Power. Why, the next thing he may deny the authority of King George himself, who is divinely appointed. He is a dangerous man, the most dangerous man in all the colony."

Old Mr. Calamity warned the people against the innovations of this dangerous man.

One day, as he was resting under the great trees on the Schuylkill, there was brought to him grievous news. A clerk in the Pennsylvania Assembly came up to him and asked:

"Do you know what has been done? The Assembly has appointed Franklin as agent to London; he is to go as the agent of all the colonies."

"Sho! What do the colonies want of an agent in London? Don't the king know how to govern his colonies? And if we need an agent abroad, why should we send a printer and a lightning-rod man? Clerk, sit down! That man Franklin is a dangerous leader. 'An agent of the colonies in London!' Why, I have seen him carrying printing paper in a wheelbarrow. A curious man that to send to the court of England's sovereign, whose arms are the lion and the unicorn."

"But there is a movement in England to tax the colonies."

"And why shouldn't there be? If the king thinks it is advisable to tax the colonies for their own support, why should not his ministers be instructed to do so? The king is a power divinely ordained; the king can do no wrong. We ought to be willing to be taxed by such a virtuous and gracious sovereign. Taxation is a blessing; it makes us realize our privileges. Oh, that Franklin! that Franklin! there is something peculiarsome about him; but the end of that man is to fall. First carrying about printing paper in a wheelbarrow, then trifling with the lightning in a thunderstorm, and now going to the court of England as a representative of the colonies. The world never saw such an amazing spectacle as that in all its history. Do you know what the king may yet be compelled to do? He may yet have to punish his American colonies. Clouds are gathering—I can see. Well, let Franklin go, and take his wheelbarrow with him! What times these are!"

Franklin was sent to England again greatly to the discomfort of Mr. Calamity.

The English Parliament passed an act called the Stamp Act, taxing the colonies by placing a stamp on all paper to be used in legal transactions. It was passed against the consent of the colonies, who were allowed to have no representatives in the foreign government, and the measure filled the colonies with indignation. There were not many in America like Mr. Calamity who believed the doctrine that the king could do no wrong. King George III approved of the Stamp Act, not only as a means of revenue, but as an assertion of royal authority.

The colonies were opposed to the use of the stamped paper. Were they to submit to be governed by the will of a foreign power without any voice in the measures of the government imposed upon them? Were their lives and property at the command of a despotism, without any source of appeal to justice?

The indignation grew. The spirit of resistance to the arbitrary act of tyranny was everywhere to be met and seen.

From the time of his arrival in London, in 1764, at the age of fifty-nine, Franklin gave all his energies for a long time to opposing the Stamp Act, and, after it had passed, to securing its repeal. He was, as it were, America in London.

The Stamp Act, largely through his influence, was at last repealed, and joy filled America. Processions were formed in honor of the king, and bonfires blazed on the hills. In Boston the debtors were set free from jail, that all might unite in the jubilee.

Franklin's name filled the air.

Old Mr. Calamity heard of it amid the ringing of bells.

"Franklin, Franklin," he said on the occasion, turning around in vexation and taking a pinch of snuff, "why, I have seen him carrying printing paper in a wheelbarrow!"

Philadelphia had a day of jubilee in honor of the repeal of the Stamp Act, and Mr. Calamity with cane and snuffbox wandered out to see the sights. The streets were in holiday attire, bells were ringing, and here and there a shout for Franklin went up from an exulting crowd. As often as the prudent old gentleman heard that name he turned around, pounding his cane and taking a pinch of snuff.

He went down to a favorite grove on the banks of the Schuylkill. He found it spread with tables and hung with banners.

"Sir," he said to a local officer, "is there to be a banquet here?"

"Yes, your Honor, *the* banquet is to be here. Have you not heard?"

"What is the banquet to be for?"

"In honor of Franklin, sir."

Mr. Calamity turned round on his cane and took out his snuffbox.

There was an outburst of music, a great shout, and a hurrying of people toward the green grove.

Something loomed in air.

The old gentleman, putting his hand over his eye as a shade, looked up in great surprise.

"What—what is that?"

What indeed!

"A boat sailing in the air?" He added, "Franklin must have invented that!"

"No," said the official, "that is the great barge."

"What is it for?"

"It will exhibit itself shortly," said the official.

It came on, covered with banners that waved in the river winds.

The old man read the inscription upon it—"*Franklin.*"

"I told you so," he said.

"It will thunder soon," said the official. "Don't you see it is armed with guns?"

The barge stopped at the entrance of the grove. A discharge of cannon followed from the boat, which was forty feet long. A great shout followed the salute. The whole

city seemed cheering. The name that filled the air was
"*Franklin*."

Mr. Calamity turned around and around, planting his cane
down in a manner that left a circle, and then taking out of his
pocket his snuffbox.

He saw a boy cheering.

" Boy! "

" Sir? "

" What are *you* shouting for? "

" For the Stamp Act, sir! "

" That is right, my boy."

" No, for Franklin! "

" For Franklin? Why, I have seen him carrying a lot of
printing paper through the streets in a wheelbarrow! May
time be gracious to me, so that I may see him hanged! Boy,
see here——"

But the banners were moving into the green grove, and the
boy had gone after them.

Benjamin Franklin returned to Philadelphia the most popular man in the colonies, and was elected a delegate to the Continental Congress.

" Only Heaven can save us now," said troubled Mr. Calamity. "There's treason in the air! "

The old gentleman was not a bad man; he saw life on the
side of shadow, and had become blind to the sunny side of life.
He was one of those natures that are never able to come out of
the past.

The people amid the rising prosperity ceased to believe in
old Mr. Calamity as a prophet. He felt this loss of faith in

him. He assumed the character of the silent wise man at times. He would pass people whom he had warned of the coming doom, shaking his head, and then turning around would strike his cane heavily on the pavement, which would cause the one he had left behind to look back. He would then lift his cane as though it were the rod of a magician.

"Old Mr. Calamity is coming," said a Philadelphia school-boy to another, one new school day in autumn. "See, he is watching Franklin, and is trying to avoid meeting him."

Their teacher came along the street.

"Why, boys, are you watching the old gentleman?"

"He is trying to avoid meeting Mr. Franklin, sir."

"Calamity comes to avoid Industry," said the teacher, as he saw the two men. Franklin was the picture of thrift, and his very gait was full of purpose and energy. I speak in parable," said the teacher, "but that old gentleman is always in a state of alarm, and he seems to find satisfaction in predicting evil, and especially of Mr. Franklin. The time was when the young printer avoided him—he was startled, I fancy, whenever he heard the cane on the pavement; he must have felt the force of the suggestion that Calamity was after him. Now he has become prosperous, and the condition is changed. Calamity flees from him. See, my boys, the two men."

They stopped on the street.

Mr. Calamity passed them on the opposite side, and Mr. Franklin came after him, walking briskly. The latter stopped at the door of his office, but the old gentleman hurried on. When he reached the corner of the street he planted his cane down on the pavement and looked around. He saw the popular printer standing before his office door on the street. The two looked at each other. The old man evidently felt uncomfortable. He turned the corner, out of sight, when an extraordinary movement appeared.

Mr. Calamity reached back his long, ruffled arm, and his cane, in view of the philosopher, the teacher, and the boys, and shook the cane mysteriously as though he were writing in the air. He may have had in mind some figure of the ancient prophets. Up and down went the cane, around and around, with curves of awful import. It looked to those on the street he had left as though the sharp angle of the house on the corner had suddenly struck out a living arm in silent warning.

The arm and cane disappeared. A head in a wide-rimmed hat looked around the angle as if to see the effect of the writing in the air. Then the arm and cane appeared again as before. It was like the last remnant of a cloud when the body has passed.

The teacher saw the meaning of the movement.

"Boys," said he, "if you should ever be pursued by Mr. Calamity in any form, remember the arm and cane. See Franklin laugh! Industry in the end laughs at Calamity, and Diligence makes the men who 'stand before kings.' It is the law of life. Detraction is powerless before will and work, and as a rule whatever any one dreams that he may do, he will do."

The boys had received an object lesson, and would long carry in their minds the picture of the mysterious arm and cane.

In a right intention one is master of the ideal of life. If circumstances favor, he becomes conscious that life is no longer master of him, but that he is the master of life. This sense of

power and freedom is noble; in vain does the shadow of
Calamity intrude upon it; the visions of youth become a part
of creations of the world; the dream of the architect is a mansion now; of the scientist, a road, a railway over rivers and
mountains; of the orator and poet, thoughts that live.   Even
the young gardner finds his dreams projected into his farm.   So
ideals become realities, and thoughts become seeds that multiply.   Mr. Calamity may shake his cane, but it will be behind a
corner.   Happy is he who makes facts of his thoughts that were
true to life!

CHAPTER XXXIV.

OLD MR. CALAMITY AND THE TEARING DOWN OF THE KING'S ARMS.

Our gentlemanly friend Mr. Calamity was now very, very old, long past the milestone of eighty. As Philadelphia grew, the streets lengthening, the fine houses rising higher and higher, he began to doubt that he was a prophet, and he shunned Benjamin Franklin when the latter was in the country.

One day, long before the Stamp Act, he passed the Gazette office, when the prosperous editor appeared.

"It's coming," said he, tap, tapping on. "What did I tell you?"

"What is coming?" asked our vigorous king of prosperity.

"War!" He became greatly excited. "Indians! they're coming with the tommyhawk and scalping knife, and we'll need to be thankful if they leave us our heads."

There were indeed Indian troubles and dire events at that time, but not near Philadelphia.

Time passed. He was a Tory, and he heard of Concord and Lexington, and he ceased to read the paper that Franklin printed, and his cane flew scatteringly as it passed the office door. To him that door was treason.

One evening he lifted his cane as he was passing.

"The king will take the puny colonies in his mighty arms and dash them against the high rock of the sea. He will dash them in pieces 'like a potter's vessel.' What are we to the throne of England!"

He heard of Bunker Hill, and his old heart beat free again.

"What did I tell you?" he said. "King George took the rebels in his arms and beat them against Bunker Hill. He'll plant his mighty heel on Philadelphia some day, and may it fall on the head of Benjamin Franklin, for of all rebels he is the most dangerous. Oh, that Franklin! He is now advocating the independence of the colonies!"

The Provincial Congress began to assemble, and cavalcades went out to meet the members as they approached the city on horseback. The Virginia delegation were so escorted into the city with triumph. The delegates were now assembling to declare the colony free. Independence was in the air.

Terrible days were these to Mr. Calamity. As often as he heard the word "independence" on the street his cane would fly up, and after this spasm his snuffbox would come out of his pocket for refreshment. His snuffbox was silver, and on it in gold were the king's arms.

He was a generous man despite his fears. He was particularly generous with his snuff. He liked to pass it around on the street, for he thereby displayed the king's arms on his snuffbox.

When the Massachusetts delegates came, the city was filled with joy. But Samuel Adams was the soul of the movement for independence, and after his arrival independence was more and more discussed, which kept poor old Mr. Calamity's cane continually flying. But his feelings were terribly wounded daily by another event of common occurrence. As he passed the snuffbox to the Continentals he met, and showed the royal arms upon it, they turned away from him; they would not take snuff from the royal snuffbox. These were ominous times indeed.

The province of Pennsylvania had decreed that no one should hold any office derived from the authority of the king. For a considerable period there was no government in Pennsylvania, no authority to punish a crime or collect a debt, but all things went on orderly, peacefully, and well.

Old Mr. Calamity used to sit under the great elm tree at Shakamaxon in the long summer days and extend his silver snuffbox to people as they passed. The tree was full of singing birds; flowers bloomed by the way, and the river was bright; but to him the glory of the world had fled, for the people no longer would take snuff from the box with the royal arms.

One day a lady passed who belonged to the days of the Penns and the Proprietors.

"Madam Bond," said he, "comfort me."

A patriot passed. The old man held out the snuffbox. The man hesitated and started back.

"The royal arms will have to go," said the patriot.

"Where from?" said the old man excited.

"From everywhere. We are about to decree a new world."

"They will never take these golden arms from that snuffbox. Sir, do you know that box was given to the Proprietor by Queen Charlotte herself?"

"Well, the golden arms will have to come off it; they will have to come down everywhere. No—I thank you," he continued. "I can not ever take snuff again out of a snuffbox like that."

Poor old Mr. Calamity turned to the lady.

"What am I to do? Where am I to go? You do pity me, don't you?"

A little girl passed near. He held out the box. The girl ran. The poor old man began to tremble.

"I have trembling fits sometimes," said he. "Take a pinch of snuff with me; it will steady me. Take a pinch of snuff for Queen Charlotte's sake."

He shook like the leaves of the elm tree in the summer wind.

Dame Bond hesitated.

He trembled more violently. "Do you hesitate to honor the name of Queen Charlotte?" he said.

The woman took a pinch of snuff in memory of the days gone. He grew calmer.

"That strengthens me," he said. "What am I to do? The things that I see daily tear me all to pieces. It broke my heart to see that child run away. I can not cross the sea, and if they were to tear down the king's arms from the State House I would die. I would tremble until I grew cold and my breath left me. You do pity me, don't you? I sometimes grow cold now when I tremble."

It was June. A bugle rang out in the street.

17

" What is that? " he asked of a volunteer who passed by.

" It is the summons."

" For what? "

" For the assembling of the people."

" In God's name, for what? Is a royal messenger coming? "

" No. They are going to tear down the king's arms from all the buildings at six, and are going to pile them up on tar barrels and make a bonfire of them when the sun goes down. The flame will ascend to heaven. That will be the end of the reign of King George III in this province forever! "

The old man trembled again.

" I am cold," he said.—" Dame Bond, take another pinch of snuff out of the silver box with the golden arms—it helps me."

Dame Bond once more paid her respects to Queen Charlotte.

" Before God, you do not tell me, sir, that they are going to take down the king's arms from the State House? "

" The king's arms are to be torn down from all the buildings, my aged friend; from the inns, the shops, the houses, the State House, and all."

" Dame Bond, my limbs fail. I shall never go home again. Tell the family as you pass that I shall not return to tea with them. Let me pass the evening here, where Penn made his treaty with the Indians. To-night is the last of Pennsylvania. I never wish to see another morning."

At seven o'clock in the long, fiery day the great bell rang. The bugle sounded again. People ran hither and

THE DESTRUCTION OF THE ROYAL ARMS.

thither.   A rocket flared across the sky, and a great cry went up:

"Down with the arms!"

A procession headed with soldiers passed through the streets of the city bearing with them a glittering sign.   Military music filled the air.

The old man's daughter Mercy came to see him under the tree and to persuade him to go home with her.

"Mercy—daughter—what are they carrying away?"

"The king's arms from the State House; that is all, father."

"All! all!   Say you rather that it is the world!"

The roseate light faded from the high hills and the waters. The sea birds screamed, and cool breezes made the multitudinous leaves of the tree to quiver.

"Mercy—daughter—and what was that?"

"They are lighting a bonfire, father."

"What for?"

"To burn the king's arms."

"What will we do without a king?"

"They will have a Congress."

A great shout went up on a near hill.

"But, Mercy—daughter—a Congress is men.   A Congress is not a power ordained.   Oh, that I should ever live to see a day like this!   'Twas Franklin did it.   I can see it all—it was he; it was the printer boy from Boston."

Darkness fell.   It was nine o'clock now.   There was a discharge of firearms, and a great flame mounted up from the pile on the hill, and put out the stars and filled the heavens.

" Father, let us go home."

" No, let me stay here under the tree."

" Why, father? "

" The palsy is coming upon me—I can feel it coming, and here I would die."

" Oh, father, return with me, for my sake! "

" Well, help me, then."

She lifted him, and they went back slowly to the street.

The city was deserted. The people were out to the hill. There was a crackling of dry boards in the bonfire, and the flame grew redder and redder, higher and higher.

They came to the State House. The old man looked up. The face of the house was bare; the king's arms were gone.

He sank down on the step of an empty house and began to tremble. He took out his silver snuffbox and held it shaking.

" For Queen Charlotte's sake, daughter," he said.

She touched the box, to please him.

" Gone," he said; " the king's arms are gone, and I have no wish to survive them. I feel the chill coming on—'tis the last time. Take the silver box, daughter ; for my sake hide it, and always be true to the king's arms upon it. As for me, I shall never see the morning! "

He lay there in the moonlight, his eyes fixed on the State House where the king's arms had been.

The people came shouting back, bearing torches that were going out. Houses were being illuminated.

He ceased to tremble. They sent for a medical man and for his near kin. These people were among the multitude.

They came late and found him lying in the moonlight white and cold.

The bells are ringing. Independence is declared. The king's rule in the province is gone forever. Benjamin Franklin's name commands the respect of lovers of liberty throughout the world. He is fulfilling the vision of Uncle Benjamin, the poet. He has added virtue to virtue, intelligence to intelligence, benevolence to benevolence, faith to faith. So the ladder of success ascends. Like his great-uncle Tom, his influence has caused the bells to ring; it will do so again.

Franklin heard of his great popularity in America while in England.

"Now I will call for the pamphlets," he said. He again walked alone in his room. He faced the future. "Not yet, not yet," he added, referring to the pamphlets. "The struggle for liberty has only begun. I will order the pamphlets when the colonies are free. The hopes in them will then be fulfilled, and not until then."

JENNY AGAIN.

FRANKLIN was suddenly recalled to America.

He stood at Samuel Franklin's door.

Samuel Franklin was an old man now.

"I have come to Boston once more," said Benjamin Franklin. "I would go to my parents' graves and the grave of Uncle Ben. But they are in the enemy's camp now. Samuel, I found your father's pamphlets in London."

"Is it possible? Where are they now?"

"I will return them to you when the colonies shall be free. The reading of them shall be a holiday in our old lives."

"I may never live to see that day. Benjamin, I am an old man. I want that you should will those pamphlets to my family."

The old men went out and stood by the gate late in the evening. The moon was rising over the harbor; it was a warm, still night. Sentries were pacing to and fro, for Boston was surrounded by sixteen thousand hostile men in arms.

The nine o'clock bell rang.

"I must go back to the camp," said Franklin, for he had met Samuel within the American lines.

"Cousin Benjamin, these are perilous times," said Samuel. "Justice is what the world needs. Make those pamphlets live, and return them with father's name honored in yours to my family."

"I will do so or perish. I am in dead earnest."

He ascended the hill and looked down on the British camps in Boston town.

Franklin had been sent to Cambridge as a commissioner to Washington's army at this time. It was October, 1775.

He longed to see his sister Jane—"Jenny"—once more. His sister was now past sixty years of age. Foreseeing the siege of Boston, he had written to her to come to Philadelphia and to make her home with him. But she was unwilling to remove from her own city and old home, though she was forced to find shelter within the lines of the American army.

One night, after her removal from Boston, there came a gentle knock at the door of her room. She opened it guardedly, and looked earnestly into the face of the stranger.

"Jenny!"

"My own brother!—do I indeed see you alive? Let me put my hand into yours once more."

He drew her to him.

"Jenny, I have longed for this hour."

"But what brings you here at this time? You did not come wholly to see me? Sit down, and let us bring up all the past again."

He sat down beside her, holding her hand.

"Jenny, you ask what brings me here. Do you remember Uncle Ben?"

"Whose name you bear? Never shall I forget him. The memory of a great man grows as years increase."

"Jenny, I've heard the bells in Ecton ring, and I found in Nottinghamshire letters from Uncle Benjamin, and they coupled your name when you was a girl with mine when I was a boy; do you remember what he said to us on that showery summer day when all the birds were singing?"

"Yes, Ben—I must call you 'Ben'—he said that 'more than wealth, more than fame, more than anything, was the power of the human heart, and that that power grows by seeking the good of others.'"

"What he said was true, but that was not all he said."

"He told you to be true to your country—to live for the things that live."

"Jenny, that is why I am here. He told you to be true to your home. You have been that, Jenny. You took care of father when he was sick for the last time, and you anticipated all his wants. I love you for that, Jenny."

"But it made me happy to do it, and the memory of it makes me happy now."

"And mother, you were her life in her old age. They are gone, both gone, but your heart made them happy when their steps were retreating. O Jenny, Jenny, your hair is turning gray, and mine is gray already. You have fulfilled Uncle Benjamin's charge under the trees. You have been true to your home."

"I only wish that I could have done more for our folks; and you, Ben—I can see you now as you were on that summer day—you have been true to your country."

"Jenny, do you remember the old writing-school master, George Brownell? You do? Well, I have a great secret for you. I used to tell my affairs to you many years ago. I am in favor of the *independence* of the colonies; and when Congress shall so declare, I shall put my name, that the old schoolmaster taught me to write, to the Declaration."

"Ben, it may cost you your life!"

"Then I will leave Uncle Ben's name in mine to the martyrs' list. I must be true to my country as you have been to your family—I must live for the things that live. I am Uncle Ben's pamphlet, Jenny. I know not what may befall me. This may be the last time that I shall ever visit Boston town—my beloved Boston—but I have found power with men by seeking their good, and my prayer is that I may one day meet you again, and have you say to me that I have honored Uncle Ben's name. I would rather have that praise from you than from any other person in the world: 'More than wealth, more than fame, more than anything, is the power of the human heart.'"

It was night. The camp of Washington was glimmering far away. Boston Neck was barricaded. There was a ship in the mouth of the Charles. A cannon boomed on Charlestown's hills.

"Jenny, I must go. When shall we meet again? Not until I have put Uncle Ben's name to the declaration of American liberty and independence is won. I must prepare the minds of the people to resolve to become an independent nation. My sister, my own true sister, what events may pass before we shall see each other again! When you were younger I made you a present of a spinnnig-wheel; later I sent you finery. I wish to leave you now this watch. The hours of the struggle for human liberty are at hand. Count the hours!"

They parted at the gate. The leaves were falling. It was the evening of the year. He looked back when he had taken a few steps. He was nearly seventy years of age. Yet his great work of life was before him—it was yet to do, while white-haired Jenny should count the hours on the clock of time.

Sam Adams had grasped the idea that the appeal to arms must end in the independence of the colonies. Franklin saw the rising star of the destiny of the union of the colonies to secure justice from the crown. He left Boston to give his whole soul to this great end.

The next day they went out to Tuft's Hill and looked down on the encamped town, the war ships, and the sea. It was an Indian summer. The trees were scarlet, the orchards were laden with fruit, and the fields were yellow with corn.

Over the blue sea rose the Castle, now gone. The smoke from many British camps curled up in the still, sunny air.

The Providence House Indian (now at the farm of the late Major Ben Perley Poore) gleamed over the roofs of the State House and its viceregal signs, which are now as then. Boston was three hills then, and the whole of the town did not appear as clearly from the hills on the west—the Sunset Hills—as now.

"Jenny, liberty is the right of mankind, and the cause of liberty is the cause of mankind," said Franklin. "Why should England hold provinces in America to whom she will allow no voice in her councils, whose people she may tax and condemn to prisons and death at the will of the king? I have told you my heart. America has the right of freedom, and the colonies must be free!"

They walked along the cool hill ways, and he looked longingly back at the glimmering town.

"Beloved Boston!" he said. "So thou wilt ever be to me!" He turned to his sister: "I used to tell my day dreams to you— they have come true, in part. I have been thinking again. If the colonies could be made free, and I were to be left a rich man, I would like to make a gift to the schools of Boston, whose influence would live as long as they shall last. Sister, I was too poor in my boyhood to answer the call of the school bells. I would like to endow the schools there with a fund for gifts or medals that would make every boy happy who prepares himself well for the work of life, be he rich or poor. I would like also to establish there a fund to help young apprentices, and to open public places of education and enjoyment which would be free to all people."

"You are Silence Dogood still," said Mrs. Mecom. "Day dreams in your life change into realities. I believe that all you now have in your heart to do will be done. Benjamin, these are great dreams."

"It may be that I will be sent abroad again."

"Benjamin, we may be very old when we meet again. But the colonies will be made free, and you will live to give a medal to the schools of Boston town. I must prophesy for you now, for Uncle Benjamin is gone. I began life with you—you carried me in your arms and led me by the hand. We used to sit by the east windows together; may we some day sit down together by the windows of the west and review the book of life, and close the covers. We may then read in spirit the pamphlets of Uncle Ben."

There was a thunder of guns at the Castle. War ships were coming into the harbor from the bay. Franklin beheld them with indignation.

"The people must not only have justice," he said, "they must have liberty."

They returned by the Cambridge road under the bowery elms. It would be a long time before they would see each other again.

In such beneficent thoughts of Boston the Franklin medal had its origin. It was coined out of his heart, that echoed wherever it went or was destined to go, "Beloved Boston!"

CHAPTER XXXVI.

THE DECLARATION OF INDEPENDENCE.—A MYSTERY.

The fame of Benjamin Franklin now filled America. On the continent of Europe he was held to be the first citizen of America. In France he was ranked among the sages and philosophers of antiquity, and his name associated with the greatest benefactors of the human race. It was his electrical discovery that gave him this solid and universal fame, but his Poor Richard's proverbs, which had several times been translated into French, were greatly quoted on the continent of Europe, and made his popularity as unique as it was general.

The old Boston schoolmaster who probably taught little Ben to flourish with his pen could have little dreamed of the documents of state to which this curious characteristic of the pen would be attached. Four of these documents were papers that led the age, and became the charters of human freedom and progress and began a new order of government in the world. They were the Declaration of Independence, the Alliance with France, the Treaty of Peace with England, and the draft of the Constitution of the United States.

In his service as agent of the colonies and as a member of the Continental Congress his mind clearly saw how valuable to the American cause an alliance with France and other Continental powers would be.   While in Europe as an agent of the colonies he gave his energy and experience to assisting a secret committee to negotiate foreign aid in the war.   It was a time of invisible ink, and Franklin instructed this committee how to use it.   He saw that Europe must be engaged in the struggle to make the triumph of liberty in America complete and permanent.

It was 1776.   Franklin was now seventy years old and was in America.   The colonies had resolved to be free.   A committee had been chosen by the Continental Congress in Philadelphia to prepare a draft for a formal Declaration of Independence, a paper whose principles were destined to emancipate not only the united colonies but the world.   The committee consisted of Thomas Jefferson, Benjamin Franklin, John Adams, Robert R. Livingston, and Roger Sherman.   Mr. Jefferson was appointed by this committee to write the Declaration, and he made it a voice of humanity in the language of the sages.   He put his own glorious thoughts of liberty into it, and he made these thoughts trumpet tones, and they, like the old Liberty Bell, have never ceased to ring in the events of the world.

When Jefferson had written the inspired document he showed it to Franklin and Adams, and asked them if they had any suggestions to offer or changes to make.

Franklin saw how grandly and adequately Jefferson had done the work.   He had no suggestion of moment to offer. But the composition was criticised in Congress, which brought out Franklin's wit, as the following story told by an eye-witness will show:

"When the Declaration of Independence was under the consideration of Congress, there were two or three unlucky expressions in it which gave offense to some members. The words 'Scotch and other foreign auxiliaries' excited the ire of a gentleman or two of that country. Severe strictures on the conduct of the British king in negativing our repeated repeals of the law which permitted the importation of slaves were disapproved by some Southern gentlemen, whose reflections were not yet matured to the full abhorrence of that traffic. Although the offensive expressions were immediately yielded, these gentlemen continued their depredations on other parts of the instrument. I was sitting by Dr. Franklin, who perceived that I was not insensible to ('*that I was writhing under*,' he says elsewhere) these mutilations.

"'I have made it a rule,' said he, 'whenever in my power, to avoid becoming the draughtsman of papers to be reviewed by a public body. I took my lesson from an incident which I will relate to you. When I was a journeyman printer, one of my companions, an apprenticed hatter, having served out his time, was about to open shop for himself. His first concern was to have a handsome signboard, with a proper inscription. He composed it in these words, *John Thompson, Hatter, makes and sells Hats for ready Money*, with a figure of a hat subjoined. But he thought he would submit it to his friends for their amendments. The first he showed it to thought the word *hatter* tautologous, because followed by the words *makes hats*, which showed he was a hatter. It was struck out. The next observed that the word *makes* might as well be omitted, because his customers would not care who made the hats; if good and to their mind they would buy, by whomsoever made. He struck it out. A third said he thought the words *for ready money* were useless, as it was not the custom of the place to sell on credit. Every one who purchased expected to pay. They were parted with; and the inscription now stood, 'John Thompson sells hats.' '*Sells* hats?' says his next friend; ' why, nobody will expect you to give them away. What, then, is the use of that word?' It was stricken out, and *hats* followed, the rather as there was one painted on the board. So his inscription was reduced ultimately to *John Thompson*, with the figure of a hat subjoined.' "

" We must all hang together," said Mr. Hancock, when the draft had been accepted and was ready to be signed.

" Or else we shall hang separately," Franklin is reported to have answered.

John Hancock, President of the Congress, put his name to the document in such a bold hand that " the King of England might have read it without spectacles." Franklin set his signature with its looped flourish among the immortals. In the same memorable month of July Congress appointed Franklin, Jefferson, and Adams to prepare a national seal.

The plan submitted by Franklin for the great seal of the United States was poetic and noble. It is thus described:

" Pharaoh sitting in an open chariot, a crown on his head and a sword in his hand, passing through the divided waters of the Red Sea in pursuit of the Israelites. Rays from a pillar of fire in the cloud, expressive of the Divine presence and command, beaming on Moses, who stands on the shore, and, extending his hand over the sea, causes it to overflow Pharaoh. Motto: 'Rebellion to tyrants is obedience to God.'"

This device was rejected by Congress, which decided upon a more simple allegory, and the motto *E Pluribus Unum*.

It was a time of rejoicing in Philadelphia now, and of the great events Jefferson was the voice and Franklin was the soul.

The citizens, as we have shown, tore down all the king's arms and royal devices from the government houses, court-rooms, shops, and taverns. They made a huge pile of tar barrels and placed these royal signs upon them. On a fiery July night they put the torch to the pile, and the flames curled up, and the black smoke rose in a high column under the moon and stars, and the last vestige of royalty disappeared in the bonfire.

Franklin heard the Liberty Bell ring out on the adoption of the Declaration of Independence by Congress. He saw the bonfire rise in the night of these eventful days, and heard the shouts of the people. He had set his hand to the Declaration. He desired next to set it to a treaty of alliance with France. Would this follow?

A very strange thing had happened in the colonies some seven months or more before—in November, 1775. A paper was presented to Congress, coming from a mysterious source, that stated that a stranger had arrived in Philadelphia who brought an important message from a foreign power, and who wished to meet a committee of Congress in secret and to make a confidential communication.

Congress was curious, but it at first took no official notice of the communication. But, like the Cumæan sibyl to Tarquin,

18

the message came again. It was not received, but it made an unofficial impression. It was repeated. Who was this mysterious stranger? Whence came he, and what had he to offer?

The curiosity grew, and Congress appointed a committee consisting of John Jay, Dr. Franklin, and Thomas Jefferson to meet the foreigner and to receive his proposition.

The committee appointed an hour to meet the secret messenger, and a place, which was one of the rooms of Carpenters' Hall.

At the time appointed they went to the place and waited the coming of the unknown ambassador.

There entered the room an elderly man of dignified appearance and military bearing. He was lame; he may have been at some time wounded. He spoke with a French accent. It was plainly to be seen that he was a French military officer.

Why had he come here? Where had he been hiding?

The committee received him cautiously and inquired in regard to the nature of his mission.

" His Most Christian Majesty the King of France," said he, " has heard of your struggle for a defense of your rights and for liberty. He has desired me to meet you as his representative, and to express to you his respect and sympathy, and to say to you in secrecy that should the time come when you needed aid, his assistance would not be withheld."

This was news of moment. The committee expressed their gratitude and satisfaction, and said:

" Will you give us the evidence of your authority that we may present it to Congress? "

His answer was strange.

"Gentlemen," said he, drawing his hand across his throat, "I shall take care of my head."

"But," said one of the committee, "in an event of such importance we desire to secure the friendly opinion of Congress."

"Gentlemen," making the same gesture, "I shall take care of my head." He then said impressively: "If you want arms, you may have them; if you want ammunition, you may have it; if you want money, you may have it. Gentlemen, I shall take care of my head."

He went out and disappeared from public view. He is such a mysterious character in our history as to recall the man with the Iron Mask. Did he come from the King of France? None knew, or could ever tell.

Diplomacy employed secret messengers at this time. It was full of suggestions, intrigues, and mysteries.

But there was one thing that this lame but courtly French officer did: he made an impression on the minds of the committee that the colonies had a friend in his "Most Christian Majesty the King of France," and from him they might hope for aid and for an alliance in their struggle for independence. Here was topic indeed for the secret committee.

On the 26th of September, 1776, Congress elected three ambassadors to represent the American cause in the court of France; they were Silas Deane, Arthur Lee, and Benjamin Franklin. Before leaving the country Franklin collected all the money that he could command, some four thousand pounds, and lent it to Congress. Taking with him his two grandsons, he arrived at Nantes on the 7th of December of that year, and he received in that city the first of the many ovations that his long presence in France was destined to inspire. He went to Paris, and took up his residence at Passy, a village some two miles from the city, on a high hill overlooking the city and the Seine. It was a lovely place even in Franklin's day. Here have lived men of royal endowments—Rossini, Bellini, Lamartine, Grisi. The arrival of Franklin there, where he lived many years, made the place famous. For Franklin, as a wonder-worker of science and as an apostle of human liberty, was looked upon more as a god than a man in France—a Plato, a Cato, a Socrates, with the demeanor of a Procion.

His one hope now was that he would be able to set the signature which he had left on the Declaration of Independence on a Treaty of Alliance between the States of America and his Most Christian Majesty the King of France. Will he, O shade of the old schoolmaster of Boston town?

Jamie the Scotchman, the type of the man who ridicules and belittles one, but claims the credit of his success when that one is successful, was very old now. Fine old Mr. Calamity, who could only see things in the light of the past, would prophesy no more. A young man with a purpose is almost certain to meet men like these in his struggles. Not all are able to pass such people in the Franklin spirit. He heard what such men had to say, tried to profit by their criticism, but wasted no time or energy in dispute or retaliation. The seedtime of life is too short, and its hours are too few, to spend in baffling detraction. Time makes changes pleasantly, and tells the truth concerning all men. A high purpose seeking fulfillment under humble circumstances is sure to be laughed at. It is that which stands alone that looks queer.

After Samuel Adams, Franklin was among the first of those leaders whose heart sought the independence of the colonies. The resolution for independence, passed on July 4, 1776, set ringing the Liberty Bell on the State House of Philadelphia. Couriers rode with the great news of the century and of the ages to Boston, which filled the old town with joy.

They brought a copy of the Declaration with them, and a day was appointed for the reading of it from the front window of the State House, under the shadow of the king's arms, the classic inscription, and the lion and the unicorn.

Old, tottering Jamie the Scotchman was among those who heard the great news with an enkindled heart. He, who had so laughed at little Ben's attempts for the public welfare, now claimed more and more to have been the greatest friend of the statesman's youth. It was the delight of his ninety or more years to make this claim wherever he went, and when the courier brought the news of the Declaration, we may see him going to Jane Mecom's house.

"You all know what a friend I was to that boy, and how I encouraged him, a little roughly it may be, but I always meant well. Jane, on the day the Declaration is read in public I want you to let me go with you to hear it."

They go together; she a lusty woman in full years, and he who had longed outlived his generation.

The street in front of the old State House is filled with people. The balcony window is thrown up, and out of the Council Chamber, now popularly known as the Sam Adams

room, there appears the representative of Sam Adams and of
five members of the Boston schools who had signed the Declaration. The officers of the State are there, and over the street
shines the spire of the South Church and gleams the Province
House Indian. The children are there; aged idlers who loi-
tered about the town pump; the women patriots from Spring
Lane. The New England flag, of blue ground with the cross
of St. George on a white field, floats high over all.

A voice rends the clear air. It read:

"When in the course of human events," and it marches on
in stately tones above the silence of the people. At the words
"all men are created free and equal," the name of Franklin
breaks upon the stillness. Jamie the Scotchman joins in the
rising applause, and he proudly turns to Jane Mecom and
says:

"Only to think what a friend I was to him, too!"

They return by the Granary burying ground. A tall, gray
monument holds their attention. It is one that the people
loved to visit then, and that touches the heart to-day. At the
foot of the epitaph they read again, as they had done many
times before:

"Their youngest son,

in filial regard to their memory,

places this stone."

"His heart was true to the old folks." said Jamie.

It was the monument that Benjamin Franklin had erected
to his parents.

CHAPTER XXXVII.

SOME years ago I stood on the battlements of Metz, once
a French but now a German town.   Below the town, with its
grand esplanade, on which is a heroic statue of Marshal Ney,
rolls the narrow Moselle, and around it are the remains of fortifications that are old in legend, song, and story.

It was here, near one of these old halls, that a young Frenchman saw, as it were, a vision, and the impression of that hour
was never lost, but became a turning point in American history.

There had come a report to the English court that Washington had been driven across the Jerseys, and that the American cause was lost.

There was given at this time a military banquet at Metz.
The Duke of Gloucester, brother of George III, was present,
and among the French officers there was a marquis, lately married, who was a favorite of the French court.   He had been
brought up in one of the heroic provinces of Auvergne, and he
had been associated with the heroes of Gatinais, whose motto
was *Auvergne sans tache.*   The Auvergnese were a pastoral people, distinguished for their courage and honor.   In
this mountainous district was the native place of many eminent
men, among them Polignac.

The young French marquis who was conspicuous at the banquet on this occasion was named Lafayette.

The Duke of Gloucester was in high spirits over his cups on this festal night.

"Our arms are triumphant in America!" he exclaimed. "Washington is retreating across the Jerseys."

A shout went up with glittering wine-cups: "So ever flee the enemies of George III!"

"Washington!" The name rang in the young French officer's ears. He had in his veins the blood of the mountaineers, and he loved liberty and the spirit of the motto *Auvergne sans tache*.

He may never have heard the name of Washington before, or, if he had, only as of an officer who had given Braddock unwelcome advice. But he knew the American cause to be that of liberty, and Washington to be the leader of that cause.

And Washington "was retreating across the Jerseys." Where were the Jerseys? He may never have heard of the country before.

He went out into the air under the moon and stars. There came to him a vision of liberty and a sense of his duty to the cause. The face of America, as it were, appeared to him. "When first I saw the face of America, I loved her," he said many years afterward to the American Congress.

Washington was driven back in the cause of liberty. Lafayette resolved to cross the seas and to offer Washington his sword. He felt that liberty called him—liberty for America, which might mean liberty for France and for all mankind.

About this time Benjamin Franklin began to receive letters

from this young officer, filled with the fiery spirit of the mountaineers. The officer desired a commission to go to America and enter the army. But it was a time of disaster, and faith in the American cause was very low. The marquis resolved to go to America at his own expense.

He sailed for that country in May, 1777. He landed off the coast of the Carolinas in June, and made his memorable ride across the country to Philadelphia in that month. Baron de Kalb accompanied him.

On landing on the shores of the Carolinas, he and Baron de Kalb knelt down on the sand, at night under the stars, and in the name of God dedicated their swords to liberty.

The departure of these two officers for America filled all France with delight. Lafayette had seen that it would be so; that his going would awaken an enthusiasm in the circles of the court and among the people favorable to America; that it would aid the American envoys in their mission. It was the mountain grenadiers that made the final charges at the siege of Yorktown under the inspiring motto of *Auvergne sans tache* (Auvergne without a stain).

Franklin now dwelt at beautiful Passy on the hill, and his residence there was more like a princely court than the house of an ambassador. He gave his heart and life and influence to seeking an alliance between France and the States. The court was favorable to the alliance. but the times and the constitution of the kingdom made the king slow, cautious, and diplomatic.

The American cause wavered. The triumphs of Lord Howe filled England with rejoicing and Passy with alarm.

In the midst of the depression at Passy there came a messenger from Massachusetts who brought to Franklin the news of Burgoyne's surrender. When Dr. Franklin was told that this messenger was in the courtyard of Passy, he rushed out to meet him.

"Sir, is Philadelphia taken?"

"Yes, sir."

Franklin clasped his hands.

"But, sir, I have other news. Burgoyne and his army are prisoners of war!"

Great was the rejoicing at Passy and in Paris. The way to an alliance appeared now to open to the envoys.

"O Mr. Austin," Dr. Franklin used to say to the young messenger from Massachusetts, "you brought us glorious news!"

The tidings was followed by other news in Passy. December 17, 1777, was a great and joyful day there. A minister came to the envoys there to announce that the French Government was ready to conclude an agreement with the United States, and to make a formal treaty of alliance to help them in the cause of independence.

The cause was won, but the treaty was yet delayed. There were articles in it that led to long debates.

But in these promising days Franklin was a happy man. He dressed simply, and he lived humbly for an envoy, though his living cost him some thirteen thousand dollars a year. He did not conform to French fashions, nor did the French expect them from a philosopher. He did not even wear a wig, which most men wore upon state occasions. Instead of a wig he. wore a fur cap, and one of his portraits so represents him.

While the negotiations were going on, a large cake was sent one day to the apartment where the envoys were assembled.   It bore the inscription *Le digne Franklin* (the worthy Franklin).   On reading the inscription, Mr. Silas Deane, one of the ambassadors, said, "As usual, Franklin, we have to thank you for our share in gifts like these."

"Not at all," said Franklin.   "This cake is designed for all three of us.   Don't you see?—Le (Lee) Digne (Deane) Franklin."

He could afford to be generous and in good humor.

February 6, 1778, was one of the most glorious of all in Franklin's life.   That day the treaties were completed and put upon the tables to sign.   The boy of the old Boston writing school did honor to his schoolmaster again.   He put his name now after the conditions of the alliance between France and the United States of America.

The treaty was celebrated in great pomp at the court.

The event was to be publicly announced on March 20, 1778.   On that day the envoys were to be presented to the king amid feasts and rejoicings.

Would Franklin wear a wig on that great occasion? His locks were gray and thin, for he was seventy-two years old, and his fur cap would not be becoming amid the splendors of Versailles.

He ordered one. The hairdresser came with it. He could not fit it upon the philosopher's great head.

"It is too small," said Franklin. "Monsieur, it. is impossible."

"No, monsieur," said the perruquier, "it is not that the wig is too small; it is that your head is too large!"

What did Franklin need of a wig? He dressed for the occasion in a plain suit of black velvet, with snowy ruffles and silver buckles. When the chamberlain saw him coming, he hesitated to admit him. Admit a man to the royal presence in his own head alone? But he allowed the philosopher to go on in his velvet, ruffles, and silver buckles, and his independent appearance filled the court with delight.

There was another paper that he must now have begun to see in his clear visions. The treaty of alliance would lead to the triumph of the American cause. That end must be followed by a treaty of peace between Great Britain and the United States. Would he sign that treaty some day and again honor the old Boston schoolmaster? We shall see.

But how did young Lafayette meet his duties in the dark days of America—he whose motto was "Auvergne without a stain?"

The day of his test came again at a banquet. It was at York. Let us picture this pivotal scene of his life and of American history.

After the triumphs of Gates at Saratoga, Washington became unpopular, and Congress appointed a Board of War, whose object it became to place Lafayette at the head of the Northern army, and thus give him a chance to supersede his chief.

The young Frenchman was loyal to Washington, and the motto *Auvergne sans tache* governed his life.

Let us suppose him to meet his trusty old friend Baron de Kalb, the German temperance general, at this critical hour.

"Baron de Kalb, we stood together side by side at Metz, and we knelt down together that midsummer night when we first landed on Carolina's sands, and then we rode together across the provinces. These are events that I shall ever love to recall. To-night we stand together again in brotherhood of soul. Baron, the times are dark and grow more perilous, and it may be I now confide in thee for the last time."

"Yes, Lafayette," answered De Kalb, "I myself feel 'tis so. You may live and rise, but I may fall. But wherever I may go I shall draw this sword that I consecrated with thine to liberty. It may be ours to meet by chance again, but, Lafayette, we shall never be as we are now. Thou well hast said the hour is dark. Open thy soul, then, Lafayette, to me."

"Baron, it burns my brain and shrinks my heart to say that the hour is dark not only for the cause but for our chief, for Washington. In halls of state, in popular applause, the rising star is Gates. Factions arise, cabals combine, and this new Board of War has sent for me. In some provincial room that flattery decorates they are to make for me a feast. What means the feast? 'Tis this: to offer me the Northern field. And why? To separate my sword from Washington. 'If thy right hand offend thee, cut it off!' I'm loyal to the cause, and must obey this new-made Board of War; but on that night, if so it be that I have the opportunity, I shall arise, and, against all flatteries, take my stand. I then and there will proclaim in clear-cut words my loyalty to Washington. He is the cause;

in him it stands or falls; to gain a world for self, my heart could never be untrue to him. Day after day, month after month, year after year, he leads the imperiled way, yet holds his faith in God and man. The hireling Hessians roll their drums through ports and towns; the wily Indian joins the invader; his army is famine-smitten and thinned with fever, and drill in rags, while Congress meets in secret halls but to impede his plans and criticise; and while he holds the scales and looks toward the end, and makes retreat best serve the cause, what rivals rise! See brilliant Gates appear! Does he not know this rivalry and hear the plaudits that surround the name of Saratoga? I've shared my thoughts with Washington, young as I am, and he has honored me with his esteem. I have heard him say: "O Lafayette, I stand alone in all the world! I dream no dreams of high ambition. I love the farm more than the field—my country home more than the halls of state I serve. In a cause like this I hold that it is not unsubstantial victories but generalship that wins.'

"One day he spoke like this: ' Marquis, I stood one winter night upon a rocking boat and crossed the Delaware. It was a bitter night; no stars were in the sky; the lanterns' rays scarce fell upon the waters; the oars rose and fell, though they were frozen, for they were plied by strong and grizzly fishermen; the snow fell pitiless, with hail and sleet and rain. The night was wind, and darkness was the air. The army followed me, where I could not see. Our lips were silent. These stout and giant men, from Cape Ann and from wintry wharfages of Marblehead, knew their duty well, and safe we crossed the tide.' In that lone boat, amid the freezing sleet and darkness deep, the new flag of the nation's hope marched in darkness.

"Baron de Kalb, there is a spirit whose pinions float upon the wings of time. She comes to me in dreams and visions in such hours as these. I saw her on the fortress walls of Metz; I knew her meaning and her mission saw. Where liberty is, there is my country, and all I am I again offer to her cause. Hear me this hour; the presence of that spirit falls on me now as at Metz. I go to the feast that is waiting for me; there my soul must be true and speak the truth, and for the truth there is no judgment day. At Metz I left myself for liberty; at York I shall be as true to honor. I hold unsullied fame to be more than titles—*Auvergne sans tache.* My resolution makes my vision clear. Baron de Kalb, mark you my words in this prophetic hour: the character of Washington will free one day the world, and lead the Aryan race and liberty and peace. It is not his genius—minds as great have been; it is not his heart—there have been hearts as large; it is not his sword, for swords have been as brave, but it is himself that makes sure the cause. He shall win liberty, and give to men their birthright and to toil a field of hope; to industry the wealth that it creates, and to the toiler his dues. So liberty to brotherhood shall lead, and brotherhood to peace, and brotherhood and peace shall bring to unity all human families, and men shall live no more in petty strife for gain, but for the souls of men. The destinies then, as in Virgil's eye, shall spin life's web, and to their spindles say, 'Thus go forever and forever on!' He is the leader appointed by Heaven for sublime events. I am sent to him as a knight of God. I go to York.

I was true at Metz to liberty, and in the council hall I shall be true, whatever is offered me, to Washington, our Washington beloved! to the world's great commoner! Farewell."

The feast for Lafayette was spread at York in a blazing hall; red wine filled the crystal cups. Silken banners waved and disclosed the magic name of "Lafayette." The Board of War was there, proud Gates, and the men of state. The *Fleur de lis* was there and blew across the national banners. Lafayette came. A shout arose as he appeared. The Board of War was merry, and the wine was spilled and toasts were drunk to all the heroes of the war except Washington. The name of Lafayette was hailed with adulation; then all was still. The grand commissioner had waved his hand. He bowed, and gave to Lafayette a sealed paper; he raised his cup, and rose and bowed, and said, " Now drink ye all to him, our honored guest, commander of the Army of the North." The oak room rang with cheers; the glasses clinked and gleamed.

The board and guests sat down. There, tall and grand above the council, towered the form of Lafayette. He stood there silent, then raised a crystal cup, and said: " I thank you, friends, and I would that I were worthier of your applause. You have honored many worthy names, but there is one name that you have omitted in your many toasts, and that one name to me stands above all the other heroes of the world! *I* drink to him!" He lifted high the cup, and said, " I pledge my honor, my sword, and all I am to Washington!"

He stood in silence; no other cup with his was raised. He

left the hall, and walked that night the square of York beneath the moon and stars as he had done at Metz.

He poured forth his soul, thinking again the thoughts of Metz, and making again the high resolves that he had made on Carolina's sands with Baron de Kalb:

"O Liberty! the star of hope that lights each noble cause, uniting in one will the hearts of men, and massing in one force the wills of men. The stars obey the sun; the earth, the stars; the nations, those who rise o'er vain ambitions and become the cause. Thou gavest Rome the earth and Greece the sea; thou sweepest down the Alps, and made the marbles bloom like roses, for thy heroes' monuments! I hear thy voice, and I obey, as all the true have bowed who more than self have loved mankind!"

The coming of Franklin to Passy and the going of Lafayette from Metz were among the great influences of the age of liberty. Count Rochambeau followed Lafayette after the alliance, and brought over with him among his regiments the grenadiers of Auvergne—*Auvergne sans tache*, which motto they honored at Yorktown.

Jenny's heart beat with joy as she heard of the coming of Lafayette. In these years of the great struggle for human liberty she looked at the watch and counted the hours.

Franklin had long been the hope of the country. America looked to him to secure the help of France in the long struggle for liberty. Into this hope humble Jane Mecom entered with a sister's confidence and pride.

She awaited the news from Philadelphia, which was the seat of government, with the deepest concern. The nation's affairs were her family affairs. She heard it said daily that if Franklin secured the aid of the French arms, the cause of liberty in America would be won. It was the kindly hand that led her when a girl that was now moving behind these great events.

One July day, at the full tide of the year, she was standing in the bowery yard of her simple home, thinking of her brother and the hope of the people in him. She moved, as under a spell of thought, out of the gate and toward Beacon Hill. She met Jamie the Scotchman on her way.

"An' do you think that he will be able to do it?" said Jamie. By "it" he meant the alliance of France with the colonies. "Surely it is a big job to undertake, but if he should succeed, Jane, I want you always to remember what a friend I was to him. Where are you going, Jane?"

"To the old tree on Beacon Hill, where Uncle Ben used to talk to me in childhood."

"May I go with you, Jane? They say that a fleet has been sighted off Narragansett Bay. We shall know when the post comes in."

"Yes, Jamie, come with me. I love to talk of old times with you."

"And what a friend I was to *him*."

It was a fiery day. Cumulus clouds were piling up in the fervid heats. The Hancock House gardens, where now the State House is, were fragrant with flowers, and the Common below was a sea of shining leaves.

A boom shook the air.

"What was that, Jane?"

"It came from the Castle."

“ Perhaps there is news.”

Another boom echoed from the Dorchester Hills, and a puff of smoke rose from the Castle.

“ There is news, Jamie; the Castle is firing a salute.”

“ I think the French fleet has arrived; if so, *his* work is behind it, and I always was such a friend to him, too! ”

The Castle thundered. There was news.

A magistrate came riding over the hills on horseback, going to the house of John Hancock.

“ Hey! ” cried Jamie, “ an’ what is the news? ”

“ The French fleet has arrived at Newport. Count Rochambeau is landing there. Hurrah! this country is free! ”

Jane sat down under the old tree, as she had done when a girl in Uncle Benjamin’s day. She saw the flag of the Stripes and Stars leap, as it were, into the air over the Hancock gardens. She had always revered John Hancock since he had heroically written to Washington at the time of the siege, “ Burn Boston, if there is need, and leave John Hancock a beggar! ”

Who was that hurrying up from the broad path of the Common toward the Hancock mansion? Jane rose up and looked. It was Samuel Adams, the so-called “ last of the Puritans,” a man who had almost forgotten his own existence in his efforts to unite the colonies for the struggle for liberty, and who had said to an agent of General Gage who offered him bribes if he would make his peace with the king, “ I have long ago made my peace with the King of kings, and no power on earth can make me recreant to my duties to my country.”

The Castle thundered on from the green isle in the harbor.

People were hurrying to and fro and gathering about the grounds of the first President of the Provincial Congress. Business stopped. The hearts of the people were thrilled. The independence of the American colonies now seemed secure.

There went up a great shout in front of the Hancock house. It was—

"Franklin! Rochambeau! Franklin!"

Jamie the Scotchman echoed the cheer from his lusty lungs.

"Franklin!" he cried, waving his hat, "Franklin now and forever!"

His face beamed. "Only think, Jane, what a friend I used to be to him! What do you suppose gave his hand such power in these affairs of the nation?"

"It was his heart, Jamie."

"Yes, yes, Jane, that was it—it was the heart of Franklin—of Ben, and don't you never forget what a friend I used to be to him."

The coming of Rochambeau, under the influence of the poor tallow chandler's son, was a re-enforcement that helped to gain the victory of liberty. When Cornwallis was taken, Jane Mecom heard the Castle thunder again over the sea; and when Rochambeau came to Boston to prepare for the re-embarkation of the French army, she saw her brother's hand behind all these events, and felt like one who in her girlhood had been taken into the counsels of the gods. Her simple family affairs had become those of the nation.

She knew the springs of the nation's history, and she loved to recall the days when her brother was Silence Dogood, which he had never ceased to be.

CHAPTER XXXVIII.

THE surrender of Lord Cornwallis at Yorktown brought
the war to an end. The courier from the army came flying
into Philadelphia at night. The watchman called out, "Past
twelve o'clock, and all is well!" "Past one o'clock, and all is
well!" and "Past two o'clock, and Cornwallis is taken!" The
people of the city were in the streets early that morning. Bells
pealed; men saluted each other in the name of "Peace."

Poor George III! He had stubbornly sought to subdue
the colonies, and had honestly believed that he had been divinely appointed to rule them after his own will. No idea that
he had ever been pigheaded and wrong had ever been driven
into his dull brain. His view of his prerogative was that whatever he thought to be best was best, and they were ungrateful
and stiff-necked people who took a different view, and that it
was his bounden duty to punish such in his colonies for their
obstinacy.

It was November 25th in London—Sunday. A messenger
came flying from the coast to Pall Mall. He was bearing exciting news. On he went through London until he reached
the house of George Germain, Minister of American Affairs.

The messenger handed to Lord George a dispatch. The minister glanced at it and read the fate of the New World, and must have stood as one dazed:

"Cornwallis has surrendered!"

Lord Walsingham, an under-Secretary of State, was at the house. To him he read the stunning dispatch. The two took a hackney coach and rode in haste to Lord Stormont's.

"Mount the coach and go with us to Lord North's. Cornwallis is taken!"

Lord Stormont mounted the coach, and the three rode to the office of the Secretary of State.

The prime minister received the news, we are told, "as he would have taken a ball into his heart."

"O God, it is all over!" he exclaimed, pacing up and down the room, and again and again, "O God, it is over!"

The news was conveyed to the king that half of his empire was lost—that his hope of the New World was gone. How was the king affected? Says a writer of the times, who gives us a glance at this episode:

"He dined on that day," he tells us, "at Lord George Germain's; and Lord Walsingham, who likewise dined there, was the only guest that had become acquainted with the fact. The party, nine in number, sat down to the table. Lord George appeared serious, though he manifested no discomposure. Before the dinner was finished one of his servants delivered him a letter, brought back by the messenger who had been dispatched to the king. Lord George opened and perused it; then looking at Lord Walsingham, to whom he exclusively directed his observation, 'The king writes,' said he, 'just as he always does, except that I observe he has omitted to note the hour and the minute of his writing with his usual precision.' This remark, though calculated to awaken some interest, excited no comment; and while the ladies, Lord George's three daughters, remained in the room, they repressed their curiosity. But they had no sooner withdrawn than Lord George, having acquainted them that from Paris information had just arrived of the old Count de Maurepas, first minister, lying at the point of death, 'It would grieve me,' said he, 'to finish my career, however far advanced in years, were I first minister of France, before I had witnessed the termination of this great contest between England and America.' 'He has survived to see that event,' replied Lord George, with some agitation. Utterly unsuspicious of the fact which had happened beyond the Atlantic, he conceived him to allude to the indecisive naval action fought at the mouth of the Chesapeake early in the preceding month of September between Admiral Graves and Count de Grasse, an engagement which in its results might prove most injurious to Lord Cornwallis. Under this impression, 'My meaning,' said he, 'is, that if I were the Count de Maurepas I should wish to live long enough to behold the final issue of the war in Virginia.' 'He has survived to witness it completely,' answered Lord George. 'The army has surrendered, and you may peruse the particulars of the capitulation in that paper,' taking at the same time one from his pocket, which he delivered into his hand, not without visible emotion. By his permission he read it aloud, while the company listened in profound silence. They then discussed its contents as affecting the ministry, the country, and the war. It must be confessed that they were calculated to diffuse a gloom over the most convivial society, and that they opened a wide field for political speculation.

" After perusing the account of Lord Cornwallis's surrender at Yorktown, it was impossible for all present not to feel a lively curiosity to know how the king had received the intelligence, as well as how he had expressed himself in his note to Lord George Germain, on the first communication of so painful an event. He gratified their wish by reading it to them, observing at the same time that it did the highest honor to his Majesty's fortitude, firmness, and consistency of character. The words made an impression on his memory, which the lapse of more than thirty years has not erased; and he here commemorates its tenor as serving to show how that prince felt and wrote under one of the most afflicting as well as humiliating occurrences of his reign. The billet ran nearly to this effect:

" ' I have received with sentiments of the deepest concern the communication which Lord George Germain has made me of the unfortunate result of the operations in Virginia. I particularly lament it on account of the consequences connected with it, and the difficulties which it may produce in carrying on the public business, or in repairing such a misfortune. But I trust that neither Lord George Germain, nor any member of the cabinet, will suppose that it makes the smallest alteration in those principles of my conduct which have directed me in past time, and which will always continue to animate me under every event in the prosecution of the present contest.' Not a sentiment of despondency or of despair was to be found in the letter, the very handwriting of which indicated composure of mind."

Franklin was still envoy plenipotentiary at beautiful Passy. He received the thrilling news, and wondered what terms the English Government would now seek to make in the interests of peace.

The king was shaken in mind and becoming blind. He was opposed to any negotiations for peace, and threatened to abdicate. He sank into a pitiable state of insanity some years after, was confined in a padded room, and even knew not when the battle of Waterloo was fought, and when his own son died he was not called to the funeral ceremonies.

But negotiations were begun, or attempted, with Dr. Franklin at Paris. Passy was again the scene of great events.

Mr. Adams, as a representative of the United States, arrived in Paris. Mr. Gay, another representative, was there; conference after conference was held with the English ambassador, and the final conference was held with the English ministers on November 29, 1782.

On the 18th of January, 1782, at Versailles, the representatives of England, France, and Spain signed the preliminaries of peace, declaring hostilities suspended, in the presence of Mr. Adams and Dr. Franklin. These preliminaries were finally received as a definitive treaty of peace, and on Wednesday, September 3, 1783, this Treaty of Peace was signed in Paris.

When the preliminary treaty was signed, Franklin rushed into the arms of the Duc de la Rochefoucault, exclaiming:

"My friend, could I have hoped at my age to enjoy such happiness?" He was then seventy-six years old.

So again the handwriting of the old Boston school appeared in the great events of nations. It was now set to peace.

It would not seem likely that it would ever again adorn any like document. Franklin was old and gray. He had signed the Declaration, the Treaty of Alliance, and now the Treaty of Peace. He had done his work in writing well. It had ended well. Seventy-six years old; surely he would rest now at Passy, or return to some Philadelphia seclusion and await the change that must soon fall upon him.

But this glorious old man has not yet finished the work begun by Silence Dogood. Those are always able to do the most who are doing many things. It is a period of young men now; it was a time of old men then. People sought wisdom from experience, not experiment.

The peace is signed. The bells are ringing, and oppressed peoples everywhere rejoice. There is an iris on the cloud of humanity. The name of Franklin fills the world, and in most places is pronounced like a benediction.

From a tallow-chandler's shop to palaces; from the companionship of Uncle Ben, the poet, to that of royal blood, people of highest rank, and the most noble and cultured of mankind; from being laughed at, to being looked upon with universal reverence, love, and awe.

CHAPTER XXXIX.

THE TALE OF AN OLD VELVET COAT.

WHEN Franklin appeared to sign the Treaty of Peace between England and the United States, he surprised the ministers, envoys, and his own friends by wearing an old velvet coat. What did his appearance in this strange garment mean?

We must tell you the story, for it is an illustration of his honorable pride and the sensitiveness of his character. There was a time when all England, except a few of his own friends, were laughing at Franklin. Why?

Men who reach honorable success in life always pass through dark days—every sun and star is eclipsed some day—and Franklin had one day of eclipse that burned into his very soul, the memory of which haunted him as long as he lived.

It was that day when he, after a summons, appeared before the Council of the Crown as the agent of the colonies, and was openly charged with dishonor. It is the day of the charge of dishonor that is the darkest of all life. To an honorable man it is the day of a false charge of dishonor that leaves the deepest sting in memory.

> " My life and honor both together run :
> Take honor from me. and my life is done."

But how came Franklin, the agent of the colonies in London, to be called before the Privy Council and to be charged with dishonor?

While he was in London and the colonies were filled with discontent and indignation at the severe measures of the crown, there came to him a member of Parliament who told him that these measures of which the colonies complained had been brought about by certain men in the colonies themselves; that the ministry had acted upon the advice of these men, and had thought that they were acting justly and wisely. Two of the men cited were Lieutenant-Governor Hutchinson and Andrew Oliver, both belonging to most respected and powerful families in the colonies.

Franklin could not believe these statements against his countrymen, and asked for the proof. The member of Parliament brought to him a package of letters addressed to public men on public affairs, written by Lieutenant-Governor Hutchinson and Mr. Oliver, which proved to him that the severe action of the ministry against Boston and the province had been brought about by Bostonians themselves. Franklin asked permission to send these letters to Boston in the interests of justice to the ministry. The request was granted. The letters were sent to Boston, and were read in private to the General Assembly of the province. As an agent of the colonies, Franklin could not have done less in the interests of justice, truth, and honorable dealing.

But the use of these letters angered the ministry, and Franklin was called before the Privy Council to answer the charge of surreptitiously obtaining private correspondence and using it for purposes detrimental to the royal government.

To persons whose whole purpose of life is to live honorably such days as these come and develop character. Every one has some lurking enemy eager to misinterpret him to his own advantage. The lark must fly to the open sky when he sees the serpent coiling among the roses, or he must fight and dare the odds. Woe be to the wrongdoer who triumphs in such a case as this! He may gain money and ease, and laugh at his adversary, but when a man has proved untrue to any man for the sake of his own advantage, it may be written of him, " He went out, and it was night." A short chapter of a part of a biography or history may be an injustice, and seem to show that there is no God in the government of the world, but a long chapter of full history reveals God on the high throne of his power, and justice as his strength and glory. The Roman emperors built grand monuments to atone for their injustice, cruelty, and vice-seeking lives, but these only blackened their names by recalling what they were, and defeated their builders' ends. In this world all long chapters of history read one way: that character is everything, and that time tells the truth about all things. Justice is the highest expectation of life; it is only wise so to live that one's " expectation may not be disappointed." The young man can not be too soon led to see that " he that is spiritual judgeth all things, and that no man judgeth him."

It was the year 1773, when Franklin was sixty-eight years of age, that this dark and evil day came. A barrister named Wedderburn, young in years and new to the bar, a favorite of

Lord North, and one who was regarded as "a wonderfully smart young man," was to present the case of the government against him.

The case filled all England with intense interest. The most notable men of the kingdom arranged to be present at the hearing. Thirty-five members of the Privy Council were present, an unusual number at such an assembly. Lord North was there; the Archbishop of Canterbury; even Dr. Priestley was there.

Dr. Franklin appeared on this memorable day in a velvet coat. He took a place in the room in a recess formed by a chimney, a retired place, where he stood motionless and silent. The coat was of Manchester velvet, and spotted.

Wedderburn addressed the Council. He was witty, brilliant, careless of facts. His address on that occasion was the talk of all England in a few days, and it led him to a career of fame that would have been success had it had the right foundation. But nothing lasts that is not sincere. Everything in this world has to be readjusted that is not right.

"How these letters," said he, "came into the possession of any one but the right owners is a mystery for Dr. Franklin to explain."

He then spoke of Mr. Whatley, to whom the letters were first consigned, and proceeded thus:

"He has forfeited all the respect of societies and of men. Into what companies will he hereafter go with an unembarrassed face, or the honest intrepidity of virtue? Men will watch him with a jealous eye; they will hide their papers from him, and lock up their escritoires. He will henceforth esteem

it a libel to be called *a man of letters;* this man of *three* letters.
(*Fur*—a thief.)"

The manner of the orator thrilled the august company. It
is thus described by Jeremy Bentham:

"I was not more astonished at the brilliancy of his lightning than astounded by the thunder that accompanied it. As
he stood, the cushion lay on the council table before him; his
station was between the seats of two of the members, on the
side of the right hand of the lord president. I would not, for
double the greatest fee the orator could on that occasion have
received, been in the place of that cushion; the ear was stunned
at every blow; he had been reading perhaps in that book in
which the prince of Roman orators and rhetoric professors in-
structs his pupils how to make impression. The table groaned
under the assault. Alone, in the recess on the left hand of the
president, stood Benjamin Franklin, in such position as not
to be visible from the situation of the president, remaining the
whole time like a rock, in the same posture, his head resting on
his left hand; and in that attitude abiding the pelting of the
pitiless storm."

Franklin, the agent of the colonies, stood in his humble
place, calm and undisturbed to all outward appearance, but he
was cut to the quick as he heard this assembly of representative
Englishmen laughing at his supposed dishonor.

Says one of that day, "At the sallies of the orator's sarcas-
tic wit all the members of the Council, the president himself
not excepted, frequently laughed outright."

Benjamin Franklin went home, and put away his spotted
velvet coat. He might want it again. It would be a re-

minder to him—a lesson of life. He might wear it again some day.

The next day, being Sunday, the eminent Dr. Priestley came to take breakfast with him.

Dr. Franklin said: "Let me read the arraignment twice over. I have never before been so sensible of the power of a good conscience. If I had not considered the thing for which I have been so much insulted the best action of my life, and which I certainly should do again under like circumstances, I could not have supported myself."

Franklin held an office under the crown. On Monday morning a letter was brought to him from the postmaster-general. It read:

"The king finds it necessary to dismiss you from the office of deputy postmaster-general in America."

Dismissed in disgrace at the age of sixty-eight! And England laughing. He had nothing left to comfort him now but his conscience—that was the everything.

The old spotted velvet coat; he brought it out on the day of the treaty. It was some nine or more years old now. He stood like a culprit in it one day; it should adorn him now in the hour of his honor.

He was facing eighty years.

He prepared to leave France, where his career had been one of such honor and glory that his fame filled the world.

The court made him a parting present. It was a portrait of the king set in a frame of *four hundred diamonds!*

CHAPTER XL

It has been said that Franklin forgot to be old. Verging upon eighty, he had asked to be recalled from France, and he dreamed of quiet old age among his grandchildren on the banks of the Schuylkill, where so many happy years of his middle life had been spent. He was recalled from France, but, as we have before stated, this was an age in America when men sought the councils of wisdom and experience.

Pennsylvania needed a President or Governor who could lay the foundations of early legislation with prudence, and she turned to the venerable Franklin to fill the chair of state. He was nominated for the office of President of Pennsylvania, and elected, and twice re-elected; and we find him now, over eighty years of age, in activities of young manhood, and bringing to the office the largest experience of any American.

He was among the first of most eminent Americans to crown his life after the period of threescore and ten years with the results of the scholarship of usefulness.

We have recently seen Gladstone, Tennyson, King William, Bismarck, Von Moltke, Whittier, Holmes, and many other men of the enlightened world, doing some of their strongest and most impressive work after seventy years of age, and some of these setting jewels in the crown of life when past eighty. We have seen Du Maurier producing his first great work of fiction at sixty, and many authors fulfilling the hopes of years at a like age.

We have a beautiful pen picture of Franklin in these several years, in his youth's return when eighty years were past. It shows what is possible to a life of temperance and beneficence, and it is only such a life that can have an Indian summer, a youth in age.

"Dr. Franklin's house," wrote a clergyman who visited him in his old age, "stands up a court, at some distance from the street. We found him in his garden, sitting upon a grass-plot, under a very large mulberry tree, with several other gentlemen and two or three ladies. When Mr. Gerry introduced me, he rose from his chair, took me by the hand, expressed his joy at seeing me, welcomed me to the city, and begged me to seat myself close to him. His voice was low, but his countenance open, frank, and pleasing. I delivered to him my letters. After he read them he took me again by the hand, and, with the usual compliments, introduced me to the other gentlemen.

"Here we entered into a free conversation, and spent our time most agreeably until it was quite dark. The tea table was spread under the tree, and Mrs. Bache, who is the only daughter of the doctor and lives with him, served it out to the company. She had three of her children about her. They seemed to be excessively fond of their grandpa. The doctor showed me a curiosity he had just received, and with which he was much pleased. It was a snake with two heads, preserved in

FRANKLIN'S LAST DAYS.

a large vial. It was taken near the confluence of the Schuylkill with the Delaware, about four miles from this city. It was about ten inches long, well proportioned, the heads perfect, and united to the body about one fourth of an inch below the extremities of the jaws. The snake was of a dark brown, approaching to black, and the back beautifully speckled with white. The belly was rather checkered with a reddish color and white. The doctor supposed it to be full grown, which I think is probable; and he thinks it must be a *sui generis* of that class of animals. He grounds his opinion of its not being an extraordinary production, but a distinct genus, on the perfect form of the snake, the probability of its being of some age, and there having been found a snake entirely similar (of which the doctor has a drawing, which he showed us) near Lake Champlain in the time of the late war. He mentioned the situation of this snake if it was traveling among bushes, and one head should choose to go on one side of the stem of a bush and the other head should prefer the other side, and neither of the heads would consent to come back or give way to the other. He was then going to mention a humorous matter that had that day occurred in the convention in consequence of his comparing the snake to America, for he seemed to forget that everything in the convention was to be kept a profound secret. But this secrecy of convention matters was suggested to him, which stopped him and deprived me of the story he was going to tell.

"After it was dark we went into his house, and he invited me into his library, which is likewise his study. It is a very large chamber and high studded. The walls are covered with bookshelves filled with books; besides, there are four large alcoves extending two thirds of the length of the chamber, filled in the same manner. I presume this is the largest and by far the best private library in America.

" He seemed extremely fond, through the course of the visit, of dwelling on philosophical subjects, and particularly that of natural history, while the other gentlemen were swallowed up with politics. This was a favorable circumstance for me, for almost the whole of his conversation was addressed to me; and I was highly delighted with the extensive knowledge he appeared to have of every subject, the brightness of his memory, and the clearness and vivacity of all his mental faculties, notwithstanding his age. His manners are perfectly easy, and everything about him seems to diffuse an unrestrained freedom and happiness. He has an incessant vein of humor, accompanied with an uncommon vivacity, which seems as natural and involuntary as his breathing. He urged me to call on him again, but my short stay would not admit. We took our leave at ten, and I retired to my lodgings."

The convention to frame a Constitution for the United States assembled at this time in Philadelphia. Dr. Franklin was elected to bring his ripe statesmanship into this great work.

He was a poet in old age. When past eighty he fulfilled one of the hopes of Uncle Ben. When the Constitution had been adopted by a majority of the States, the event was celebrated by a grand festival in Philadelphia. There were a long procession of the trades, an oration. the booming of cannon, and the ringing of bells. Some twenty thousand people joined in the festivities. They wanted a poet for the joyful occasion.

Poets were not many in those days. Who should appear? It was Silence Dogood, the Poor Richard of a generation gone.

To the draft of the Constitution of the United States Benjamin Franklin placed his signature, and thus again honored his Boston writing-master of seventy years ago.

But he gave to this august assembly an influence as noble as his signature to the document that it produced. Franklin had been skeptical in his youth, and a questioner of religious teachings in other periods of his life. Mature thought had convinced him of the glory of the Christian faith, of the doctrine of immortality and the power of prayer. The deliberations in the Constitutional Assembly were long, and they were sometimes bitter. In the midst of the debates, the divisions of opinion and delays, Dr. Franklin arose one day—it was the 28th of June, 1787—and moved

"That henceforth prayers, imploring the assistance of Heaven and its blessing on our deliberations, be held in this Assembly every morning before we proceed to business; and that one or more of the clergy of this city be requested to officiate in that service."

In an address supporting this resolution he said: "I have lived, sir, a long time, and the longer I live the more convincing proofs I see of this truth: *That* GOD *governs in the affairs of men!* And if a sparrow can not fall to the ground without his notice, is it probable that an empire can rise without his aid? We have been assured, sir, in the Sacred Writings, that 'except the Lord build the house, they labor in vain that build it.' I firmly believe this; and I also believe that without his concurring aid we shall succeed in this political building no better than the building of Babel; we shall be divided by our partial local interests, our projects will be confounded, and we ourselves shall become a reproach and a byword down to future ages. And, what is worse, mankind may hereafter from this unfortunate instance despair of establishing government by human wisdom, and leave it to chance, war, and conquest."

To consummate the American Government now only one thing was lacking—a power to interpret the meaning of the Constitution, and so to decide any disputes that should arise among the States.

In Mr. Vernon's garden, after the controversy between the fishermen of Maryland and Virginia, a plan to settle such disputes was produced. It was a high court of final appeal.

So rose the Supreme Court. And this court to decide questions of controversy arising among the States, we may hope, was the beginning of a like body, a Supreme Court of the nations of the world that shall settle the questions in dispute among nations, without an appeal to war or the shedding of human blood.

These were glorious times, and although Dr. Franklin was not actively engaged in this last grand movement for the government of the people, he lived to give his influence to make George Washington President, and see the new order of a popular government inaugurated. He entered the doors of that golden age of liberty, equality, and progress, when the destinies might say to their spindles, " Thus go on forever! "

CHAPTER XLI.

JANE'S LAST VISIT.

IT was midsummer. Benjamin Franklin, of fourscore
years, President of Pennsylvania, had finished a long, three-
story ell to his house on Market Street, and in this ell he had
caused to be made a library which filled his heart with pride.
He had invented a long arm with which to take down books
from the high shelves of this library—an invention which came
into use in other libraries in such a way as to make many libra-
rians grateful to him.

He was overburdened with care, and suffered from chronic
disease.

In his days of pain he had been comforted by letters from
Jenny, now long past seventy years of age. She had written
to him in regard to his sufferings such messages as these:

"Oh, that after you have spent your whole life in the
service of the public, and have attained so glorious a conclusion, as I thought, as would now permit you to come home and
spend (as you say) the evening with your friends in ease and
quiet, that now such a dreadful malady should attack you! My
heart is ready to burst with grief at the thought. How many
hours have I lain awake on nights thinking what excruciating

pains you might then be encountering, while I, poor, useless, and worthless worm, was permitted to be at ease! Oh, that it was in my power to mitigate or alleviate the anguish I know you must endure!"

When she heard of his arrival in Philadelphia she wrote:

"I long so much to see you that I should immediately seek for some one that would accompany me, but my daughter is in a poor state of health and gone into the country to try to get a little better, and I am in a strait between two; but the comfortable reflection that you are at home among all your dear children, and no more seas to cross, will be constantly pleasing to me till I am permitted to enjoy the happiness of seeing and conversing with you."

The tenderness and charity of Franklin for the many members of his own family still revealed his heart. "I tenderly love you," he wrote to Jane—Jenny—"for the care of our father in his sickness."

One of his sisters, Mrs. Dowse, whose family had died, insisted upon living alone, on account of her love for the place that had been her home. Many other men would have compelled her removal, but there is nothing more beautiful in all Franklin's letters than the way that he advised Jenny how to treat this matter. He had been told that this venerable woman would have her own way.

"As *having their own way* is one of the greatest comforts of life to old people, I think their friends should endeavor to accommodate them in that as well as anything else. When they have long lived in a house, it becomes natural to them; they are almost as closely connected with it as the tortoise with his shell; they die if you tear them out. Old folks and old trees, if you remove them, 'tis ten to one that you kill them, so let our good old sister be no more importuned on that head; we are growing old fast ourselves, and shall expect the same kind of indulgences; if we give them, we shall have a right to receive them in our turn."

Jane Mecom—the " Jenny " of Franklin's young life—had one great desire as the years went on: it was, to meet her brother once more and to review the past with him.

" I will one day go to Philadelphia and give him a great surprise," the woman used to say.

Let us picture such a day.

Benjamin Franklin sat down in his new library. His books had been placed and his pictures hung.

Among the pictures were two that were so choice that we may suppose them to be hung under coverings. One of them was the portrait of the King of France in its frame of four hundred brilliants, and the other was his own portrait with, perhaps, Turgot's famous inscription.

It was near evening when he sat down and asked to be left alone.

He opened his secretary, and took from it a letter from Washington. It read:

" Amid the public gratulations on your safe return to America after a long absence, and many eminent services you have rendered it, for which as a benefited person I feel the obligation, permit an individual to join the public voice in expressing a sense of them, and to assure you that, as no one entertains more respect for your character, so no one can salute you with more sincerity or with greater pleasure than I do on the occasion."

He took from his papers the resolution of the Assembly of Pennsylvania and began to read:

" We are confident, sir, that we speak the sentiments of the whole country when we say that your services in the public councils and negotiations have not only merited the thanks of the present generation, but will be recorded in the pages of history to your immortal honor."

He dropped the paper on the table beside the letter of Washington and sank into his armchair, for his pains were coming upon him again.

He thought of the past—of old Boston, of Passy, of all his struggles—and he wished that he might feel again the sympathetic touch of the hand of his sister who had been so true to him, and who had loved him so long and well.

It was near sunset of one of the longest days of the year when he heard a carriage stop before the door.

" I can not see any one," he said. " I must have rest—I must have rest."

There came a mechanical knock on his door. He did not respond.

A servant's voice said outside, " There is a woman, master, that asks to see you."

" I can not see any one," answered the tortured old man.

" She is an old woman."

" I could not see the queen."

He heard an echo of the servant's voice in the hall.

" He says that he could not see the queen."

"Well, tell him that I am something more than that to him. He will see me, or else I will die at his door."

There came a tap on the door, very gentle.

"Who is there?"

"It is Jane."

"What Jane—who?"

"She who folded the hands of your father for the last time. Open the door. There can be no No to me."

The door opened.

"Jenny!"

"Ben—let all titles pass now—I have come to give you a surprise."

The old woman sank into a chair.

"I have come to visit you for the last time," she said, "and to number with you our mercies of life. Let me rest before I talk. You are in pain."

"Jenny, my pains have gone. I had sat down in agony in this new room; my head ached as well as my body. I am happy now that you have come."

She moved her chair to his, and he took her hand again, saying:

"My sister's hand—your hand, Jenny, as when we were children. They are gone, all gone."

He looked in her face.

"Jenny, your hair is gray now, and mine is white. I have been reading over again this letter from Washington."

"Read it to me while I rest, then we will talk of old times."

He read the letter.

“ Here are the resolutions of the Assembly of Pennsylvania passed on my return.”

“ Read them to me, brother, for I must rest longer before we talk of old times.”

He read the resolutions.

“ Jenny, let me uncover this. It is not vanity that makes me wish to do it now, but on account of what I wish to say.”

He uncovered the portrait of the French king. The last light of the sun fell into the room and upon the frame, causing the four hundred diamonds to gleam.

“ That was presented to me by the court of France.”

“ I never saw anything so splendid, brother. But what is the other picture under the cover? ”

He drew away the screen.

“ It is my portrait, Jenny.”

“ But, brother, what are those words written under it? ”

Franklin read, “ *Eripuit cœlo fulmen, sceptrumque tyrannis.*”

“ Brother, what does that mean? ”

“ ‘ He snatched the thunderbolts from heaven, and the scepter from the tyrants.’ ”

“ Who, brother? ”

“ Jenny, let us talk of these things no longer. Do you remember Uncle Ben? ”

“ He has never died. He lives in you. You have lived out his life. You have lived, Ben, and I have loved. Brother, you have done well. He who does his best does well.”

“ Jenny, can you repeat what Uncle Ben said under the

tree on the showery day when the birds sang, nearly seventy years ago?"

"Let us repeat it together, brother. You have made that lesson your life."

"'More than wealth, more than fame, or any other thing, is the power of the human heart, and it is developed by seeking the good of others. Live for the things that live.'"

"Jenny, my own true sister, I have something else to show you—something that I value more than a present from a throne. I have here some 'pamphlets,' into which Uncle Ben put his soul before he sought to impress the same thoughts upon me. I want you to have them now, to read them, and give them to his family."

He went to his secretary and took from it the pamphlets.

"Here are the thoughts of a man who told me when I was a poor boy in Boston town that I had a chance in the world.

"He told me not to be laughed down. .

"He told me that diligence was power.

"He told me that I would be helped in helping others.

"He told me that justice was the need of mankind.

"He told me that to have influence with men I must over-come my conscious defects.

"He was poor, he was empty-handed, but Heaven gave to him the true vision of life. He committed that vision to me, and what he wished to be I have struggled to fulfill. These pamphlets are the picture of his mind, and that picture deserves to be hung in diamonds, and is more to me than the portrait of the king. Blessed be the memory of that old man, who taught my young life virtue, and gave it hope!

" Jenny, I have tried to live well."

" You have been ' Silence Dogood,' the idea that Uncle Benjamin printed on your mind."

" Jenny, I have heard the church bells—Uncle Tom's bells—of Nottingham ring. I found Uncle Benjamin's letters there—those that he wrote to his old friends from America. He lovingly described you and me. What days those were! Father was true to his home when he invited Uncle Benjamin to America. You have been true to your home, and my heart has been, through your hands. Jenny, I have given my house in Boston to you."

The old woman wept.

" Jenny, you have loved, and your heart has been better than mine. Let me call the servants. These are hours when the soul is full—my soul is full. I ask for nothing more."

CHAPTER XLII.

FOR THE LAST TIME.

SILENCE DOGOOD is an old man now—a very old man. He looks back on the spring and summer and autumn of life—it is now the time of the snow. But there are sunny days in winter, and they came to him, though on the trees hang the snow, and the nights are long and painful.

What has Silence Dogood done in his eighty years now ending in calm, in dreams and silence? Let us look back over the past with him now. What a review it is!

He had founded literary and scientific clubs in his early life that had made not idlers, but men. He had founded the first subscription library in America. It had multiplied, and in its many branches had become a national influence.

He made a stove that was a family luxury, and showed how it might be enjoyed without a smoky chimney.

He had shown that lightning was electricity and could be controlled, and had disarmed the thunder cloud by a simple rod.

He had founded the High School in Pennsylvania.

He had encouraged the raising of silk.

He had helped found the Philadelphia Hospital, and had founded the American Philosophical Society.

He had promoted the scheme for uniting the colonies.

He had signed the Declaration of Independence, the Treaty of the Alliance with France, the Treaty of Peace between England and the United States, and the draft of the Constitution of the United States.

We may truly say, " Well done, thou good and faithful servant." But there remains yet one paper to sign. It is his will. The influence of that paper is felt in the world to-day, but nowhere more than in Boston. In this will he made provision for lending the interest of great bequests to poor citizens, he left the fund for the Franklin Silver Medal in Boston schools, and he sought to be a benefactor to the children of Boston after a hundred years. This will has the following words:

" If this plan is executed, and succeeds as projected without interruption for one hundred years, the sum will then be one hundred and thirty-one thousand pounds, of which I would have the managers of the donation to the town of Boston then lay out, at their discretion, one hundred thousand pounds in public works, which may be judged of most general utility to the inhabitants, such as fortifications, bridges, aqueducts, public buildings, baths, pavements, or whatever may make living in the town more convenient to its people, and render it more agreeable to strangers resorting thither for health or a temporary residence. The remaining thirty-one thousand pounds I would have continued to be let out on interest, in the manner above directed, for another hundred years, as I hope it will have been found that the institution has had a good effect on the conduct of youth, and been of service to many worthy characters and useful citizens. At the end of this second term, if no unfortunate accident has prevented the operation, the sum will be four millions and sixty-one thousand pounds sterling; of which I leave one million sixty-one thousand pounds to the disposition of the inhabitants of the town of Boston, and three millions to the disposition of the government of the State, not presuming to carry my views farther."

He put his signature to this last paper, and for the last time did honor to his old writing-master, George Brownell.

He died looking upon a picture of Christ, and he was buried amid almost unexampled honors, France joining with the United States in his eulogies.

But in a high sense he lives. There is one boy who has never ceased to attend the Boston Latin School, and will not for generations to come. It is Silence Dogood.

Virtue to virtue, intelligence to intelligence, benevolence to benevolence, faith to faith! So ascend the feet of worth on the ladder of life; so reaches a high purpose a place beyond the derision of the world.

The bells of the nation tolled when he died. "He was true to his country!" said all men; but aged Jenny, "He was true to his home!"

The influence of Uncle Benjamin in his godson had lived, but it was not ended.

On September 17th, in the year 1856, the city of Boston stopped business to render homage to the memory of her greatest citizen. On that day was inaugurated the Franklin statue, by Horatio Greenough, that now stands in front of the City Hall. On that day the graves of Josiah and Abiah Franklin in

21

the Granary burying ground were covered with evergreens and flowers, and we hope that the grave of Uncle Ben, the poet, which is near by, was not forgotten.

The procession was one of the grandest that the city has ever seen, for it was not only great in numbers, but it blossomed with heart tributes. The trades were in it, the military, the schools. Orators, poets, artists, all contributed to the festival. Boston was covered with flags, and her halls were filled with joyous assemblages.

There was one house that was ornamented by a motto from Franklin's private liturgy. It was:

> "Help me to be faithful to my country,
>
> Careful for its good,
>
> Valiant for its defense,
>
> And obedient to its laws."

Conspicuous among the mottoes were:

"Time is money," "Knowledge is power," "Worth makes the man," and, queerly enough, "*Don't give too much for the whistle,*" the teaching of an experience one hundred and fifty years before.

The bells rang, and the influence of the old man who slept beside the flower-crowned grave of Josiah Franklin and Abiah Franklin was in the joy; the chimes of Nottingham were ringing again. Good influences are seeds of immortal flowers, and no life fails that inspires another.

Franklin Park, Boston, which will be one of the most beautiful in the world, will carry forward, in its forests, fountains, and flowers, these influences for generations to come.

CHAPTER XLIII.

It was the day of the award of the Franklin medals in the old Boston Latin School, a day in June, and such a one as James Russell Lowell so picturesquely describes. We say "old" Boston Latin School, not meaning old Boston in England, but such an association would not be an untrue one; for the Boston Latin School in Boston, Massachusetts, which was founded under the influence of Governor John Winthrop and Rev. John Cotton, and that numbers five signers of the Declaration of Independence among its pupils, was really begun in Boston, England, in 1554, or in the days of Queen Mary. It has the most remarkable history of any school in America; it has been the Harrow of Harvard, and for five or more generations has sent into life many men whose character has shed luster upon their times.

To gain the Franklin medal is the high aim of the Boston schoolboy. It is to associate one's name with a long line of illustrious men, among them John Collins Warren, Wendell Phillips, Charles Sumner, Phillips Brooks, S. F. Smith, and many others.

But one of the boys who had won the Franklin medal to-

311

day had done so amid the ridicule of his people at home and after very hard work. Boston Latin boys are too well bred to laugh at the humble gifts of any one, but those of this period could hardly have failed to notice the natural stupidity and the strong, silent purpose and will of this lad. His name we will call Elwell—Frank Elwell. He came from a humble home, where he was not uncommonly taunted as being the "fool of the family."

He first attracted attention at this school of brilliant pupils by a bold question which he asked his teacher one day that commanded instant respect. After hard study he had made a very poor recitation. He was reproved by his teacher, who was a submaster, but a kindly, sensitive, and sympathetic man. He lifted his eyes and looked into the teacher's face, and said:

"Why do you reprove me? I am doing the best I can, sir."

The teacher knew the words to be true. The boys that heard the question turned with a kind of chivalrous feeling toward their dull companion, who was doing his best against poverty, limited gifts, and many disadvantages in life. The old school of Charles Sumner, Wendell Phillips, and Phillips Brooks is not wanting in true sympathy with any manly struggle in life.

The teacher answered: "Master Elwell, I have done wrong in reproving you. He does well who does his best. You are doing well."

Frank Elwell won the Franklin medal by doing his best. On the evening after his graduation he stood before his teacher and asked:

"Master Lowell" (for so we will call the teacher, and use

the old term in the vocative case), "Master Lowell, did you ever know any boy to struggle against defects like mine?"

"Yes, my boy, I have."

"Did he succeed in life?"

"He did. He became the first citizen of Boston, and is so regarded still."

"Who was it, sir?"

"Look at your medal. It was Benjamin Franklin himself."

Reader, Frank Elwell perhaps is *you.*

"More than wealth, more than fame, more than any other thing, is the power of the human heart." Live for influences— live for the things that live, and let the best influences of the Peter Folgers and Benjamin Franklins of your family live on in you, and live after you. You will do well in life and will succeed in life if you do your best; and if your ideal seems to fail in you, it will not fail in the world, in whose harvest field no good intention perishes.

Be true to those who have faith in you, and *to* their faith in you, and help others by believing in the best that is in them. Those who have the most faith in you are your truest friends. An Uncle Benjamin and a Jenny are among the choicest characters that can enter the doors of life, and we will see it so at the end.

Do good, and you can not fail.

> "Do thou thy work; it shall succeed
> In thine or in another's day,
> And if denied the visitor's meed,
> Thou shalt not miss the toiler's pay."

APPENDIX.

"FRIENDS," said the old auctioneer, "the taxes are indeed very heavy. If those laid on by the government were the only ones we had to pay, we might more easily discharge them; but we have many others, and much more grievous to some of us. We are taxed twice as much by our idleness, three times as much by our pride, and four times as much by our folly; and from these taxes the commissioners can not ease or deliver us by allowing an abatement. However, let us hearken to good advice, and something may be done for us. God helps them that help themselves, as Poor Richard says.

"I. It would be thought a hard government that would tax its people one tenth part of their time to be employed in its service; but idleness taxes many of us much more; sloth, by bringing on diseases, absolutely shortens life. Sloth, like rust, consumes faster than labor wears; while the used key is always bright, as Poor Richard says. But dost thou love life? then do not squander time, for that is the stuff life is made of, as Poor Richard says. How much more than is necessary do we spend in sleep, forgetting that The sleeping fox catches no poultry, and that There will be sleeping enough in the grave? as Poor Richard says.

314

"If time be of all things the most precious, wasting time must be, as Poor Richard says, the greatest prodigality, since, as he elsewhere tells us, Lost time is never found again, and what we call time enough always proves little enough. Let us, then, be up and doing, and doing to the purpose; so by diligence shall we do more with less perplexity. Sloth makes all things difficult, but industry all ease; and He that riseth late must trot all day, and shall scarce overtake his business at night; while Laziness travels so slowly that Poverty soon overtakes him. Drive thy business, let not that drive thee; and, Early to bed and early to rise makes a man healthy, wealthy, and wise, as Poor Richard says.

"So, what signifies wishing and hoping for better times? We make these times better if we bestir ourselves. Industry need not wish, and he that lives upon hopes will die fasting. There are no gains without pains; then help, hands, for I have no lands; or, if I have, they are smartly taxed. He that hath a trade hath an estate; and he that hath a calling hath an office of profit and honor, as Poor Richard says; but then the trade must be worked at, and the calling followed, or neither the estate nor the office will enable us to pay our taxes. If we are industrious we shall never starve; for, At the workingman's house Hunger looks in but dares not enter; for, Industry pays debts, while despair increases them. What though you have no treasure, nor has any rich relation left you a legacy; Diligence is the mother of good luck, and God gives all things to industry. Then plow deep while sluggards sleep, and you shall have corn to sell and to keep. Work while it is called to-day, for you know not how much you may be hindered to-morrow. One to-day is worth two to-morrows, as Poor Richard says; and further, Never leave that till to-morrow which you can do to-day. If you were a servant, would you not be ashamed that a good master should catch you idle? Are you, then, your own master? Be ashamed to catch yourself idle, when there is so much to be done for yourself, your family, your country, your king. Handle your tools without mittens; remember that The cat in gloves catches no mice, as Poor Richard says. It is true there is much to be done, and perhaps you are weak-handed; but stick to it steadily, and you will see great effects; for, Constant dropping wears away stones, and By diligence and patience the mouse ate in two the cable; and Little strokes fell great oaks.

"Methinks I hear some of you say, Must a man afford himself no leisure? I will tell thee, my friend, what Poor Richard says: Employ thy time well, if thou meanest to gain leisure; and since thou art not sure of a minute, throw not away an hour. Leisure is time for doing something useful; this leisure the diligent man will obtain, but the lazy man never; for A life of leisure and a life of laziness are two things. Many, without labor, would live by their wits only, but they break for want of stock; whereas, industry gives comfort, and plenty, and respect. Fly pleasures, and they will follow you. The diligent spinner has a large shift; and now I have a sheep and a cow, every one bids me good-morrow.

"II. But with our industry we must likewise be steady and careful, and oversee our own affairs with our own eyes, and not trust too much to others; for, as Poor Richard says:

> " I never saw an oft-removed tree,
>   Nor yet an oft-removed family,
>   That throve so well as those that settled be."

And again, Three removes are as bad as a fire; and again, Keep thy shop, and thy shop will keep thee; and again, If you would have your business, go; if not, send.   And again,

> " He that by the plow would thrive,
>   Himself must either hold or drive."

And again, The eye of the master will do more work than both his hands; and again, Want of care does us more damage than want of knowledge; and again, Not to oversee workmen is to leave them your purse open.   Trusting too much to others' care is the ruin of many; for, In the affairs of this world men are saved not by faith but by the want of it; but a man's own care is profitable, for, If you would have a faithful servant, and one that you like, serve yourself.   A little neglect may breed great mischief: for want of a nail the shoe was lost; for want of a shoe the horse was lost; and for want of a horse the rider was lost, being overtaken and slain by the enemy—all for want of a little care about a horseshoe nail.

" III. So much for industry, my friends, and attention to one's own business; but to these we must add frugality, if we would make our industry more certainly successful.   A man may, if he knows not how to save as he gets, keep his nose all his life to the grindstone, and die not worth a groat at last.   A fat kitchen makes a lean will; and

> " Many estates are spent in the getting,
>   Since women forsook spinning and knitting.
>   And men for punch forsook hewing and splitting.
>   If you would be wealthy, think of saving as well as of getting."

The Indies have not made Spain rich, because her outgoes are greater than her incomes.

"Away, then, with your expensive follies, and you will not then have so much cause to complain of hard times, heavy taxes, and chargeable families; for

"Women and wine, game and deceit,
Make the wealth small and the want great."

And, further, What maintains one vice would bring up two children. You may think, perhaps, that a little tea or a little punch now and then, diet a little more costly, clothes a little finer, and a little entertainment now and then, can be no great matter; but remember, Many a little makes a mickle. Beware of little expenses; A small leak will sink a great ship, as Poor Richard says; and again, Who dainties love shall beggars prove; and, moreover, Fools make feasts and wise men eat them.

"Here you are all got together at this sale of fineries and knickknacks. You call them goods; but if you do not take care, they will prove evils to some of you. You expect they will be sold cheap, and perhaps they may for less than they cost; but if you have no occasion for them, they must be dear to you. Remember what Poor Richard says: Buy what thou hast no need of, and ere long thou shalt sell thy necessities. And again, At a great pennyworth pause awhile. He means that perhaps the cheapness is apparent only, and not real; or the bargain, by straitening thee in thy business, may do thee more harm than good; for in another place he says, Many have been ruined by buying good pennyworths. Again, It is foolish to lay out money in a purchase of repentance; and yet this folly is practiced every day at auctions for want of minding the almanac. Many, for the sake of finery on the back, have gone with a hungry belly and half starved their families. Silks and satins, scarlet and velvets, put out the kitchen fire, as Poor Richard says.

"These are not the necessaries of life; they can scarcely be called the conveniences; and yet, only because they look pretty, how many want to have them! By these, and other extravagances, the genteel are reduced to poverty, and forced to borrow of those whom they formerly despised, but who through industry and frugality have maintained their standing; in which case it appears plainly that A plowman on his legs is higher than a gentleman on his knees, as Poor Richard says. Perhaps they have a small estate left them which they knew not the getting of; they think, It is day, and it never will be night; that a little to be spent out of so much is not worth minding; but Always taking out of the meal-tub, and never putting in, soon comes to the bottom, as Poor Richard says; and then, When the well is dry, they know the worth of water. But this they might have known before, if they had taken his advice. If you would know the value of money, go and try to borrow some; for, He that goes a-borrowing goes a-sorrowing, as Poor Richard says; and, indeed, so does he that lends to such people, when he goes to get it again. Poor Dick further advises, and says:

> " Fond pride of dress is sure a very curse ;
> Ere fancy you consult, consult your purse."

And again, Pride is as loud a beggar as Want, and a great deal more saucy. When you have bought one fine thing, you must buy ten more, that your appearance may be all of a piece; but

Poor Dick says, It is easier to suppress the first desire than to satisfy all that follow it. And it is as truly folly for the poor to ape the rich, as for the frog to swell in order to equal the ox.

> " Vessels large may venture more,
> But little boats should keep near shore."

It is, however, a folly soon punished; for, as Poor Richard says, Pride that dines on vanity, sups on contempt. Pride breakfasted with Plenty, dined with Poverty, and supped with Infamy. And, after all, of what use is this pride of appearance, for which so much is risked, so much is suffered? It can not promote health, nor ease pain; it makes no increase of merit in the person; it creates envy; it hastens misfortune.

" But what madness must it be to run in debt for these superfluities! We are offered by the terms of this sale six months' credit; and that, perhaps, has induced some of us to attend it, because we can not spare the ready money, and hope now to be fine without it. But, ah! think what you do when you run in debt: you give to another power over your liberty. If you can not pay at the time, you will be ashamed to see your creditor; you will be in fear when you speak to him; you will make poor, pitiful, sneaking excuses, and, by degrees, come to lose your veracity, and sink into base, downright lying; for, The second vice is lying, the first is running in debt, as Poor Richard says; and again, to the same purpose, Lying rides upon Debt's back; whereas, a free-born Englishman ought not to be ashamed nor afraid to see or speak to any man living. But poverty often deprives a man of all spirit and virtue. It is hard for an empty bag to stand upright.

" What would you think of that prince, or of that government, who should issue an edict forbidding you to dress like a gentleman or gentlewoman on pain of imprisonment or servitude? Would you not say that you were free, have a right to dress as you please, and that such an edict would be a breach of your privileges, and such a government tyrannical? And yet you are about to put yourself under such tyranny when you run in debt for such dress. Your creditor has authority, at his pleasure, to deprive you of your liberty, by confining you in jail till you shall be able to pay him. When you have got your bargain you may perhaps think little of payment; but, as Poor Richard says, Creditors have better memories than debtors; creditors are a superstitious sect, great observers of set days and times. The day comes round before you are aware, and the demand is made before you are prepared to satisfy it; or, if you bear your debt in mind, the term, which at first seemed so long, will, as it lessens, appear extremely short. Time will seem to have added wings to his heels as well as his shoulders. Those have a short Lent who owe money to be paid at Easter. At present, perhaps, you may think yourselves in thriving circumstances, and that you can bear a little extravagance without injury; but

> "For age and want save while you may;
> No morning sun lasts a whole day."

Gain may be temporary and uncertain, but ever, while you live, expense is constant and certain; and It is easier to build two chimneys than to keep one in fuel, as Poor Richard says; so, Rather go to bed supperless than rise in debt.

> "Get what you can, and what you get, hold;
> 'Tis the stone that will turn all your lead into gold."

And when you have got the philosopher's stone, surely you will no longer complain of bad times or the difficulty of paying taxes.

"IV. This doctrine, my friends, is reason and wisdom; but, after all, do not depend too much upon your own industry and frugality and prudence, though excellent things; for they may all be blasted, without the blessing of Heaven; and, therefore, ask that blessing humbly, and be not uncharitable to those that at present seem to want it, but comfort and help them. Remember, Job suffered, and was afterward prosperous.

"And now, to conclude, Experience keeps a dear school, but fools will learn in no other, as Poor Richard says, and scarce in that; for, it is true, we may give advice, but we can not give conduct. However, remember this: They that will not be counseled can not be helped; and further, that, If you will not hear Reason, she will surely rap your knuckles, as Poor Richard says."

THE END.

9 783337 343972